Sexcapades
Torn in Transit

By: Sonja D. King

Dedication

I dedicate this book to God, Dorcas, Melessia, and Victoria.

Acknowledgment

First and foremost, I give thanks to Elohim—the Maker of heaven and earth, the Keeper of my soul, the Author and Finisher of my faith. He is the one true and living God, holy and almighty. He is the very breath I breathe and the source of every good thing in my life. It was He who promised that my gifts would make room for me—and here I stand, living proof of that promise.

To my parents, Willie Clay and Linda Canion—thank you. Daddy, you nicknamed me "Phenomenal" after hearing Dr. Maya Angelou's famous poem, never realizing that I would grow into the very woman she described. Mama, you told me in my thirties that I needed to write this book. You always cared for me, reminding me I was fragile—even when I didn't understand what you meant. I do now. I believe you've found a way to still be here with me, because my roommate, Melessia (Shug), is just like you—always looking out for me. Mom and Dad, you are in heaven now, but I hope you're looking down and smiling at what's unfolding.

To my siblings—Dorcas, Caprice, Redmund, Shakara, Stephen, Trivias, Nicholas, and Tomesha—thank you for proving that Mama was right: we didn't need friends because we had each other. We've shown the world what a loving blended family looks like. Unless we told them, no one would know, because we've always stood together—laughing, playing, and loving one another fiercely. I love you more than you know, and I'm proud that we carry the Canion legacy forward. We are, without question, **CANION STRONG!**

A special thank you to Victoria—and no, I am still not moving to Dallas. You never stopped telling me to write this book. Well, here it is!

Finally, to Apostle Dr. Derrick R. Zachary (DRZ) and the Walking in Authority International Ministries and Fellowship of Churches—thank you. DRZ, you have been the vessel God used to teach me what true healing and forgiveness look like. I am living proof that God's method of healing works, and I could not have finished this book from a broken place. To WIA, thank you for holding me up when I wanted to quit, for letting me cry on your shoulders when DRZ and God were "doing too much," and for pushing me back out there to finish the assignment. I am forever grateful.

Table of Contents

Introduction

My name is Emileigh.

But for this moment, let me set her aside—because this is also my testimony.

I am Sonja, and I need you to know that the redemptive, miracle-working power of God is not just a line in a sermon or a lyric in a song. It is real. I have lived it.

Somewhere along this journey called life, I realized that everyone is in transit. Every one of us is headed toward something—our destiny, our purpose, the reason we were created. But here's the tragedy: before most of us ever take the wheel and decide where we're going, we've already been torn. We've already been broken. Some cracks we inherited. Some we stumbled into. Others were carved into us by the hands of people who were torn themselves.

Yet, if you're paying attention, you'll notice you're not traveling alone. There is Someone on this train with you. His name is Redemption. I call Him my Redeemer.

He met me on the ride—right in the chaos, in the noise, in the crowded car of my life. He didn't just patch me up. He healed me. Completely.

Now I'm still in transit, but I'm no longer torn. There are no cracks for shame to hide in or fear to creep through. I'm on my way to Destiny and Purpose, and I can almost hear them calling me—like Oleta Adams sings, "I don't care how you get here, just get here if you can."

And here's the truth that changed everything for me: I didn't have to get there alone. I never did. The Redeemer was always with me.

This is my journey. This is my confession. This is my *Sexcapade.*

Prologue

Before the heartbreak, before the guilt, before the coma—there was a whisper.

It wasn't audible.

It lived in my gut. A flutter. A warning. A truth I wasn't ready to face.

That something sacred was forming between Jake and me. And that I was about to destroy it.

It happened slowly—like a fog rolling in. Not all at once, but thick enough that I couldn't see clearly until I had already lost sight of who I was.

People say women like me don't fall in love. We fall into patterns. We fall into trauma. We fall into loops that look like love but are really just old wounds with new names.

But then came Jake.

He didn't try to fix me. He didn't ask for the pieces. He just stood still. Present. Unflinching.

And somehow, that scared me more than all the red flags I had grown used to chasing.

There's something deeply unsettling about a man who sees you—really sees you—and doesn't flinch. Doesn't run. Doesn't recoil at the mess. Jake was that man.

And for a while, I loved him the best way I knew how.

But I was tired. Tired in my bones. Tired of choosing wrong. Tired of being wrong. Tired of being tired.

So when Mitch showed up again, slick smile and false promises, I let the door crack open.

Not because I loved him. Not even because I wanted him.

But because chaos felt more familiar than peace. And my soul, fractured as it was, didn't know how to rest in calm waters.

This is the story of how I broke something beautiful.

This is the story of how I tried to put the pieces back together.

This is my confession.

Chapter One

I wasn't supposed to be there. Not that night. Not in that dress. And definitely not with him.

But there I was—standing in six-inch heels that defied both logic and gravity, wearing a dress that hugged my hips like it had been stitched with sin, and holding a glass of champagne I hadn't even tasted yet. The hotel banquet hall pulsed with low light, jazz, and the faint clinking of cutlery from some silent dinner service long since forgotten.

Mitch stood across the room. Tall, cocky, and magnetic in that dangerous way. The kind of man your mother warned you about and your therapist billed you for. He was talking to a group of investors, effortlessly charming, laughing at his own jokes.

I told myself I didn't care.

Jake had just texted me: *You good, babe?*

I stared at the screen too long before answering. "Yeah. Be home soon." A lie I told with the same ease I once told myself I was over Mitch.

But I wasn't over him.

And the worst part? He knew it.

Our eyes met. That was all it took.

He excused himself from the group, crossing the room like a man who already knew the answer to the question he hadn't yet asked.

"Damn, Emileigh. That dress is disobedient," he said, voice low, eyes locked on mine.

I tried to laugh. Tried to roll my eyes. Tried to remember that I was supposed to be in love with someone else.

But my body betrayed me first.

"You shouldn't be here," I whispered.

He leaned in. "Neither should you."

And just like that, I was twenty-four again, back in his passenger seat, my lipstick smudged and my boundaries blurred.

We danced around it for another hour. Polite conversation. Thinly veiled innuendos. Shared memories dressed as jokes.

But when he brushed his fingers along the small of my back as I walked past him to get another drink, I felt my legs weaken.

He didn't follow me.

He didn't have to.

He knew I'd come back.

Because chaos doesn't chase peace   , it seduces it.

And I was already slipping.

I caught my breath in the hallway, one hand braced against the cool marble wall, the other gripping my champagne flute like it could steady the storm inside me.

I hated that he still had that power.

Mitch was the kind of man who didn't need to touch you to make you feel him. He just had to look at you long enough, hard enough, and all your good intentions would start to unravel like cheap thread.

And mine were already fraying.

I should've left. Should've called an Uber. Should've gone home to Jake, who was probably watching the game and thinking about what takeout to order.

But the truth was, I didn't want to go home.

I wanted to feel something.

I wanted to be wanted.

The elevator dinged behind me. I turned to see Mitch leaning against the frame, one hand in his pocket, the other holding a room key.

"Just wanted to make sure you weren't lost," he said, voice velvet-smooth.

"I'm not."

He held out the key. "Room 1704. If you're curious."

I didn't take it. But I didn't walk away either.

He slid it onto the small table by the wall and walked away without looking back.

That should've been the end of it.

But I stood there. Ten seconds. Then twenty.

Then I picked up the key. And with trembling hands and a heart full of contradictions, I followed him upstairs.

The elevator ride felt like purgatory. Silent. Heavy. My reflection in the mirrored walls was a stranger—lips parted, eyes glassy, a woman halfway between resistance and surrender.

When the doors slid open, he didn't touch me. Just walked ahead like he trusted I'd follow.

Room 1704.

He slid the keycard into the lock and opened the door with practiced ease. The suite was dimly lit, all golden lamps and shadows. Expensive. Cold. Beautiful in the way danger often is.

I hovered at the threshold.

"You're not here for coffee," he said, slipping off his jacket and tossing it over the armchair.

"I shouldn't be here at all."

"But you are."

He crossed the room slowly, like a lion stalking prey, and stopped just short of touching me.

"I won't force you," he said. "I never had to."

That's what did it.

I stepped into the room.

I didn't undress. He didn't ask. We kissed like addicts sharing a relapse. Everything we weren't supposed to be, pouring out between gasps and grazed skin.

It wasn't love.

It was history.

It was muscle memory and emotional scar tissue.

He peeled the dress down my arms like he was unwrapping a secret he already knew too well.

And when he finally entered me, it wasn't gentle.

It was desperate.

And I let him have all of me—because it was easier than admitting how broken I still was.

Because pain has a rhythm   , and that night, I danced to it.

Afterward, I lay in silence, staring at the ceiling while Mitch snored softly beside me. The room was still, except for the slow spin of the ceiling fan and the throb of shame pressing against my chest.

My phone buzzed on the nightstand. Three messages. All from Jake.

9:47 PM: *You okay? Haven't heard from you.*

10:15 PM: *Babe?*

11:02 PM: *I'm worried. Please call me.*

I couldn't move. I couldn't respond. I just stared at the screen until the light faded.

This wasn't supposed to happen. I wasn't supposed to be this girl. Not anymore.

I slid out of bed quietly and grabbed my dress from the floor. It smelled like cologne and guilt. The shower steamed quickly, but no amount of water could wash away what I'd done.

When I stepped out, Mitch was awake, propped on one elbow, watching me.

"You always disappear after," he said, voice scratchy.

"I wasn't planning to be here at all."

"But you were."

I didn't have the strength to argue. I zipped my dress, slipped on my heels, and gave him one last look—equal parts resentment and regret.

"Goodbye, Mitch."

"You'll be back," he said, too confidently.

I didn't answer.

Because I wasn't sure if he was wrong.

I took the elevator down alone, each floor a reminder of how far I'd let myself fall.

By the time I stepped outside, the cool night air slapped my skin like penance. I stood on the curb trying to collect myself, but guilt had a way of wrapping itself around my lungs, making it hard to breathe.

I didn't call a car. I walked.

Past the velvet ropes and doormen. Past the curious eyes of strangers. Past the version of myself I thought I had outgrown.

It was nearly midnight by the time I reached Jake's place. The lights were off, but I knew he was awake. He never really slept when I was out late.

I let myself in with the spare key he insisted I keep. The apartment smelled like him—cedarwood and comfort.

He was on the couch, TV glowing in the dark, but his eyes found mine the moment I stepped inside.

"Hey," he said softly. "You okay?"

No judgment. No anger. Just a concern.

And that made it worse.

I nodded. "Long night."

He held his arms open.

And like the coward I was, I crawled into them, carrying a secret I had no intention of confessing.

Because love, real love, is quiet. Steady. Safe.

And I didn't know how to live in that kind of love.

Yet.

Jake held me like I was whole. Like I hadn't just given a piece of myself to a man who saw me as nothing more than a pastime.

He kissed the top of my head and whispered, "I missed you."

I closed my eyes and willed the tears not to fall.

The silence between us felt sacred—like a promise I didn't deserve. And yet, he gave it freely.

I spent the night in his bed, his arms wrapped around me like armor. But my mind was a war zone.

Sleep came in fragments. Images of Mitch's hands. Jake's eyes. My own reflection in the bathroom mirror, asking questions I had no honest answers for.

By morning, Jake was already in the kitchen, brewing coffee and humming some old-school R&B song. The smell of cinnamon toast filled the air, like he was trying to feed more than my body—trying to nourish whatever was broken inside me.

I leaned against the doorway, watching him, wondering what kind of man loves a woman who keeps breaking him with her silence.

"Morning, beautiful," he said, turning to me with a smile that made my chest ache.

"Morning."

I smiled back.

But it didn't reach my eyes.

Jake didn't seem to notice. Or maybe he did and chose not to say anything. That was the thing about him—he always gave me space to be what I couldn't name.

He handed me a mug of coffee, warm and sweet, just the way I liked it. I took a sip and let the quiet settle between us again.

"Anything on your agenda today?" he asked.

"Just the usual," I lied.

He nodded. "You want a ride?"

"No, I'll drive. I need the air."

He studied me for a beat too long. "Okay. Just… call me if you need anything."

I kissed his cheek and left before the truth could crawl up my throat.

The drive to work was a blur of traffic lights and self-loathing. My body was present, but my spirit lagged behind, somewhere in a hotel suite, wrapped in regret.

By the time I reached the office, I had pulled the mask back on—composed, polished, unbothered. My coworkers greeted me with smiles and compliments. I smiled back, pretending nothing about me had changed.

But inside, a storm was brewing.

And I didn't know how much longer I could keep pretending I wasn't standing in the rain.

At lunch, I sat alone in my car, picking at a salad I didn't want, staring out the windshield like it held the answers. My phone buzzed again—Jake.

"Thinking about you. Hope your day is better than it started."

I wanted to scream. To throw the phone out the window. Not because he did anything wrong, but because he did everything right. And I was the one tainting it.

Instead, I texted back a heart emoji and turned the radio up loud enough to drown my thoughts.

I made it through the day in pieces. Smiles here. Email replies there. Nods and small talk, and calendar reminders. All while my insides rotted under the weight of guilt.

By the time I got home, Jake had made dinner. Pasta, garlic bread, and a glass of red wine. He really was trying to love me into healing.

I didn't deserve him.

That night, when we lay in bed, he pulled me close and whispered, "You're all I've ever wanted, Em."

I almost confessed right then. The words sat on my tongue, thick and bitter.

But I swallowed them down.

Because I wasn't ready to lose him.

Not yet.

But secrets don't stay buried forever.

A week passed. Then two. I avoided Mitch like a habit I was trying to break. Deleted his number. Blocked his socials. Anything to convince myself that the moment of weakness was just that—a moment.

Jake remained steady. Sweet. Oblivious.

He talked about taking a trip. Just the two of us. "Maybe the mountains," he said one night while we folded laundry. "Or the beach. Somewhere quiet."

I nodded like I could picture it.

But all I could see was the hotel room. Room 1704. My heels are on the floor. Mitch's breath in my ear.

The guilt ate at me like rust.

Still, I smiled. Still, I said yes.

Still, I let him dream about a future I had already soiled.

Because that's what broken people do when they're pretending to be whole.

We perform.

And I was putting on the show of my life.

Flawless makeup. Tight routines. Hollow smiles that passed for happiness. I even started attending brunches again, letting the girls gush about their partners and planners and pregnancies, while I sipped mimosas and bit my tongue.

No one knew. Not even my best friend.

Jake kept talking about the trip. He booked the cabin. Sent me links to hiking gear. Told me he wanted to watch the stars with me and talk about forever.

I wanted to say no.

I wanted to scream that I didn't deserve forever.

But I just kissed him and said I couldn't wait.

And then one afternoon, everything changed.

I got a text.

From an unknown number.

"We both know it wasn't just a moment."

No name. No context.

But I knew.

Mitch.

My hands trembled as I deleted the message, my chest tight with panic.

The past always has a way of circling back.

And mine had just found its way to my doorstep.

I spent the rest of the day in a haze. Paranoid. Shaken. Checking my phone every few minutes, like the message might reappear or multiply.

It didn't.

But the damage was done.

By the time Jake came home, I had nearly convinced myself it was nothing. Just Mitch being Mitch. Just a scare tactic. A reminder that he still had a grip on me, even if I was clawing my way out.

Jake wrapped his arms around me in the kitchen and kissed my forehead.

"You okay?" he asked.

"Yeah, just tired."

He nodded, never pushing. He trusted me. And that trust became the sharpest blade I carried.

That night, I lay awake long after Jake had fallen asleep, staring at the ceiling with tears silently sliding down my temples.

How long before the whole truth cracked open?

How long could I keep this mask in place before it crumbled?

And when it did…

Would there be anything left of me to love?

I didn't know.

But I clung to the hope that maybe—just maybe—Jake could love the version of me I was still becoming.

The next morning, I put on a brave face and showed up to life like it hadn't just unraveled in my hands. Work. Meetings. Emails. Smiles that didn't quite reach the surface.

Until my phone buzzed again.

A photo this time.

Me. Mitch. The hotel hallway. My hand is reaching for the key.

No words. Just proof.

My stomach dropped. I ducked into the nearest bathroom stall and locked the door.

I stared at the image for a long time, heart racing, vision blurring.

How long had he been watching me?

What did he want?

I deleted the message and turned off my phone. But the dread clung to me like a second skin.

This wasn't over.

Not by a long shot.

I drove home with my phone still off, anxiety chewing at the edges of every breath. Every shadow looked like a threat. Every pair of headlights felt like Mitch's eyes following me.

When I pulled into Jake's driveway, he was on the porch waiting. Smiling.

Safe.

I wanted to fall apart in his arms. Instead, I stood tall and forced a smile back.

He opened his arms. "Rough day?"

"The worst," I whispered into his shoulder.

He didn't ask questions. Just held me. Let me sink into him like he was the only thing keeping me tethered to the ground.

Maybe he was.

We ate dinner in silence. I watched him more than I ate. The way he chewed. The way his eyes lit up when he talked about work. The way he reached for my hand without thinking.

And for a fleeting moment, I imagined telling him everything.

But fear won.

Like it always did.

So I kissed him goodnight, curled into his side, and prayed that the past wouldn't steal the one good thing I hadn't completely ruined.

But prayers whispered in guilt rarely hold back the tide.

The next morning, Jake was gone before I woke up—left a note on the counter and a thermos of coffee just the way I liked it. Sweet, strong, dependable.

Just like him.

I stood in the kitchen for a long time, clutching that thermos like it could give me courage.

My phone was back on, and the silence from Mitch's side was louder than anything he could've sent. The damage was done, and now he had the upper hand.

That scared me more than any text ever could.

I checked the locks twice before I left. Triple-checked my rearview mirror on the way to work. The paranoia was becoming ritual.

I walked into the office like nothing was wrong—because what else could I do? Confess? Implode?

No. I kept moving.

Because if I stopped, even for a second, the truth might catch up.

And I wasn't ready to face it.

Not yet.

I buried myself in work. Poured over spreadsheets. Replied to emails within seconds. Smiled at the boss's jokes even when they made my skin crawl. Anything to keep the noise down.

But the silence in my head was deceptive.

It wasn't peace—it was pressure. And pressure always builds before it breaks.

During a meeting, my phone buzzed again.

A single message.

"You still taste like regret."

I nearly dropped the device.

I excused myself from the room, muttering something about cramps, and locked myself in the restroom.

I didn't cry. I didn't scream.

I stared at myself in the mirror and said aloud, "You need to fix this."

But I didn't know what fixing it meant.

Confession?

Running?

Lying better?

All of it felt like drowning.

And I was already breathless.

I pressed a damp paper towel to the back of my neck, trying to steady the pounding in my chest. The bathroom air felt thick, like guilt had seeped into the ventilation.

I knew then that silence was no longer protection—it was poison.

But I still wasn't ready to speak.

Not to Jake.

Not to anyone.

I walked out of the bathroom like nothing had happened, my face fixed into a practiced calm. My coworkers didn't notice. Or maybe they did, but chose not to ask.

When I got home that night, Jake had flowers waiting for me on the table. Sunflowers—my favorite. A note taped to the vase read: *For being the sunshine, even on your cloudy days.*

Tears threatened to break through, but I blinked them back. I hugged him tightly, and he held me like he could feel every war I was fighting.

We had dinner. We laughed. We made love like everything was right in the world.

But when he fell asleep, I lay beside him, staring at the ceiling, wondering how long I could keep living two lives.

Because the longer I stayed silent, the more I began to disappear.

And I didn't know who I'd be when the truth finally came out.

But I knew who I used to be.

A woman who ran from the mess instead of cleaning it up.

A woman who mistook survival for healing. Lust for love. Silence for strength.

Now I was all of them at once—and none of them completely.

The next morning, I woke before the alarm. The air in Jake's apartment felt heavy, like it knew something I didn't.

He stirred beside me and pulled me closer, pressing a kiss to my shoulder. "You okay?"

"Yeah," I whispered. "Just thinking."

"About what?"

"Everything."

He held me a little tighter, like he could hold the truth at bay with his arms alone.

We didn't talk much that morning. But when I left for work, he kissed me like it might be the last time.

And maybe, in a way, it was.

Because that day, everything started to unravel.

Mitch showed up.

In the parking lot.

Leaning against his car like he had every right to be there. Like my unraveling was his favorite show.

And I knew—whatever control I thought I had left, I was about to lose it.

He smiled like a man who knew my secrets, like he had tucked them in his back pocket and was waiting for the perfect moment to unfold them.

I didn't get out of my car right away.

He waited.

I could feel my pulse in my throat as I finally stepped out, determined not to give him the power of my fear.

"Mitch, what the hell are you doing here?" I snapped, lowering my voice but not my fire.

"Just saying hello."

"This isn't the place."

He shrugged, like boundaries were suggestions.

"I missed you," he said. "And I figured, why keep pretending?"

My stomach twisted.

"You need to leave."

He stepped closer. "I will. But not before I remind you who you really are when you're with me."

I stepped back. "You don't get to define me anymore."

He leaned in, voice low. "Then why are you still lying to him?"

I didn't answer. I couldn't.

He smirked, turned, and walked away like he'd already won.

And maybe, in that moment, he had.

Because I was shaking.

Because I couldn't breathe.

Because the truth was no longer content to stay buried—and neither was he.

Back at my desk, I couldn't focus. Words blurred, deadlines slipped past me like shadows. My hands trembled each time I reached for the mouse, and I flinched every time the office door creaked open.

Jake called around noon. I let it go to voicemail.

I knew if I heard his voice, I might break.

And I couldn't afford to break.

Not yet.

When I finally left work, I took the long way home. Past the old bookstore where Jake and I had our first real date. Past the diner where we shared fries and too many dreams.

Past every place that held a memory I wasn't sure I deserved anymore.

The sun was setting when I pulled into the driveway. Jake's car wasn't there. I exhaled with relief and dread.

I needed time.

Time to figure out how to tell the truth without losing the one thing that still made me feel like I was worth saving.

Because the truth was coming.

I could feel it rising like a storm.

And this time, I didn't know if I'd survive the fallout.

Chapter Two

Jake got home late.

I was curled on the couch in one of his hoodies, nursing a half-empty glass of wine I couldn't taste and scrolling aimlessly through a movie menu I had no intention of watching.

When he walked through the door, his presence filled the room like a warm front. He dropped his bag by the door, loosened his tie, and smiled at me like I was the most consistent part of his day.

"Hey, baby," he said, leaning down to kiss my forehead.

"Hey."

He studied me for a moment. "You okay?"

I nodded. "Just tired."

That lie was becoming second nature.

He didn't press. Just walked to the kitchen and started fixing a plate of leftovers like we were the kind of couple who had it all figured out.

And for a moment, I let myself believe we were.

But the truth had started knocking, and I could feel the door splintering.

I watched him eat, his face lit by the soft kitchen light, his eyes flickering between the food and whatever thoughts filled his head.

He looked peaceful.

And I hated that I was about to destroy that.

I took a deep breath, held it, and let it go slow. My palms were sweating, and my throat felt tight. But the words wouldn't come. Not yet.

So instead, I stood and walked over to him, wrapping my arms around his shoulders from behind.

He leaned into my touch.

"Long day?" I asked, my voice softer than I meant it to be.

He nodded. "Meetings all afternoon. Nothing new."

I kissed the top of his head and tried to memorize the way he smelled—clean soap and cinnamon spice.

Jake didn't know it, but I was collecting memories, just in case everything fell apart.

"I was thinking," he said, turning slightly to face me, "maybe this weekend we could go up to the cabin. Just us. No phones. No work. Just quiet."

My stomach twisted.

That's what he always gave me—quiet. Safety. Escape.

And I'd brought chaos into it.

"Yeah," I said, forcing a smile. "That sounds perfect."

He grinned and kissed me. "Good. It's already booked."

Of course it was. Jake planned for the future like it were a guarantee.

I wasn't sure I had a future with him anymore.

But I wanted to believe I did.

So I kissed him again—deeper this time—and let myself pretend.

Pretend that secrets didn't rot foundations.

Pretend that love could survive betrayal.

Pretend that I wasn't already drowning in what I hadn't said.

Because tonight, I needed the lie more than I needed the truth.

We made love in that quiet, deliberate way Jake had about him—like he was reading me instead of rushing me. He kissed my collarbone like it was sacred, held my waist like he was anchoring me, and whispered things that sounded too beautiful to be meant for someone like me.

And I let him.

I let him love me in a way that made me ache—because part of me believed it might be the last time.

Afterward, we lay tangled in sheets and silence. He traced circles on my arm, and I stared at the ceiling, waiting for peace that wouldn't come.

"Hey," he said after a while, voice low. "Do you ever think we'll get married?"

The question hit me like a slap.

Not because I hadn't thought about it.

But because I had.

Too many times.

I turned to look at him. He was serious, hopeful even. Eyes soft, mouth curved in the hint of a smile that knew no betrayal.

"I do," I whispered.

And I meant it.

Even if I didn't deserve it.

He kissed me again, then pulled me closer, and just like that, the conversation ended.

But the lie didn't.

It grew roots.

It seeped into my morning coffee, clung to my clothes, followed me like perfume I couldn't wash off. Every I love you, every future plan, every kiss goodnight layered over the truth I had buried too deep to dig out without bleeding.

Jake didn't notice. Or maybe he didn't want to.

He started talking more about the cabin trip—hikes, fire pits, maybe even taking some engagement photos if we were feeling bold. My stomach flipped every time he said *we*.

I nodded and smiled and pretended to be excited, but inside I was shrinking.

Mitch hadn't reached out again. Not directly.

But I still felt him. In the silence. In the corners. In the tight spaces of my mind where shame likes to hide.

I checked my phone obsessively, expecting another photo, another message, another threat dressed as flirtation.

Nothing came.

And somehow that made it worse.

Because now, I wasn't just hiding what happened.

I was waiting.

Waiting for the moment it all came crashing down.

And when it did, I had no idea who would survive the wreckage—me or the man I swore I'd never lie to.

The cabin was only two days away now.

Jake had packed the car twice already just to make sure everything fit—snacks, blankets, firewood, and a camera he borrowed from his brother. He was beaming, like we were heading into the best weekend of our lives.

And maybe we were.

Or maybe it would be the beginning of the end.

The night before we left, he curled up beside me and whispered, "I've never loved anyone like this before."

I didn't speak.

Because anything I said would feel like betrayal.

I just kissed him—soft, slow, like maybe I could transfer my apology through the way my lips trembled against his.

I don't know if he felt it.

But I did.

The next morning, we hit the road before sunrise. The mountains waited like open arms, ready to hold whatever pieces we brought with us.

And God knows, I brought mine in a fragile box of silence.

Wrapped in guilt.

Tied with trembling hands.

We drove in comfortable silence, the kind that only exists between two people who believe they've made it through the worst.

Jake reached for my hand somewhere between the interstate and the trees, and I gave it to him without hesitation, though inside, my grip was slipping.

The cabin was more beautiful than I remembered. Woodsy and warm, tucked into the slope of a mountain like it had been carved there by time.

Jake unloaded the car with the excitement of a man unwrapping the life he had always dreamed of. I followed him inside, trying to mimic his joy, trying not to look too long in the mirrors.

He built a fire. I unpacked the wine. We settled into the rhythm of something that almost felt like peace.

That night, we sat on the deck wrapped in blankets, watching stars blink into view.

"You feel far away," Jake said softly.

I froze.

"Not on purpose," I whispered.

He nodded. "I know. I just miss you. The version of you who laughs with her whole body."

I looked away. "She's still in here."

"I believe you."

And somehow, that hurt more than doubt ever could.

I stood up and walked to the railing, needing the cold air more than I needed the warmth of his arms. The stars above us shimmered, unbothered by the weight of my deception.

Jake stayed quiet. He always gave me room when he sensed I was unraveling.

The silence stretched long between us until I finally whispered, "What if I'm not who you think I am?"

He looked at me, brow furrowed but soft. "Then I'll love whoever you are. Even if it's not who I expected."

I nearly collapsed under the weight of that grace.

But grace without truth is just another lie.

And I'd had enough of those.

I opened my mouth to speak, but the words lodged in my throat.

Jake crossed the deck and wrapped his arms around me from behind. "You don't have to carry whatever it is alone."

Tears welled in my eyes, but I blinked them away.

Not yet.

I wasn't ready to lose him.

Even if I'd already broken us.

So I leaned into him instead, letting the silence say what I couldn't.

And the stars kept watching.

Quiet witnesses to a woman standing on the edge of her own confession.

We stayed that way for a while—his chest against my back, his hands folded over my middle like a promise. Like an anchor.

And yet, I still felt adrift.

Eventually, we went inside. Jake stoked the fire while I poured two glasses of wine we wouldn't finish.

We curled up on the rug, half-tangled in a blanket, and watched the flames dance without speaking.

There was something holy about the hush between us. Something I didn't want to desecrate.

But secrets have weight, and mine was starting to smother all that softness.

Jake reached for my hand again.

"I'm happy you're here," he said.

I nodded, unable to speak.

He pressed his forehead to mine and whispered, "I love you, Em."

I swallowed hard. "I love you too."

And in that moment, it was the truest lie I'd ever told.

Because I did love him.

And that's what made it unforgivable.

Not the act.

Not the guilt.

But the fact that I could look into the eyes of the one man who never failed me and still let the lie settle between us like it belonged there.

I barely slept that night.

Jake, on the other hand, slept like he had nothing to fear.

He held me close, our legs tangled, his breath warm against my neck—an unspoken vow that I was safe here.

But safety didn't exist where deception lived.

And by morning, I knew something had to change.

I made coffee while he showered, the cabin filling with the scent of roasted beans and slow-burning regret.

The air was thinner that day, the wind louder. Maybe it was just my conscience roaring louder than usual.

Jake came down smiling, hair damp, hoodie slung over his shoulder. "Let's take a hike after breakfast," he said. "I found a trail online—secluded, quiet. Perfect."

I nodded, though everything in me screamed.

Because quiet trails didn't just echo your footsteps.

They echoed your truths.

And I wasn't sure mine was ready to be heard out loud.

We ate breakfast in near silence—just the sound of silverware against ceramic and the occasional hum from Jake as he packed a small day bag. He didn't seem to notice I barely touched my food.

Or maybe he did.

And like always, he gave me space to unravel.

We set off just after nine. The trail wound through a canopy of gold and rust-colored leaves, each step cushioned by the softness of late-autumn earth. It should have felt peaceful.

It didn't.

Every branch that cracked underfoot made me flinch. Every breeze felt like it whispered, *Tell him.*

Half an hour in, we came to a clearing. Jake dropped his bag, stretched his arms, and looked at me with a kind of tenderness that made my stomach turn.

"This," he said, gesturing around us, "feels like the rest of our life."

I looked away.

"It could be," I murmured.

He walked over, brushing hair from my face. "Em... I know something's been off. You don't have to say it now. But when you're ready, I'm here."

My chest ached.

This was the moment.

I opened my mouth—

And a scream split the forest.

Not mine.

Farther off. Female. Panicked.

Jake's eyes widened. He grabbed his bag and bolted toward the sound.

And just like that, the confession was gone.

Swallowed by the trees.

I stood frozen for a heartbeat, every nerve in my body screaming to run after him—but my legs refused. Fear anchored me to the spot, not just of what the scream meant, but of the timing.

Why now?

Why here?

It felt like a divine interruption. Or karmic delay.

Eventually, instinct overrode hesitation, and I took off in the direction Jake had gone, branches whipping at my arms and ankles as the woods swallowed me, too.

I followed the sound of his voice.

"Hey! We're coming! Are you okay?"

Another cry echoed through the trees. Closer this time.

I broke through a thicket and into another small clearing. Jake was kneeling beside a woman, probably mid-thirties, her leg twisted at a sickening angle beneath her. Tears streaked her dirt-smudged face.

"I think I stepped off the trail," she sobbed. "I heard something and just—"

Jake looked up at me. "Call for help. There's no signal here. Try back up the hill."

I nodded, breathless, and turned to climb back.

But before I left the clearing, I glanced back.

Jake was holding her hand.

Gentle. Steady. Present.

The way he always was.

And in that moment, I realized the confession could wait a little longer.

Because the truth might've been mine to tell.

But he was still everyone's hero.

It was in his nature to show up, to anchor chaos with calm, to offer his steadiness without ever asking for anything in return.

And maybe that's what scared me most.

Because eventually, he would ask for the one thing I'd already broken: trust.

I hiked back to higher ground, every step an internal argument. My phone finally lit up with a weak signal and a faint bar of hope. I called 911, gave them our coordinates, and turned back before they could ask for too many details.

By the time I made it back, Jake had wrapped the woman's ankle in his jacket and was talking to her in that soft, assured tone I knew too well. She was still crying, but now it was from pain—not fear.

He looked up as I approached. "They're on their way?"

"Yeah," I nodded. "Maybe twenty minutes."

"Good."

We waited with her in silence, and even then, his hand never left hers.

The paramedics arrived and carried her off the trail. Jake offered to ride along, but they assured him she'd be okay.

As we made our way back to the cabin, the air between us felt different—thinner, heavier.

He didn't ask about the moment I'd almost confessed.

And I didn't offer it.

Because now there was another lie to carry:

That my silence wasn't selfish.

That it was survival.

That's what I kept telling myself, anyway.

As the days passed, the memory of the injured woman faded, but the weight of my unspoken truth did not. It sat with me at breakfast. Followed me down the trails. Lingered behind Jake's every smile.

He was still planning a future.

And I was still hiding from it.

We spent one last night at the cabin before heading home. The fire crackled. Jake played some old soul record he found in the closet, and we slow-danced in the middle of the living room, barefoot and swaying like we hadn't been carrying a secret between us the entire trip.

"Don't ever leave me," he whispered against my ear.

I held him tighter.

"I don't plan to."

Another truth. Another lie.

We drove back in silence that felt like surrender. Not heavy, not light—just settled.

And that scared me.

Because settled things crack quietly.

And I was beginning to break.

Little things started slipping. Missed calls. Half-finished thoughts. Moments where I'd zone out in the middle of a sentence, and Jake would tilt his head and ask if I was okay.

I always said yes.

But my reflection told the truth. Dark circles. Tighter shoulders. That nervous twitch in my jaw, I thought I'd outgrown.

It didn't help that Mitch had gone silent again.

No texts.

No cryptic messages.

Just a vacuum where tension used to be. And somehow, that was worse.

Because silence, in the wrong hands, is a strategy.

One night, Jake brought home takeout and a bottle of wine. He lit candles. Played music. Tried to bring back the version of us that wasn't haunted by everything unsaid.

"Tell me something real," he said as we sat cross-legged on the living room floor.

I looked at him—really looked at him.

And my mouth opened.

But again, the words didn't come.

Because the closer I got to the truth, the more I felt like I'd shatter under it.

So instead, I leaned forward, kissed him slow, and whispered, "I love you."

He smiled.

And for a moment, I almost believed myself.

But belief without confession is just a delay of consequence.

And mine was coming.

Jake left early the next morning to help his sister move. I stayed behind, claiming I needed to catch up on some writing.

What I really needed was stillness—some kind of divine clarity to tell me how to fix the hole I'd torn through everything good.

The house was too quiet. My guilt echoed louder in that silence.

I sat at the kitchen table, phone in hand, heart racing.

And then I did something stupid.

I texted Mitch.

"What do you want?"

The reply was instant.

"You."

Three letters. One weapon.

I stared at the screen, not breathing.

"Leave me alone." I typed.

But I didn't send it.

Instead, I deleted the thread.

I tossed my phone across the table and buried my face in my hands.

I was unraveling.

And the worst part was—I didn't know if I wanted to stop.

There was something addictive about the chaos, the sharp edge of danger that made the quiet feel suffocating.

Jake's love was a lullaby.

Mitch's attention was a scream.

And somewhere inside me, the scream was winning.

I got up from the table and paced the living room, adrenaline prickling beneath my skin like a thousand invisible splinters.

I didn't want Mitch.

I wanted the version of myself I used to be when I had nothing to lose. The girl who didn't know better. The one who thought survival meant surrendering to whichever man roared loudest.

But I wasn't her anymore.

Or maybe I still was.

The front door opened.

I jumped.

But it was only Jake—back early, smiling, arms full of groceries and a bottle of wine.

"Thought I'd surprise you," he said.

And God, did he.

I forced a smile as he kissed my cheek.

"Everything okay?" he asked, reading my face like a familiar book.

I nodded.

Lied.

And prayed he wouldn't read the next chapter.

Because that chapter was soaked in guilt.

It smelled like hotel linens and regret. It tasted like wine and deception. It pulsed beneath my skin every time Jake touched me, gentle and trusting, the way a man loves when he has no idea he's bleeding.

We made dinner together.

Pasta. Garlic bread. His favorite playlist hums low in the background.

He talked about his sister's new place, how happy she looked. I nodded, stirred the sauce, and laughed in the right places. Performed love like it was a role I'd rehearsed a thousand times.

But I felt hollow.

Like I was a house with no foundation—pretty on the outside, but one tremor away from collapse.

After dinner, we curled up on the couch, his arm around me, my head on his chest. The world should've felt soft. Safe.

Instead, every heartbeat I heard in his chest made mine stutter.

I wanted to tell him.

So badly.

But the silence had become its own kind of comfort.

And I wasn't sure who I was without it.

The silence had become a second skin—thin, fragile, but just thick enough to hide the truth.

And I wore it like armor.

Jake fell asleep with his hand resting on my hip, his breath slow and even, like he was sure I'd still be there in the morning.

I stared at the ceiling.

The darkness felt louder than usual, like it was waiting for something to break.

And maybe I was.

Because all I could think about was what it would feel like to be free of it—to say the words, to take whatever came next and finally stop living in the space between betrayal and redemption.

But when I turned to face him, he looked so peaceful.

And peace, I realized, was the one thing I could never give him again.

So I closed my eyes.

And for one more night, I chose silence.

Again.

And for one more night, I chose silence.

Again.

The next morning, I watched Jake pack his gym bag, towel draped over one shoulder, humming as if nothing in our world was cracked. And maybe to him, nothing was.

He kissed me on the forehead before he left. "Back in an hour."

I nodded, pretending to sip my coffee.

The door clicked shut.

And that's when I exhaled.

Not just breath—but guilt. Fear. The weight of one more secret layered onto the last.

I set the mug down and walked into the bathroom. Stared at myself in the mirror. The woman looking back didn't flinch. She didn't cry.

She was just tired.

Of hiding.

Of lying.

Of loving someone who deserved so much better.

I walked back into the bedroom and grabbed my phone from the nightstand.

No texts from Mitch.

No threats.

No clues that he was anywhere near.

And yet, the tension in my body told a different story.

Because absence isn't always peace.

Sometimes, it's a setup.

And I had a feeling the next chapter was already being written—

With or without my permission.

The rest of the morning moved like fog. I cleaned things that weren't dirty. Rearranged picture frames. Folded blankets that were already neat. All the small, desperate rituals of a woman trying to feel in control.

By the time Jake returned, sweaty and glowing from his workout, I had composed myself back into the version of me he recognized.

He wrapped his arms around me from behind and kissed my neck. "Miss me?"

"Always," I said, without hesitation.

And again, it wasn't a lie.

Just not the whole truth.

We showered. Made brunch. Talked about nothing. It was all so painfully normal that I nearly convinced myself I hadn't texted Mitch at all.

Until the doorbell rang.

Jake looked at me. "You expecting someone?"

I shook my head.

He walked to the door and peeked through the window.

Then turned back, confused.

"It's just a package."

Relief flooded me—until he bent to pick it up and paused.

He stared at the label.

"Why does this have your maiden name?"

My heart stuttered.

"I—I don't know."

But I did.

And as he brought it inside, setting it on the table, my hands trembled.

Because I hadn't ordered anything.

And I had a terrible feeling Mitch just had.

I stared at the box sitting on the table like it was ticking.

My name—my maiden name—printed in bold across the label. No return address. No note. Just weight and implication.

Jake tore the tape open casually, like he was unwrapping something harmless.

But my stomach was already in knots.

Inside was a smaller box. Black. Matte. Wrapped in a blood-red ribbon.

Jake tilted his head. "You sure this isn't for you?"

I didn't answer. Couldn't.

He untied the ribbon and opened it.

Inside was a single item.

A key.

Attached to it was a photo.

Jake picked it up slowly, flipping it over. I stepped forward instinctively, my pulse hammering.

He froze.

His eyes locked on mine.

"Emileigh… what is this?"

I didn't need to look.

I already knew.

It was the photo from the hotel hallway.

Me. Reaching for the key. Mitch was in the background, watching like he owned me.

The room spun.

And just like that, silence was no longer an option.

Jake held the photo like it was on fire—like it burned just to touch it.

"Emileigh," he said again, quieter this time. "What is this?"

I opened my mouth, but no words came.

He stepped back.

"Is that you?"

I nodded.

"And that's… Mitch?"

Another nod.

He looked down at the photo again, then at the key, as if it held answers I wouldn't give him.

"Tell me this isn't what it looks like," he said, voice cracking.

But it was.

It was exactly what it looked like.

I took a step forward, then stopped.

"I was going to tell you," I whispered.

"When?" he asked, louder now. "When were you planning to tell me you were back with him? That you were sneaking around behind my back?"

"It wasn't like that."

He laughed bitterly. "Then what was it like, Em? Because from where I'm standing, it looks like betrayal."

I covered my mouth as tears slipped down my cheeks. "It was one night."

Jake turned away, pacing, dragging a hand through his hair.

"One night," he repeated. "Like that makes it better."

"It was a mistake."

"Yeah," he said, spinning back toward me. "And now it's mine to live with, isn't it?"

I reached for him. "Jake—"

But he backed away like my touch was poison.

"I need to go."

And just like that, he walked out the door.

And this time, I didn't think he was coming back.

The door slammed, but the echo felt louder than the sound.

I stood there for what felt like hours, staring at the space where he had just been, the air still warm from his anger.

My knees gave out.

I collapsed onto the floor, the photo still sitting on the table like a taunt, like proof that my worst fear had finally caught up to me.

And it had.

Because Jake was gone.

For real this time.

Not just for a drive to clear his head. Not just to cool off.

Gone.

I reached for the key—the one from the photo—and held it in my palm.

It was cold. Heavy. The kind of object that shouldn't mean anything, but suddenly meant everything.

A door. A room. A memory I couldn't erase.

My phone buzzed.

A text.

From Mitch.

"Told you he couldn't handle the truth. You ready to come home now?"

I stared at the screen, numb.

I didn't respond.

I couldn't.

Because for the first time in a long time, I wasn't sure where home was.

Or if I had one left.

I sat on the floor until the light changed.

Morning slipped into afternoon. Afternoon bled into dusk. Still, I didn't move. Not when the sun disappeared. Not when the chill crept through the windows. Not even when the house went dark.

Grief will do that to you—steal your sense of time, of direction, of self.

My phone buzzed again.

I ignored it.

Eventually, I stood. Legs shaky, heart heavier than it had ever been. I walked to the sink and splashed cold water on my face, hoping it would wash away everything I couldn't say.

But nothing could touch that kind of shame.

I changed clothes. Braided my hair. Slipped on my coat and grabbed my keys.

There was only one place I could go.

Not to Mitch.

Never to Mitch.

But to the only person who might understand what it meant to ruin the very thing you prayed for.

I drove in silence.

No music. No radio. Just my thoughts scraping against each other like rusted blades.

When I pulled into the driveway, the porch light was on.

Mama always said she'd leave it on for me.

Even when I didn't deserve it.

Especially when I didn't.

I stepped onto the porch and knocked.

And for the first time in days, I let myself cry.

Because I was finally somewhere I didn't have to pretend.

Mama opened the door like she'd been standing on the other side of it all along.

She didn't ask questions.

She just pulled me in and held me—tight, silent, and strong in the way only a mother can be.

I crumbled in her arms.

She led me to the couch, wrapped a blanket around my shoulders, and sat beside me like she was guarding me from the world.

After a while, she said softly, "Jake?"

I shook my head.

Her lips pressed into a line, but she didn't push.

Instead, she stood, walked into the kitchen, and returned with a cup of tea and a slice of the pound cake she always baked when her heart was heavy.

I took a bite and almost sobbed.

Because it tasted like forgiveness.

"Baby," she said, sitting beside me again, "whatever it is, it's not the end unless you let it be."

"But what if it feels like it is?" I asked, voice cracking.

She brushed my hair behind my ear. "Then you sit in that feeling. And when you're ready, you get up and fight for what's left."

I nodded slowly, tears slipping down my cheeks again.

Because I didn't know what was left.

But I knew I wanted to try.

Even if it was just for me.

Even if Jake never came back.

Even if the only person I could save now… was myself.

Chapter Three

The morning after, Mama's couch felt different.

Not because the grief was gone. But because, for the first time in days, it wasn't alone. It shared space with something quieter—resolve.

I sat on the porch with a blanket wrapped around my shoulders and a chipped mug of coffee in my hands. The sky was still bruised with dawn, and everything smelled like pine and dew and second chances.

I wasn't sure what came next.

But I knew what couldn't continue.

Lying. Hiding. Shrinking.

Jake may have walked away, but he didn't take my voice with him.

And for the first time, I was ready to use it.

Mama came outside, wrapped in her own shawl, and sat beside me without a word. We didn't need them. She knew.

After a long pause, she said, "You still love him?"

I nodded. "With everything I have left."

"Then don't let silence be your ending."

I looked at her. "Even if he never forgives me?"

She smiled, soft and knowing. "Then at least you'll know you tried. That matters too."

I took a deep breath and let it out slowly.

Today, I   will start making things right.

Not just for Jake.

But for me.

I left Mama's house just after noon.

The sun was higher, warmer, as if the sky itself was giving me permission to try again.

I didn't have a plan—just a conviction.

I wouldn't beg.

But I would show up. Own it. Apologize in full, not in fragments.

Jake deserved that.

I drove by his place twice before I worked up the nerve to park. His car was there. Good. Terrifying. But good.

My hands trembled as I rang the bell.

No answer.

I knocked.

Still nothing.

I backed away from the door, heart sinking, when it opened behind me.

Jake stood there.

His face was unreadable. Tired. Hurt. Guarded.

He didn't say anything.

Neither did I.

Until I did.

"I'm not here to fix it," I said. "Because I know I can't. I'm just here to say the things I should've said before everything fell apart."

His arms were crossed, but he didn't interrupt.

"I was wrong," I continued. "For letting Mitch in. For lying. For staying silent when you gave me every reason not to be. I broke something sacred. And I don't expect you to forgive me. But I needed you to hear it from me—not from a photo. Not from a box. From my mouth. My heart."

A long silence followed.

Jake looked at me like he was trying to remember who I used to be.

And maybe wondering if I could ever be her again.

He stepped aside.

Not with a word, but with a gesture. An invitation.

My feet hesitated, but my heart answered for them.

I crossed the threshold, breath caught in my throat. Everything looked the same—but it didn't feel the same. The weight in the room was different.

Jake didn't sit. Neither did I.

He leaned against the wall, arms folded again.

"I don't know what to say," he finally admitted.

"You don't have to say anything," I said. "Not yet."

He exhaled. "That's the problem. I've got too much to say and no idea where to start."

"Then don't start with the pain," I said. "Start with whatever's still true."

He looked at me—really looked—and something in his eyes softened. Only a little, but it was enough.

"I loved you," he said.

My chest tightened. "Past tense?"

"I don't know."

I nodded. Fair.

"I never stopped loving you," I said. "Even when I was being the worst version of myself. Even when I betrayed what we had   , that love never left."

Jake pushed off the wall and walked toward me. Slowly. Carefully.

When he stopped in front of me, he asked, "Why did you do it?"

And this time, I told him the truth.

"Because I didn't believe I deserved you."

The words fell out before I could take them back.

Jake blinked.

"I kept waiting for you to leave," I continued. "For the moment, you realized I was too broken, too complicated, too much. And when it didn't happen—when you stayed—I panicked."

He didn't speak. His silence didn't feel cold. It felt like he was listening.

"I let Mitch in because he was familiar. Predictable. Toxic in a way I understood. And I hated that part of me still responded to him. But I hated even more that I didn't believe I was worthy of what you were giving me."

Jake's jaw flexed, but he said nothing.

"I self-sabotaged," I whispered. "Because it was easier than waiting for the other shoe to drop."

"You didn't even give me a chance to prove I wouldn't drop it," he said, voice low.

"I know," I said, tears slipping down. "And I'll regret that for the rest of my life."

A long pause stretched between us.

Then, softly, he asked, "Do you still want this? Us?"

"Yes," I said, without hesitation. "But I won't ask you to want me back. Not until you're ready. If ever."

He nodded slowly, like he needed to hear it out loud.

"Thank you," he said.

Not for the apology.

But for the truth.

And that—maybe more than anything—felt like the first piece of us being put back in place.

We sat in the quiet, surrounded by everything that had once felt unshakable.

And somehow, in that fragile stillness, something new began to stir.

Jake motioned toward the couch. I sat first. He followed, leaving just enough space between us for honesty to breathe.

"I don't know how to be near you without remembering," he said.

"You don't have to forget," I replied. "Just don't let it keep you from seeing what's still here."

He leaned forward, elbows on knees, head in his hands. "I didn't just love you, Emileigh. I trusted you with everything I had left."

"I know."

"And when I saw that photo—" he stopped himself, jaw tight. "It felt like someone punched a hole through the life I thought we were building."

I reached for him, gently. My fingers brushed his, light enough for him to pull away.

But he didn't.

"I'm not here to beg," I said again. "But if there's anything—anything at all—that we can salvage, I'll fight for it. Even if it takes everything I have."

Jake finally looked at me. His eyes were glassy, tired.

"I need time," he said.

"You can have it."

"And space."

"Take all you need."

He gave a faint nod.

Then he stood, walked to the door, and opened it.

A gentle dismissal.

I stood too, heart aching but strangely hopeful.

Because he didn't slam the door this time.

He held it open.

The air outside felt different—sharper, like it knew something sacred had just cracked open inside me.

I didn't cry.

Not because it didn't hurt. But because somewhere deep in my gut, I knew this wasn't the end.

I drove without music again, just the hum of the tires and the rhythm of my breath filling the silence.

But this time, the silence didn't feel empty.

It felt like a room.

Room to grow. To grieve. To become.

I passed Mitch's name on my phone screen twice.

Didn't answer.

Didn't need to.

He was part of the past I was done dragging into my future.

Instead, I parked in front of the old bookstore on Ashbury—one of the only places that had always felt safe.

I stepped inside, the smell of ink and dust welcoming me like an old friend.

I wasn't sure what I was looking for.

Until I found it.

A blank journal.

The kind with thick pages and a leather cover that smelled like courage.

I bought it without hesitation.

Because if I was going to rebuild my life, I needed to start with the truth.

My truth.

And this time, I wasn't going to write it for anyone else.

Just me.

Back at home, I lit a candle and opened the journal.

The first page stared at me—clean, untouched, waiting.

And for the first time in what felt like forever, I didn't feel the need to perform.

I picked up my pen and wrote:

Day One: I don't know who I am without the damage. But I'm ready to find out.

The ink bled into the page, but the shame didn't.

Each word after that came easier. Not perfect. Not polished. Just real.

I wrote about Jake.

About the moment I fell for him—not the night he first kissed me, but the time he watched me fall apart over burnt spaghetti and offered to order pizza like it was a love language.

I wrote about Mitch.

Not to justify. But to release.

I wrote about   myself.

Not the curated version I showed the world, but the woman beneath the masks—the one who still flinched at loud voices and second-guessed every compliment.

The woman was learning, slowly, that worth didn't come from who stayed or who left.

But from who she was when no one was watching.

I didn't know where this story was going.

But for the first time in a long time, I was willing to be the author again.

The next morning, I woke up before the sun.

Not out of anxiety. Not from restlessness.

But from something else entirely—peace.

It was fragile, unfamiliar. But it was mine.

I poured a cup of coffee, opened the window, and let the crisp morning air wrap itself around me. For once, I didn't check my phone. I didn't brace for a message that might shatter me. I just breathed.

Halfway through my second cup, the doorbell rang.

My heart leapt.

Not Jake. It was too soon for that.

I opened the door to find a small white envelope resting on the welcome mat.

No name.

No return address.

Just my initials—E.J.—written in Jake's handwriting.

My fingers trembled as I picked it up.

Inside was a single card. Blank, except for one line in the center:

"Healing isn't linear. But I see you trying."

Tears welled in my eyes.

No promises.

No apologies.

Just acknowledgment.

And somehow, that mattered more than all the words we hadn't said.

I pressed the card to my chest and whispered to no one in particular:

"I'm trying."

And this time, I meant it.

The card stayed on my nightstand.

I didn't reread it often. I didn't need to.

The words had already rooted themselves deep inside me, blooming every time I felt like slipping back into old habits.

That afternoon, I dusted off my old running shoes.

Not for the body.

For the mind.

I laced them tight, stepped outside, and let the pavement teach me something about pacing.

The first block was rough. My lungs protested. My legs screamed. My pride took a hit.

But I kept going.

Not to outrun my guilt.

To move with it. To make peace with the parts of me that had stalled in shame.

When I made it back home, sweaty and spent, I laughed. Out loud.

It felt ridiculous.

It felt good.

I stood in front of the mirror, cheeks flushed, hair a mess, and smiled at the reflection staring back.

She looked more like herself.

More like the woman Jake fell in love with.

But more importantly   , more like the woman I wanted to be.

Whole. Honest. Still healing. Still here.

Later that evening, I found myself staring at my phone again.

Not waiting.

Just... wondering.

Wondering if Jake was doing the same. Wondering if healing looked as brutal on him as it felt on me. Wondering if he still believed we had a chance.

I didn't text.

Didn't call.

Instead, I opened my journal and wrote a letter I never planned to send.

Jake,

I miss your silence more than I miss anyone's words. I miss the way you breathed beside me—like the world made sense, even when I didn't. I miss the questions you asked when I wasn't ready to be honest, and how you still waited for the answers anyway.

If you're wondering whether it mattered—this thing we had—it did. It does. It always will.

But I'm not writing this to beg. I'm writing it because I don't want to be a woman who keeps her truth locked away anymore.

So here's mine: I love you. Still. Deeply. Messily. Honestly. And whether or not you ever say it back, I needed to say it out loud.

For me.

I closed the journal slowly, the final word lingering in the room like incense.

And for once, I didn't cry.

Because sometimes, truth is its own form of healing.

Even when no one hears it but you.

The next day, I went back to work.

It wasn't glamorous—just emails, schedules, small talk in the break room—but it grounded me.

Normalcy felt like rebellion against the chaos I'd been drowning in.

Tina from accounting complimented my outfit. I didn't deflect.

Micah from marketing cracked a joke that made me laugh louder than I intended.

And for the first time in weeks, I didn't feel like I was playacting at being okay.

I wasn't fully okay.

But I was present.

During lunch, I walked outside and sat on the bench near the fountain. The breeze was soft. The sky was clear. I closed my eyes and let it wash over me.

I didn't think about Mitch.

I didn't obsess over Jake.

I thought about myself.

Who I wanted to be.

What I was finally ready to let go of.

I reached into my purse and pulled out my journal. Flipped to a fresh page.

Today I was not perfect. But I was honest. And kind. And brave. And that has to count for something.

I closed it, not with finality—but with quiet pride.

I was learning to celebrate the small wins.

And for a woman who once measured her worth by how well she held it all together, that felt like a revolution.

The next morning, I woke up to rain.

Not a storm—just a steady drizzle tapping the windows like a soft reminder: even growth needs water.

I sat by the window, knees pulled to my chest, coffee in hand, and watched the drops race down the glass.

It felt symbolic.

Everything did lately.

There was a quiet power in watching something fall and knowing it would nourish what came next.

My phone buzzed once on the counter.

I didn't rush to check it.

But when I did, my breath caught.

It was Jake.

A single message.

"Lunch?   "

No punctuation.

No context.

But everything in me knew—this wasn't just about food.

This was a beginning.

Or maybe... a continuation.

I stared at the screen for a full minute before typing back.

"Yes.   "

And for the first time in a long time, I didn't feel afraid.

I felt ready.

I met him at our old spot—the corner café with the mismatched chairs and the window seat we always fought over.

He was already there when I arrived, hands wrapped around a mug, eyes lost in the steam.

I stood in the doorway a moment longer than I should've.

He looked up. Our eyes met.

No smile.

But no scowl either.

Just… recognition.

I walked over slowly. He didn't stand, but he pulled out the chair across from him.

A peace offering.

I sat.

"Thanks for coming," he said, voice low but steady.

"Thanks for asking," I replied.

The silence that followed wasn't tense. It was layered— with history, with questions, with the kind of restraint that comes from two people trying not to drown each other in their truths.

"I've been reading your notes," Jake finally said.

My brows lifted. "Notes?"

He reached into his coat pocket and pulled out three small folded scraps of paper—pages from my journal I must have torn out and left tucked between things at his place. Or maybe I dropped them on purpose. I couldn't remember.

"You kept them? "

"I read them, " he said, eyes on me now. "More than once. "

My throat tightened. "And? "

He leaned back in his chair, eyes never leaving mine.

"They didn't fix anything. But they made something clear. You're not running anymore. "

I nodded.

He nodded back.

"That matters. "

And somehow, it did.

More than any apology ever could.

A waitress came by, breaking the spell. We both ordered without thinking—like muscle memory. He got the grilled cheese with tomato soup. I got the spinach salad with extra olives.

The same as always.

"You still don't eat fries? " he asked, a ghost of a smile flickering across his face.

"Only when I'm stealing yours, " I replied.

His laugh was short. Familiar. A little painful.

Our food came. We ate slowly, like the meal was part of the conversation.

Eventually, Jake set his spoon down. "I'm not saying I'm over it."

"I'm not asking you to be."

He nodded, seeming to appreciate that.

"But I do miss you," he added, almost reluctantly. "And not just the idea of us. I miss you."

I swallowed hard. "I miss you too."

"I need time."

"I know."

"But I don't want distance."

I looked up, surprised.

"We don't have to rush into anything," he said. "But maybe we can just... start seeing each other for real. No pretending we're fine when we're not. No hiding behind old habits."

"No disappearing into silence?"

He reached across the table, gently brushing his fingers against mine.

"No silence," he said.

My heart ached with hope.

It wasn't a clean slate.

But it was a choice.

And that was enough for now.

We lingered after the check was paid, neither of us ready to be the one to say goodbye.

The sky outside had turned gray again, the rain from earlier threatening to return. Jake looked out the window, then back at me.

"Do you want a ride? "

I shook my head gently. "No. I think I need to walk. "

He nodded, understanding. "Will you call me later? "

"I will. "

He stood first. I followed. We stepped outside together, shoulders nearly touching but not quite.

He opened his umbrella, held it above us both for a beat.

Then he smiled—soft, tentative.

"I'll see you soon. "

"Yeah, " I said. "You will. "

And for the first time in what felt like forever, I believed it.

I turned and walked in the opposite direction, my steps steady, the drizzle light against my skin.

I didn't look back.

Because I didn't need to.

Whatever came next, I wasn't walking into it with fear.

I was walking into it with truth.

And maybe—just maybe—with love again.

Chapter Four

The days that followed felt lighter—not because everything was fixed, but because I had stopped carrying it alone.

I settled into a rhythm. Morning journaling. Midday walks. Evening check-ins with myself.

Jake and I didn't talk every day, but when we did, it wasn't about the past. Not yet. It was about what we were reading, what we were eating, and how the sky looked that day.

It was soft. Intentional.

And I realized that sometimes, rebuilding doesn't start with construction.

It starts with quiet.

By showing up.

With listening.

One night, after a long shower and a cup of peppermint tea, I sat on the couch and replayed the sound of his voice in my head. How steady it had become again. How present.

I didn't know what we were yet.

But it felt like we were both choosing.

Choosing to stay in the room.

Choosing to hold space for the unknown.

And in a life marked by chaos and running, that felt revolutionary.

I turned off the lights, crawled into bed, and whispered to the dark:

"Thank you.   "

For the quiet.

For the healing.

For another chance to get it right—one honest step at a time.

The next morning, I woke to sunlight creeping through the blinds—soft and warm, like a blessing.

I stretched, lingered in bed for a few extra minutes, then reached for my journal.

Day Twenty-Seven: I don't want the old version of us back. I want something new. Something rooted in truth, not illusion. I'm not the woman I was. And he's not the man who walked away. Maybe that's a gift.

After coffee and a quick shower, I threw on a denim jacket over my favorite sundress and walked to the farmer's market.

It was bustling with weekend energy—kids running, couples laughing, vendors calling out the day's specials. I took my time, letting the moment unfold without rushing.

By the flower stall, I paused.

Jake once bought me a bouquet of sunflowers and lavender "because they looked like summer and peace."

I bought them for myself this time.

The vendor smiled knowingly. "Someone special?"

"Yes," I said, smiling back. "Me."

And I meant it.

I carried the bouquet home like it was sacred.

Because maybe it was.

A small offering to the woman I was becoming.

One who no longer waited for someone else to choose her.

One who had finally, bravely, chosen herself.

That night, I placed the sunflowers and lavender in a mason jar on the kitchen table. They stood tall, radiant—like they belonged there all along.

I made dinner for myself. Not a reheated leftover or a rushed salad. A real meal. Grilled salmon, roasted vegetables, jasmine rice. I played music—something soft, soulful—and let it fill the empty spaces.

I lit a candle.

Set the table.

Sat down across from the open journal like I was sharing the meal with the most honest version of me.

And I was.

Midway through dinner, my phone buzzed again.

Jake: *You made today feel normal again. Thank you.*

I stared at the message for a long time before replying.

Me: *Today wasn't normal. It was new. And I think I liked it that way.*

He didn't respond right away.

He didn't have to.

Some connections don't need constant conversation to stay alive.

Some just need honesty.

And presence.

After the dishes were washed and the music faded into quiet, I curled up on the couch and opened my journal one last time that day.

Day Twenty-Seven (continued): Maybe healing isn't about becoming someone else. Maybe it's about remembering who I was before the world told me I had to be anything less.

The next day brought rain.

Not a storm—just a quiet, steady drizzle that softened everything it touched.

I opened the windows anyway, letting the scent of petrichor and peace settle in my space.

There was something sacred about rainy days—like the world giving permission to slow down.

I brewed tea, wrapped myself in a blanket, and reread my journal entries from the past few weeks.

They were raw. Messy. Beautiful.

A breadcrumb trail back to myself.

Mid-morning, Jake called.

Not a text. A call.

"Hey," I answered, surprised by how steady I sounded.

"Hey," he said, his voice just above a whisper. "You busy?"

"Not really. Just being still."

"I like that," he replied. "Mind if I join you?"

The pause was short, but meaningful.

"Only if you bring the stillness with you."

He chuckled. "Deal."

When he arrived, we didn't talk much.

He sat on the floor beside the couch, head leaned back, eyes closed. I handed him a cup of tea. He didn't ask for sugar. He never did.

And there, in the quiet, with nothing to prove and everything to feel, I realized something.

This was intimacy.

Not the kind forged in heat or haste—but in stillness. In breath. In being known, even in silence.

And I think—for the first time—I truly felt safe.

He stayed for hours.

We barely moved.

Every now and then, I'd glance down at him—eyes closed, fingers loosely wrapped around his mug—and wonder what he was thinking.

But I didn't ask.

I didn't need to know everything to feel close.

Eventually, he opened his eyes and looked up at me. "You still write poems?"

"Sometimes," I said, surprised he remembered.

"I'd like to read one. Someday."

"Someday," I agreed.

He stood then, slowly, as if waking from a dream. "I should go."

"Okay."

He didn't hug me. Didn't kiss me.

But as he walked toward the door, he paused, turned back, and said, "Thank you for letting me just... be."

I smiled. "Anytime."

When the door closed behind him, I didn't feel empty.

I felt full.

Because we were learning to love each other without losing ourselves.

And in a world that often demanded all or nothing, that felt like everything.

After he left, I stood in the doorway for a moment, listening to the soft hum of the world outside.

The rain had stopped.

The sky was still gray, but it no longer felt heavy.

I walked back into the living room, picked up his mug from the floor, and held it for a beat longer than necessary.

Still warm.

Like he left a part of himself here.

I washed it, dried it, and placed it gently on the shelf.

Then I did something I hadn't done in years.

I pulled out an old leather notebook—my poetry journal—and opened to a blank page.

Pen in hand, I hesitated. Not because I didn't know what to write.

But because I finally did.

He sat in my silence / like it was a song / and I let him hear / every word I hadn't said.

That's what it feels like / to be seen / without performing.

I closed the notebook, heart beating a little faster.

Not from fear.

From freedom.

There was still so much left to rebuild. So many chapters unwritten.

But for the first time in a long time, I wasn't afraid of the blank page.

I was excited to see what came next.

Later that evening, I lit a candle and let the flickering light fill the corners of the room.

There was something ceremonial about it—like I was marking a transition I couldn't yet name.

I turned on soft music, curled up in the oversized chair by the window, and wrapped myself in a throw blanket Jake had once left behind.

It still smelled like cedar and quiet strength.

My phone buzzed.

Jake: *What are you doing right now?*

Me: *Listening to Coltrane and pretending I have it all figured out.*

Jake: *That sounds like my kind of night.*

I smiled and set the phone down without replying.

Not because I didn't want to talk.

But because, for once, I didn't need to.

There was peace in knowing he was out there, thinking of me.

And peace in knowing I didn't need to chase it.

I sipped my tea slowly, letting the warmth center me.

Then I reached for my poetry journal again and added another line:

I don't need rescue / I need presence.

And today, mine was enough.

The next morning, I woke to sunlight—not the shy kind, but bold, golden beams that cut across my bed and kissed my shoulders.

It felt like an affirmation.

A new day.

A clean slate.

I stretched, yawned, and took a deep breath of lavender from the bouquet still blooming on my table.

The whole place felt alive. Or maybe it was just me.

I brewed coffee, toasted a bagel, and opened my journal again.

Day Twenty-Eight: Maybe healing isn't a straight line. Maybe it's a soft spiral—a return to places I thought I left behind, just to see them with new eyes.

I underlined it twice.

Jake hadn't texted again, and I hadn't expected him to. We were both finding our own rhythms now.

Around noon, I got dressed and walked to the bookstore downtown. The one with creaky floors and handwritten staff notes tucked into bestsellers.

I browsed aimlessly for a while before picking up a memoir about forgiveness and a slim book of poetry by a woman who once described grief as a house she learned to redecorate.

At the register, the cashier smiled at me.   "You look like someone who's starting over.   "

I blinked.

Then nodded.

"Yeah,   " I said.   "I guess I am.   "

And I walked out the door with stories in my hands and a strange, quiet kind of hope rising in my chest.

Later that afternoon, I curled up in my reading chair with the poetry book from the bookstore.

Each page felt like a mirror—some cracked, some whole—but all reflecting parts of myself I hadn't named yet.

One line stopped me cold:

"I stopped looking for closure and started looking for clarity."

I read it three times.

Then I whispered it out loud.

Closure had been my obsession for so long—trying to tie up the mess with a neat bow, make sense of pain, explain away the betrayals.

But maybe clarity was enough.

Clarity let me move forward without needing every answer.

I set the book down and pulled my knees to my chest.

Jake and I weren't fixed.

We weren't even defined.

But I knew where I stood.

And that was new.

The version of me who once begged for certainty would never recognize this woman—this calm, rooted, evolving woman who chose peace over proof.

I reached for my journal, flipped to the next page.

Day Twenty-Eight (continued): I don't need a conclusion. I need alignment. And today, I feel like I'm finally walking in it.

That evening, I took a long bath—lavender oil, candles, soft jazz echoing from the next room.

The water held me like an exhale I didn't know I was holding.

When I got out, I wrapped myself in a thick robe and stood in front of the mirror.

No makeup. No filters.

Just me.

And for the first time in years, I didn't rush past my own reflection.

I studied the soft curve of my jaw, the small scar on my collarbone, and the quiet in my eyes.

Not emptiness—just quiet.

A woman I was still learning to love.

A woman who didn't need someone else to validate her softness or sharpen her edges.

I whispered to the mirror, "You made it."

Then I smiled.

Not because everything was perfect.

But because everything was finally honest.

I turned off the lights, climbed into bed, and let the silence hold me.

Not as a void—but as a sanctuary.

And in the quiet, I made myself one last promise:

Never again will I apologize for taking up space in my own story.

The next morning, the sky was a perfect blue—the kind that made you believe in beginnings.

I threw on jeans and a soft cotton tee, then grabbed my journal and headed to the little coffee shop on 3rd Street. The one with the ivy climbing the brick walls and the barista who always spelled my name right.

I ordered an oat milk latte and settled into the corner booth by the window.

The world moved around me—laptops clacking, spoons stirring, voices humming in the background like music I didn't need to control.

And I wrote.

Not about Jake.

Not about the past.

But about the woman sitting in that booth.

The one who'd survived the storm.

The one who finally believed she was worth rescuing— and did it herself.

I looked up from my journal, watching as sunlight spilled across the floor and caught the edge of my cup.

I whispered, "Thank you," to no one in particular.

Because the truth was, I didn't need a grand moment or a sweeping gesture to know I was healing.

All I needed was this:

A blue sky. A warm drink. And a story I was finally proud to call mine.

As I stepped out of the coffee shop, the breeze wrapped around me like a soft promise.

I took the long way home.

Passed the bookstore, the flower stand, the mural on 9th Street where someone had painted a woman with her head tilted back and eyes closed—like she finally knew her worth.

I stopped to look at her longer than usual.

Today, she didn't feel like a stranger.

She felt like a mirror.

A few blocks later, I ran into Mariah—an old friend I hadn't seen since everything fell apart.

We hugged. She looked me up and down.

"You look... different.   "

I smiled.   "I feel different.   "

She nodded, eyes soft. "Whatever it is   , you wear it well."

We talked briefly—small things, light things—and then parted with promises to catch up soon.

I walked the rest of the way home with a strange calmness in my chest.

Not because I had all the answers.

But because I wasn't afraid of the questions anymore.

I unlocked my door, stepped inside, and set my journal on the table.

Then I whispered it again:

"Thank you."

Because healing wasn't loud.

It was consistent.

And today, I   showed up for myself again.

That evening, I sat on the floor with a cup of herbal tea, my back resting against the couch, legs stretched across the rug that still bore the faint stain of red wine from a night I'd rather forget.

Funny how things that used to haunt me now just existed—without shame, without weight.

Jake texted.

Jake: *Thinking about you. No pressure to reply. Just wanted you to know.*

I stared at the message.

No pressure. No demand. Just presence.

And for once, I didn't rush to respond.

I let myself sit with how that made me feel—wanted, not needed. Seen, not summoned.

When I finally replied, it was simple:

Me: *Thank you. That means more than you know.*

He didn't text back.

He didn't have to.

Some things live best in the quiet.

I sipped my tea and looked around the room—at the shelf of books I had promised to finish, the candle still flickering on the windowsill, the vase of wilting lavender now leaning but still fragrant.

Life didn't have to be perfectly arranged to be beautiful.

And neither did I.

So I sat with the mess and called it mine.

And for the first time, I didn't want to clean it up.

I just wanted to live in it.

The next day, I cleaned the apartment—not out of urgency, but intention.

I played music, opened the windows, and let the breeze sweep through the corners of the place like a gentle reset.

I didn't try to erase anything.

I just made space.

Space for peace. For joy. For whatever was coming next.

Halfway through folding laundry, I found an old sweatshirt of Jake's tucked behind the couch cushions—soft, worn, and still faintly scented with cedar.

I held it for a moment.

Then I pressed it to my face, breathing in the memory, the comfort, the ache.

And then I folded it and placed it in the drawer.

Not because I wanted to forget.

But because I was learning how to remember without unraveling.

Later, I stood in front of the mirror again—hair wild, face fresh, heart steady—and thought,

This is the kind of woman who survives.

Not because she's unbreakable.

But because she keeps choosing to piece herself back together.

Over and over.

And somehow, each time, she comes back stronger.

That night, I dreamed of the ocean.

Not crashing waves or violent tides—but calm, endless blue that stretched into forever.

I was standing at the edge of the shore, toes in the sand, the wind lifting my hair.

Jake stood beside me.

He didn't say anything.

He didn't have to.

We just stood there—two souls no longer running, no longer hiding.

When I woke, there were no tears.

Only a quiet fullness.

A sense that maybe we were finally finding our way—not back, but forward.

I rolled over, reached for my journal, and wrote without thinking:

Day Twenty-Nine: Healing is not always loud. Sometimes, it's just standing still in a place that used to scare you.

And I smiled.

Because today, I wasn't scared.

Not of the past.

Not of the future.

Not even the quiet between us.

Because the woman I was becoming had learned something vital:

Peace isn't the absence of struggle.

It's the presence of self.

And she had finally arrived.

Chapter Five

The first sign that something was shifting came quietly.

Jake stopped texting every day.

Not abruptly.

Not cruelly.

But gradually—like a tide pulling back from the shore.

At first, I didn't notice.

I had filled my days with poetry and long walks and lavender tea.

I was healing.

And healing, I'd learned, often feels like enough—until it doesn't.

One evening, I picked up my phone and realized it had been three days.

Three days without a message.

Three days without his name lighting up my screen.

And that old ache—the one I thought I'd buried beneath journal pages and affirmations—rose like smoke in my chest.

I whispered to myself,   "It's okay. You're okay.   "

And I believed it.

Mostly.

But grief has a way of echoing through healed places.

And in that silence, I could hear everything I hadn't said out loud.

Everything I still wanted.

Everything I was still afraid to lose.

I didn't text him.

Not because I was angry.

But because I needed to know: Would he come back on his own?

Would I still matter if I stopped reaching?

The answers, I feared, were already arriving—one quiet day at a time.

The next morning, I lingered in bed longer than usual.

The sun poured in through the windows, golden and soft, but it couldn't quite warm the quiet gnawing inside me.

I checked my phone.

Nothing.

Still nothing.

I set it back down, face   down this time, and stared at the ceiling.

I didn't cry.

Didn't spiral.

I just lay there, suspended between disappointment and resolve.

Eventually, I got up, made coffee, and sat at the kitchen table where my journal waited like a friend who never gave up.

Day Thirty: Sometimes, the people who once made the silence feel safe become the reason it feels suffocating.

I underlined it.

Then I closed the journal.

Today, I wasn't going to chase closure.

I wasn't going to beg the universe for explanations.

I was going to live.

Even in the not knowing.

Even in the space between what was and what might never be again.

Because this was still my story.

And I refused to let anyone else write the next page for me.

Later that day, I went to the bookstore.

Not because I needed another book.

But because I needed to be somewhere that reminded me of how many endings had already turned into beginnings.

The owner greeted me with a nod, and I wandered to the back corner—the poetry section.

I ran my fingers along the spines, pausing at one with a navy blue cover and gold lettering that read: *What We Carry.*

I flipped it open to a random page.

Sometimes we call it love / when really, it's just fear of being alone.

It punched the air right out of me.

I bought it.

Took it to the park.

Found a quiet bench and read for hours while children laughed in the distance and a couple argued softly behind a tree.

The world didn't stop because my heart felt fragile.

And maybe that was the point.

Healing doesn't require silence.

It just asks you to keep showing up.

So I stayed on that bench, reading and underlining and letting the sun fall on my shoulders.

And when I finally stood to leave, I felt a little steadier.

Not because the ache had gone away.

But because I was no longer afraid to carry it.

That night, I couldn't sleep.

I lay in bed staring at the ceiling, counting the seconds between each slow blink.

Every part of me felt restless—like my body was still, but my soul was pacing.

I tried all the usual things: tea, music, deep breaths.

Nothing worked.

So I got up.

Wrapped myself in a cardigan and walked barefoot into the kitchen.

The floor was cold, grounding.

I poured a glass of water, stared out the window at the dark street below.

The world felt so still, so indifferent.

And maybe that's what I needed—a reminder that my pain wasn't the center of everything.

That I could feel this deeply, and the world would keep spinning.

I opened my journal again.

Day Thirty-One: Loneliness doesn't always feel like being alone. Sometimes, it's lying next to a silence you used to find comfort in—and realizing it no longer fits.

I closed the book and leaned my forehead against the window.

Outside, a car passed by slowly.

Headlights swept across the room, casting shadows on the walls like ghosts I hadn't named yet.

And I whispered to the dark, not expecting an answer:

"Am I enough without him?　"

The silence didn't argue.

But for the first time, it didn't sting either.

It just... was.

And maybe that was an answer in itself.

The next morning, I didn't check my phone right away.

I let the sun coax me out of bed, slow and golden, warm against my skin like a silent apology for the night before.

I made breakfast—eggs, toast, strawberries—and ate on the balcony, letting the breeze comb through my hair.

Across the street, a little boy chased bubbles while his mother laughed.

It struck me, suddenly, how beautiful ordinary life could be.

How, even in the ache of missing someone, the world continued to offer small miracles.

When I finally did pick up my phone, there it was:

Jake: *Hey. Been thinking about you. You okay?*

I stared at it.

Three days.

And that was all he had to say.

Part of me wanted to scream. Another part wanted to reply immediately. But the wisest part—the one I was still learning to trust—waited.

I typed, deleted, and retyped.

Then I finally sent:

Me: *I'm finding out what okay means without you.*

He didn't respond right away.

And that, too, was an answer.

I set the phone down and picked up my journal.

Sexcapades: Torn in Transit

Day Thirty-Two: Some people come back just to make sure the door is still unlocked. Today, I chose to close it.

Later that afternoon, I took a long walk through the neighborhood.

I passed by the old church with the broken bell, the one Jake and I used to laugh about every Sunday when it chimed off-beat.

It still did.

Only now, I didn't laugh.

I just listened.

Because even broken things still made music.

At the community garden, I paused by the sunflowers—tall and wild, their heads tilted toward the light like they knew something I didn't.

I stood there for a long time, breathing in the scent of dirt and bloom.

A woman walked by with her toddler, and the little girl pointed to a butterfly perched on the tallest petal.

"Look, Mama! It's flying without trying!"

Her voice rang out like a prayer I hadn't known I needed.

I smiled.

Because that's what I wanted too.

To fly without trying.

To rest in the wind and trust I wouldn't fall.

I walked home lighter.

Not because I had let go of everything.

But because I had loosened my grip on what wasn't mine to hold anymore.

And that, I realized, was its own kind of freedom.

That evening, I lit a candle and turned on my favorite playlist—the one filled with soft piano and old R&B tracks that reminded me of my mother's kitchen and slow Sunday mornings.

The scent of vanilla and amber filled the room, and for once, I didn't feel like something was missing.

I wasn't waiting for a knock on the door.

I wasn't bracing for a text that never came.

I was here.

Fully.

Present in a way I hadn't been in years.

I opened the poetry book again, flipping to a page I'd dog-eared.

"Healing doesn't always look like joy. Sometimes, it looks like choosing not to reopen the wound just to prove it still hurts."

I ran my fingers over the words like they were scripture.

Because they were.

They reminded me that I didn't need to explain my pain to anyone.

Not even Jake.

Especially not Jake.

Tonight wasn't about him.

It was about the woman who stayed.

The one who turned her apartment into a sanctuary.

The one who chose herself again and again until the choosing became muscle memory.

I poured a glass of wine and curled up in the corner of the couch.

And for the first time, being alone didn't feel like punishment.

It felt like peace.

The next morning, I woke up before the alarm.

The sky outside was still painted in hues of soft gray and lavender—like the day itself was deciding how gently it wanted to arrive.

I pulled the covers around me and just lay there, listening to the quiet hum of my apartment, the heartbeat of a life that had finally stopped begging for chaos.

Jake still hadn't responded.

And strangely, that absence no longer felt like rejection.

It felt like clarity.

Like a truth I'd known but hadn't been ready to say out loud.

He was part of my story.

But he wasn't the whole book.

I got up, made coffee, and sat by the window with my journal.

Day Thirty-Three: Healing isn't just about mending what was broken. It's about remembering you were whole long before anyone tried to convince you otherwise.

I underlined it twice.

Then I closed the book and whispered, "Amen."

Because sometimes, the truest prayers don't come from pulpits.

They come from the quiet decision to stay with yourself.

Even when the world forgets to.

That afternoon, I ran into Mitch.

Of all the places, it was the farmer's market—the one by the old train station that only popped up twice a month.

He was holding a bag of fresh peaches and laughing with a vendor when our eyes met.

For a moment, everything froze.

Then came the smile.

That crooked, infuriating smile that once melted every defense I had.

"Emileigh,   " he said, like it was both a greeting and a confession.

I swallowed the lump rising in my throat.   "Mitch.   "

He walked over slowly, as if the air between us needed time to remember us together.

"You look... grounded,   " he said.

It wasn't what I expected.

"And you look like you still don't know how to apologize."

His smile faltered, just a little. "Maybe not. But I know how to notice when someone's changed."

I tilted my head. "I have."

"I can see that."

We stood in silence, surrounded by the smells of basil and baked bread and too many memories.

"You deserve everything good, Emileigh. Even if it's not with me."

He meant it.

For the first time, I didn't need to ask if he did.

"Take care of yourself, Mitch."

I turned to leave before the ache could catch up.

And behind me, he didn't call out.

He just let me go.

And that was his apology.

That evening, I found myself standing in front of the mirror again.

Not searching for flaws.

Not adjusting my reflection to fit some imagined version of who I thought I needed to be.

Just standing there.

Taking in the woman who had been through war and still chose softness.

Who had every reason to harden and still opened her heart.

I touched the curve of my jaw, the softness under my eyes, the place just above my collarbone where Jake used to press his lips like a benediction.

I didn't flinch.

I didn't cry.

I whispered instead:

"You are still worthy of the kind of love that stays."

Then I lit a candle—not for him, not for us, but for the version of me that almost forgot her own glow.

And I stood in that light until I believed it.

Until I became it.

The next day, the sky broke open.

Rain fell in heavy sheets, drenching the city in a gray hush.

I stayed inside, wrapped in a sweater two sizes too big, sipping coffee from a chipped mug I couldn't bring myself to throw away.

Some things hold memories too sacred to discard.

Outside, the water streamed down the windows like tears I didn't need to cry.

I pulled a blanket over my legs and opened the book of poetry again.

This time, the line that found me read:

"Grief is love's residue—what's left when the body is gone but the heartbeat still echoes."

I closed the book.

Laid my hand over my chest.

Felt the steady thump of a heart that had broken but still kept time.

Still chose rhythm.

Still chose life.

Day Thirty-Four: You are allowed to outgrow the people who once felt like home.

I stared out the window as thunder rumbled in the distance.

And for once, I didn't feel the need to chase any more storms.

I had weathered enough.

Now, I was choosing calm.

Even if it came with its own kind of loneliness.

That night, I dreamed I was underwater.

Not drowning—just suspended in stillness, the weight of everything muted by the hush of deep blue.

I could see the surface above me, rippling like glass.

But I didn't swim toward it.

I just floated, arms outstretched, eyes wide open.

And in the dream, it didn't feel like fear.

It felt like surrender.

Like finally letting go of everything I'd been holding so tightly.

When I woke, my pillow was damp with sweat—or maybe tears. It didn't matter.

I reached for my journal in the dark.

Day Thirty-Five: Some days, healing feels like swimming in grief and choosing not to sink.

I didn't need a sunrise or a silver lining.

I just needed this moment.

This breath.

This quiet awareness that I was still here.

Still trying.

Still choosing myself, even in the darkness.

Especially in the darkness.

Because maybe that's where the truest kind of love begins—with the parts of us we stop hiding from ourselves.

The following morning, I felt a shift.

It wasn't dramatic—no grand revelation or sudden clarity.

Just a small, quiet knowing.

Like something inside me had finally exhaled.

I made a cup of tea and sat by the window, watching the world stretch into a new day.

Across the street, a man held his daughter's hand as she skipped beside him, her laughter echoing through the chill.

I smiled.

Not because it filled the emptiness.

But because it reminded me that joy still existed—even if it didn't always belong to me.

And maybe that was enough for today.

Day Thirty-Six: There is beauty in letting go of timelines and simply trusting the pace of your own becoming.

I closed the journal and pressed it to my chest.

Jake was a chapter.

Mitch was a chapter.

But I was the book.

And the story wasn't finished yet.

Not even close.

Later that afternoon, I finally opened the box.

The one in the back of the closet, taped shut and wrapped in a sweatshirt I hadn't worn since the day Jake first told me he loved me.

I didn't open it to torture myself.

I opened it because I was ready.

Inside were the pieces of a life I hadn't dared to look at in months—old love notes, a playlist burned onto a CD, the Polaroid of us from that night at the jazz bar, where he said I made silence sound like music.

I held it all.

Not with sorrow.

But with gratitude.

Because it happened.

Because it mattered.

Because even the endings deserve to be honored.

Day Thirty-Seven: Closure isn't about forgetting. It's about remembering without begging the past to rewrite itself.

I folded everything back inside.

Taped the box shut again.

Not because I wanted to hide it.

But because it no longer held power over me.

And that, more than anything, felt like freedom.

That night, I went to the rooftop.

It had become my quiet place—the one spot in the city where I could hear my thoughts echo back like gentle reminders.

The stars were faint behind the haze, but they were there.

Constant. Distant. Patient.

I brought a blanket and a cup of chamomile tea, wrapped myself in both, and stared up.

I thought of everything I'd survived.

The moments I thought would break me.

The ones that almost did.

And still—I was here.

Breathing. Becoming.

Day Thirty-Eight: Strength isn't loud. Sometimes, it whispers, "Try again tomorrow," and that's enough.

I whispered thank you to the sky.

To the girl I used to be.

To the woman I was becoming.

Then I closed my eyes and let the wind carry the rest.

Whatever tomorrow held, I would meet it.

Not with fear.

But with softness.

And that would be my superpower.

The next morning, I packed a small bag and drove out of the city.

No destination in mind—just an open road, a full tank, and the need to feel movement under me.

There was something sacred about the way the highway hummed beneath the wheels, like a prayer spoken without words.

I rolled down the windows and let the wind tangle my hair.

I didn't need music.

I needed the silence between the trees, the rhythm of tires on pavement, the freedom of not knowing where I'd end up.

Hours passed.

Eventually, I pulled over at a lookout point high above the valley.

The view stole my breath.

Mountains folded into each other like secrets.

Clouds draped the peaks like lace.

I sat on the hood of my car, legs dangling, heart wide open.

Day Thirty-Nine: Sometimes the best way to find yourself is to get completely lost.

I stayed there until the sky began to blush with dusk.

Then I turned the car around and headed home.

Not because I was done searching.

But because I'd remembered something important:

I wasn't running away.

I was returning to myself.

That evening, I returned home to find a letter slipped beneath my door.

No name. No return address. Just my name written in Jake's handwriting.

My breath caught.

I stared at it for a full minute before picking it up.

I took it to the kitchen, sat at the table, and held it like it might disappear.

Then I opened it.

The paper was soft, worn at the edges, like it had been folded and unfolded too many times.

Emileigh,

I've started this letter a hundred different ways, but none of them felt right. Maybe because nothing about this is easy. Not for me. And I doubt for you, either.

I didn't call because I didn't know what to say that wouldn't come out wrong. I didn't text because I was afraid of your silence. But I never stopped thinking about you. Missing you.

You once told me love doesn't live in promises—it lives in actions. And maybe this letter is too little, too late. But it's an action. It's me showing up, even if it's just on paper.

You changed me. And I don't know if I'll ever be ready to see you again. But I hope you're healing. I hope you're happy.

You deserve that.

Always,

Jake

I read it twice. Then a third time.

And I cried.

Not because I wanted him back.

But because I finally understood that closure doesn't always come in a conversation.

Sometimes, it comes in a folded piece of paper and a whispered, "thank you. "

The next morning, I stood in the shower longer than usual, letting the water hit my back like a soft drumbeat.

It wasn't about washing away anything.

It was about making room.

Room for breath.

Room for peace.

Room for whatever came next.

I didn't need a plan. I needed presence.

And for once, I had it.

Afterward, I stood at the mirror, wrapped in my towel and didn't rush to get dressed.

I stared at myself—bare, undone, whole.

The kind of whole that comes from breaking and rebuilding, not once, but over and over again.

Day Forty: Healing is not linear. It is circular. It brings you back to lessons you thought you'd already learned— until you finally live them without pain.

I traced the outline of my reflection with my eyes and smiled.

Because I wasn't just surviving anymore.

I was living.

And for the first time, that was enough.

That afternoon, I cleaned the apartment.

Not the kind of cleaning you do when company's coming over.

The kind you do when you're ready to reclaim space.

I opened the windows, let fresh air spill in, and turned the music up loud enough to drown out old ghosts.

I dusted corners I hadn't noticed in months.

Threw out takeout menus from restaurants I no longer ordered from.

Lit a new candle and moved the furniture just enough to make the space feel like a fresh start.

It wasn't about erasing memories.

It was about making space for new ones.

For laughter that didn't carry echoes.

For peace that didn't need permission.

Day Forty-One: Decluttering is a sacred act. It is a declaration that says, "I'm making room for what serves me."

By the time the sun dipped below the skyline, the apartment smelled like lavender and lemon.

It felt like mine again.

Not ours.

Not his.

Just mine.

And I liked it that way.

That evening, I made dinner from scratch.

Nothing fancy—just lemon garlic pasta with roasted vegetables and a glass of chilled white wine.

I set the table for one.

Folded the napkin just so.

Lit the candle in the center like it was a date with someone sacred.

Because it was.

Me.

I took my time with every bite, savoring the flavors, the silence, the intimacy of being alone without feeling lonely.

No TV. No distractions. Just the clink of my fork against the plate and the hum of my own thoughts.

Day Forty-Two: Solitude isn't empty. It's full of you.

When the meal was done, I washed the dishes slowly, dried each one with care, and placed them back in their rightful places.

Ritual, I realized, was its own kind of love.

And tonight, I gave that love to myself without apology.

The next morning, I walked to the bookstore.

The air was crisp, the kind that hinted at fall just around the corner.

I wore my favorite cardigan, the one Jake used to say made me look like a poet.

This time, I wore it for me.

Inside, the smell of paper and ink greeted me like an old friend.

I wandered the aisles without a list, letting my fingers graze the spines until one called out to me.

A memoir. A woman who rebuilt her life after betrayal.

It felt like fate.

I bought it without reading the back cover.

Sometimes, stories find us when we need them most.

Day Forty-Three: The right words have a way of showing up when you stop searching for them.

On the walk home, I stopped for a lavender latte and sat by the window, book in hand.

And as I read her story, I began to rewrite my own.

Not with regret.

But with reverence.

Because I was finally learning that healing wasn't about forgetting.

It was about remembering who I was before the hurt— and becoming her again, wiser.

That afternoon, I ran into an old friend from college at the flower shop on 8th.

We hugged, exchanged updates, and laughed about how life had aged us in ways both visible and invisible.

She asked how I was doing.

I paused.

Then smiled and said, "Becoming."

She blinked, then nodded like she understood exactly what that meant.

We chose flowers together—she picked sunflowers, I picked lilies.

Before we parted, she handed me a yellow bloom. "For joy," she said.

I pressed it to my nose and breathed in the sweet promise of it.

Day Forty-Four: Healing doesn't always look like therapy sessions and journal pages. Sometimes, it looks like fresh flowers and unexpected reunions.

I walked home with the bouquet in my arms and a softness in my chest.

Sometimes, the universe sends reminders when you're not even asking for them.

And today, mine came wrapped in petals and memory.

And it felt like grace.

That evening, I finally opened the last voice message Jake had sent weeks ago.

I had kept it buried under the weight of fear and what-ifs.

But something in me was ready now.

His voice came through the speaker—soft, steady, unsure.

"Hey, Emileigh... I don't know if you'll even listen to this, but I needed to try. I miss you. I miss us. And I'm sorry ...   for all of it. For the ways I didn't show up. For the silences. For the things I said and didn't say. You didn't deserve that. I hope you know that. And wherever you are right now, I just... I hope you're okay.   "

The message ended with a pause, like he wanted to say more but ran out of bravery.

I stared at the phone in my hand for a long time.

Then I deleted the message.

Not out of anger.

But because I no longer needed it to hold space in my life.

Day Forty-Five: Letting go is not the same as forgetting. It's choosing to move forward without dragging the weight of what no longer serves you.

And with that single press of a button, I made room for what might come next.

Something still unknown.

But finally—fully—mine.

The next morning, I wrote myself a love letter.

No expectations.

No performance.

Just honesty spilled across the page.

Dear Me,

You've carried so much. Still, you rise. Still, you hope. Still, you offer kindness when the world forgets how to be gentle.

You've walked through fire and came out softer, not bitter. That is your magic.

You are allowed to take up space. To rest. To rebuild without apology.

You are not too much. You are not too broken. You are becoming. Every day. In ways the past could never imagine.

I love you.

I folded the letter and placed it in my journal.

Not to be reread—but to be remembered.

Day Forty-Six: The most important relationship you'll ever have is the one you nurture with yourself.

And I was finally learning to love her—the woman in the mirror—with the kind of tenderness I once reserved for everyone else.

That evening, I sat beneath the fairy lights on my balcony, the journal open beside me, a glass of wine in hand.

The sky was painted in hues of lavender and rose, the kind of sunset that makes you believe in second chances.

A breeze moved through the trees, soft as forgiveness.

I pulled the blanket tighter around my shoulders and watched the light fade slowly, gently.

It reminded me that endings didn't always have to be loud.

Sometimes, they arrive quietly—like a sigh, like a letting go.

Day Forty-Seven: Peace doesn't always come with answers. Sometimes, it simply comes with acceptance.

I whispered a silent prayer of gratitude.

Not for what I lost.

But for what I'd found in the wreckage.

Me.

Whole, healing, and finally at home in my own skin.

And as night settled in, I knew:

I wasn't waiting anymore.

I was living.

The next morning, I didn't check my phone.

I didn't scroll through social media or respond to texts.

Instead, I let the quiet hold me.

I brewed coffee, opened the windows, and let the morning light spill across the hardwood floors.

Barefoot, I danced.

No music—just the rhythm of my own breath, the beat of a heart finally learning how to be enough on its own.

It wasn't performative.

It was sacred.

It was mine.

Day Forty-Eight: Joy doesn't need a reason. It only needs permission.

I gave myself that permission.

To feel good.

To feel whole.

To feel free.

Because healing isn't just about mending wounds.

It's about rediscovering the parts of yourself you thought were lost forever—and realizing they never left.

They were just waiting for the light to find them again.

That afternoon, I walked to the lake.

The path was lined with golden leaves, crunching softly beneath each step.

The air smelled like cedar and change.

At the water's edge, I sat on a worn bench and watched the ripples spread like whispered secrets.

A couple walked by, hand in hand.

A child tossed pebbles into the lake and squealed with delight.

Life was happening all around me—not in grand gestures, but in the simple, steady unfolding of ordinary beauty.

Day Forty-Nine: Sometimes, the most profound moments are the ones that don't demand to be remembered.

I closed my eyes and breathed it all in.

The stillness.

The clarity.

The reminder that healing didn't mean life would be perfect—it meant I was learning to be present in the imperfect.

And in that presence, I found peace.

Not the kind that arrives with fanfare.

But the kind that settles into your bones and stays.

That night, I stood in front of the mirror, dressed in a simple black slip—the one I used to save for special occasions.

But tonight, the occasion was me.

I lit candles around the room, let soft jazz pour from the speakers, and moved like my body had finally remembered it belonged to joy.

No one was watching.

No one needed to.

This wasn't a performance.

It was a reclamation.

I danced slow, hands trailing along my waist, across my chest, down my thighs—each touch a whispered reminder: You are still here. Still beautiful. Still worthy.

Day Fifty: Sensuality doesn't belong to anyone else. It's yours. Always has been.

I fell asleep that night, tangled in silk sheets and the kind of peace that only comes when you stop waiting for permission to feel alive.

And when I woke the next morning, I wasn't ashamed.

I was radiant.

The next day, I booked a solo trip to the coast.

Just three days. Just me.

No itinerary. No expectations.

Just the ocean, a journal, and the courage to be alone with my thoughts.

I packed light—breezy dresses, my favorite sandals, and the red swimsuit I once told myself I wasn't brave enough to wear.

This time, I packed it first.

Day Fifty-One: Growth is doing the thing you used to talk yourself out of.

As the train pulled away from the station, I watched the city blur into trees and sky.

And somewhere in between the quiet hum of the engine and the sun pouring through the window, I smiled.

Not because everything made sense.

But because, for once, I wasn't running.

I was arriving.

To the coast.

To the moment.

To myself.

When I arrived at the inn, it smelled like salt and lemon.

The walls were painted seafoam green, and the windows opened wide to let in the sound of waves.

I didn't unpack right away.

I changed into that red swimsuit, grabbed a towel, and walked straight to the water.

It was colder than I expected.

But I waded in anyway.

Step by step until the chill no longer shocked me.

Until I was weightless, floating, carried.

I tilted my head back, letting the sun warm my face.

Day Fifty-Two: Sometimes healing is just letting yourself be held—by the ocean, by time, by your own resilience.

I stayed like that for what felt like hours.

And when I returned to shore, something inside me felt new.

Not fixed.

But softened.

And that was enough.

That night, I sat on the inn's balcony with a blanket over my legs and a cup of chamomile tea in my hands.

The moon hung low over the water, casting a silver path across the waves.

I thought about the woman who had arrived here this morning—the one carrying remnants of old wounds, unsure if she could ever truly set them down.

And I thought about the woman sitting here now.

Softer, yes. But also stronger.

Not because the hurt was gone, but because it no longer defined her.

Day Fifty-Three: Strength isn't the absence of pain. It's the ability to hold joy alongside it.

I pulled the blanket tighter and breathed in the salt air.

This wasn't the end of my story.

But it was the end of something.

And the beginning of something else entirely.

Chapter Six would have to wait.

Tonight, I was content to simply be here.

Chapter Six

The next morning, I woke to the sound of waves breaking against the shore—and the faint, rhythmic knock on my door.

I sat up, heart picking up pace. The robe on the back of the chair felt too thin for the way my body hummed with curiosity.

When I opened the door, a man stood there holding a tray. Tall. Broad shoulders beneath a white linen shirt, sleeves rolled just enough to reveal forearms that hinted at strength without show.

"Breakfast," he said, voice warm like morning coffee. "The inn's kitchen thought you might enjoy it on your balcony."

But his eyes said something else. Something slower.

I stepped aside, letting him pass, the scent of salt and citrus following him inside.

He set the tray down and straightened, gaze catching mine just long enough to make the air between us shift.

"Anything else you need?"

I could have said no. I could have let him walk away.

Instead, I tilted my head. "Maybe later."

His mouth curved—just slightly—before he left, closing the door behind him.

Day Fifty-Four: Sometimes the invitation isn't in the words, but in the way the world pauses around them.

I sat with my coffee, watching the steam curl up into the air, and wondered if maybe my weekend at the coast was about to become something far less quiet.

I spent the morning pretending to read, though my eyes kept drifting toward the shoreline.

He was there.

Carrying crates from a small fishing boat that had pulled up to the dock, his shirt clinging to his back, damp from the mist. Every movement was unhurried, confident—like he had nothing to prove, and yet somehow, he proved everything.

When he glanced up, our eyes met. Just for a second. Long enough for me to feel it in the pit of my stomach.

I closed my book, more aware of my own pulse than the words I wasn't reading.

By noon, the sun had burned away the morning haze, and I decided on a walk through the village. Cobblestone streets wound between cafes and small art shops, each one spilling color and music into the salt-heavy air.

Halfway down the street, I heard his voice.

"Finding your way around?"

I turned to see him leaning against the doorway of a bookstore, a small smirk on his lips.

I smiled back, a little too quickly. "Trying to."

"Then let me help," he said, pushing off the frame and falling into step beside me.

And just like that, my quiet weekend became a story I knew I'd want to read again and again.

We wandered without a map, ducking into shops that smelled of old wood and salt, sharing small discoveries like secrets. He pointed out the best place to buy fresh bread, the corner café that served coffee strong enough to wake the dead, and the pier where sunsets looked like they'd been painted just for you.

At one stall, he picked up a seashell, holding it to my ear. "Hear that?"

I nodded, smiling at the familiar rush of sound. "The ocean?"

His eyes lingered on mine. "Or maybe it's your heartbeat."

The warmth that spread through me had nothing to do with the sun overhead.

We stopped for lunch at a café with tables spilling into the street, and he ordered for both of us—fresh oysters, warm bread, crisp white wine. When I raised an eyebrow, he only said, "Trust me."

And I did.

Halfway through the meal, a drop of wine clung to my bottom lip. He leaned in, thumb brushing it away, the touch slow, deliberate.

For a moment, I forgot about the oysters, the sun, even the people passing by.

The world narrowed to the space between his hand and my skin.

Day Fifty-Five: Sometimes desire arrives quietly, slipping in between breaths until you can't remember what it felt like to breathe without it.

After lunch, we wandered toward the far end of the pier, where the crowd thinned and the sound of the waves grew louder. A breeze lifted my hair, and before I could smooth it back, he reached out, tucking the strands behind my ear.

His fingers lingered just long enough for my breath to catch.

We leaned against the weathered railing, watching the water slap against the posts below.

"Ever gone sailing?" he asked.

I shook my head. "Closest I've come is a ferry ride."

A slow smile curved his lips. "Then you've never really felt the ocean."

His voice was low, the kind that slips under your skin and stays there.

He told me about night sails under a full moon, about the way the sea smells different when no land is in sight, about the quiet that feels like it's holding its breath.

I didn't realize I was leaning toward him until our arms brushed.

Day Fifty-Six: Some moments don't ask for permission. They just happen—and change you before you even notice.

That evening, the inn hosted a small gathering on the beach—a bonfire, soft music, and the scent of grilled seafood drifting through the air.

I spotted him near the fire, speaking with the owner, his laugh low and unhurried. When his eyes found mine, it was like the rest of the world blurred out.

He walked over, offering me a drink. "Try it," he said, handing me a glass. The first sip was cool and citrusy, with a faint kick of something I couldn't place.

"Rum," he explained, watching my reaction.

We stood close enough that the heat from the flames mixed with the warmth radiating from him. Conversation flowed easily—about where we'd traveled, the strangest things we'd eaten, the songs that felt like home.

At one point, a burst of laughter from the group made me glance away, and when I looked back, his gaze was still fixed on me. Steady. Intent.

A song changed to something slower, and he offered his hand without a word.

I took it.

We moved to the edge of the firelight, the sand cool beneath our feet. His palm was warm against the small of my back, guiding me with an ease that felt both foreign and inevitable.

Day Fifty-Seven: Sometimes connection isn't built—it's recognized.

We swayed in silence, the fire a flickering backdrop to the slow pull of his body against mine. The ocean whispered just beyond the reach of the flames, the rhythm of the waves matching the beat of my heart.

When his cheek brushed mine, the faint scent of salt and smoke tangled with something warmer—him.

His thumb traced slow circles at my waist, each one sending a quiet shiver through me. My fingers curled into the fabric of his shirt, not to pull him closer, but because I wasn't sure I could let go.

The song ended, but neither of us stepped back. The world had narrowed to this—his breath near my ear, my pulse loud in my own head, the awareness of how easily this could become more.

Finally, he spoke, his voice low. "Walk with me."

I nodded, and he laced his fingers through mine, leading me toward the darker stretch of beach where the only light came from the moon.

Day Fifty-Eight: Some steps aren't planned—they're pulled from you by something you can't name yet, but already trust.

We walked until the sound of the bonfire faded into the steady hush of waves. The sand was cool beneath my feet, the moon casting silver light across the water.

He stopped near a driftwood log, turning to face me. His eyes searched mine, not hurried, not unsure—just... seeing me.

"You look like you needed this," he said softly.

I swallowed, the words catching in my throat. "Maybe I did."

He reached up, brushing a loose strand of hair from my face, his knuckles grazing my cheek. The touch was light, but it carried weight—an unspoken promise that this moment wouldn't dissolve with the tide.

When he kissed me, it wasn't tentative. It was deep, sure, and warm, pulling me under faster than the ocean ever could.

My hands slid up his chest, feeling the heat beneath the linen, the steady thrum of his heart against my palm.

We broke apart just enough for air, and I realized I was smiling.

Day Fifty-Nine: Some kisses are bookmarks—holding a place in you that you'll never forget, no matter how many chapters come after.

The kiss deepened, the cool night air a sharp contrast to the heat building between us. His hands slid to my hips, pulling me closer until there was no space left to close.

The ocean roared softly behind us, but all I could hear was the quickened cadence of our breathing.

He pulled back just enough to look at me, his thumb stroking along my jaw. "Tell me to stop," he murmured.

I didn't.

Instead, I tangled my fingers in his hair and kissed him again, harder this time, tasting the faint hint of rum on his lips.

His hands roamed lower, fingertips skimming along the backs of my thighs, and my breath caught. Every nerve in my body was awake, tuned to the places he touched and the ones he hadn't yet.

We sank down onto the driftwood, my knees bracketing his hips, the heat of him seeping through the thin fabric of my dress.

He traced the curve of my back, slow and deliberate, before resting his forehead against mine.

"This is dangerous," he said, though his hands told a different story.

Day Sixty: Sometimes the line between danger and desire is just one more kiss away.

The space for that "one more kiss" vanished before either of us could second-guess it.

His lips claimed mine again, urgent now, the kind of urgency that doesn't ask—it takes. My fingers gripped his shoulders, feeling the strength there, the promise of what could follow.

The wind tugged at my dress, and his hands followed, skimming along my sides, sliding up just enough to make my breath catch. The rough fabric of his shirt brushed my skin as I pressed closer, the world narrowing to the heat between us.

When his mouth left mine, it was only to find the hollow of my neck, his breath warm against the most sensitive places. My nails grazed the back of his neck, and he made a low sound that sent a shiver all the way down my spine.

The moonlight wrapped around us, silvering the edges of every shadow, and for a moment, I forgot everything except the way I fit against him.

Day Sixty-One: Sometimes the night doesn't need permission—it just takes you where you were already going.

His hands framed my face, his kiss deepening until the world around us dissolved into salt air and heartbeat. I shifted closer, my knees tightening around his hips, feeling the steady rise and fall of his breath against me.

When his mouth left mine, it trailed along my jaw, then lower, finding the curve where neck meets shoulder. Each slow press of his lips felt deliberate, as though he was memorizing me in the dark.

I tilted my head, giving him more space, my own hands exploring the solid line of his back beneath the thin linen. Heat pooled low in my stomach, spreading outward until every inch of me was aware of him.

The ocean stretched endless and patient beside us, but time felt condensed, the night folding in on itself until only we existed.

He pulled back just enough to meet my eyes. "You have no idea what you're doing to me."

"I think I do," I whispered, my smile slow, unhurried— like I finally understood the weight of this game.

Day Sixty-Two: Sometimes the most dangerous thing you can give someone is permission.

His mouth found mine again, harder this time—no hesitation, just heat and the kind of hunger that leaves no room for doubt. I pressed against him, feeling the tension in his body, the way he held himself in check even as his hands roamed more boldly.

His palms slid along my thighs, fingers curling just beneath the hem of my dress. My breath hitched, the cool night air brushing over skin he'd just exposed. I leaned into the sensation, the mix of salt air and his scent making my head spin.

When he pulled back, his lips hovered just above mine. "If I keep going, I'm not stopping."

I searched his face, finding no trace of jest—only raw want, threaded with restraint.

"I don't want you to stop," I said, my voice low but certain.

That was all it took. His hands gripped my hips, pulling me fully against him, and I felt the sharp intake of his breath as our bodies aligned. The night around us seemed to pulse with the same rhythm thrumming in my veins.

Day Sixty-Three: Sometimes surrender is the bravest choice you can make.

His hands slid higher, the fabric of my dress yielding to his touch until his palms splayed across my lower back, anchoring me to him. The heat between us deepened, the night air cool against flushed skin.

When his lips found mine again, they were slower this time, as though he'd decided to savor rather than rush. Each kiss was deliberate, a slow unraveling that left me trembling.

I shifted in his lap, feeling the sharp hitch of his breath, and his fingers dug into my hips. The ocean's rhythm seemed to sync with our own—steady, insistent, impossible to ignore.

His mouth trailed down to the hollow of my throat, his tongue tracing the pulse there before his teeth grazed lightly, drawing a soft gasp from me. My hands slid beneath his shirt, fingertips exploring the taut planes of muscle, the warmth of his skin electric under my touch.

He pulled back just enough to look at me, eyes dark in the moonlight. "You're making it very hard to be a gentleman."

A slow smile curved my lips. "Then don't be."

Day Sixty-Four: Sometimes the sweetest freedom is letting go of who you think you should be.

His lips crashed against mine again, the restraint from moments before dissolving into pure urgency. Our movements grew more frantic, like we were both afraid the night might steal this from us if we didn't claim it fast enough.

I could feel every line of him pressed against me, heat rising between us, every touch stoking a fire that had been building from the moment we first met. His hands roamed with purpose now, memorizing the shape of me, the sound of my breath.

When his mouth found my neck again, I arched into him, the world narrowing to sensation—the scent of salt, the whisper of the waves, the steady thrum of his heartbeat against mine.

The ocean roared louder in my ears as the moment crested, the pull between us tightening until it felt like gravity itself was bending to keep us together.

We didn't speak. We didn't need to.

Day Sixty-Five: Some moments defy language—because they aren't meant to be told, only felt.

The night settled around us in a hush, the sound of the waves smoothing out like a long exhale. My heartbeat was still wild, but softer now—less a race, more a steady echo of what we'd just shared.

He kept an arm wrapped around me, his hand tracing idle circles at the small of my back. Neither of us spoke, and for once, the silence didn't feel heavy. It felt earned.

The moon hung low, spilling silver over the sand, catching in his hair when he leaned down to press a slow, lingering kiss to my temple.

I closed my eyes and breathed him in—salt, warmth, and something that felt dangerously close to home.

He shifted slightly, tucking me closer against his chest. "You okay?" he murmured.

"More than okay," I whispered back.

For a moment, I let myself believe this could be enough—that the rest of the world could wait.

Day Sixty-Six: After the fire, there's a quiet where you can hear your own heart, and sometimes, it beats in time with someone else's.

Eventually, the chill of the night crept in, and he pulled his shirt from where it had been discarded, draping it over my shoulders. It smelled like him—warm, faintly spiced, impossibly comforting.

We started the slow walk back toward the faint glow of the bonfire, our fingers brushing until they finally laced together. The easy swing of our joined hands felt intimate in a different way, one that made my chest ache in the best possible sense.

Neither of us rushed. Each step felt like a deliberate stretch of borrowed time.

When the sound of laughter reached us from farther down the beach, he gave my hand a gentle squeeze, as though anchoring me there with him just a little longer.

"Tonight doesn't have to mean anything more than it already does," he said, his voice low, steady. "But it also doesn't have to mean less."

I met his gaze in the dim light, the weight of his words settling somewhere deep in my chest.

Day Sixty-Seven: Sometimes the meaning isn't in the promise—it's in the way someone holds your hand like they don't want to let go.

The morning came softly, sunlight slipping through the sheer curtains and casting golden lines across the sheets. I stirred, the distant crash of waves still threading through my dreams.

For a few blissful seconds, I didn't remember where I was—or that I wasn't alone.

Then his arm shifted around my waist, pulling me back against him, and the memory of the night before came rushing in, warm and steady as his breath against my shoulder.

"Morning," he murmured, voice thick with sleep.

"Morning," I echoed, my own voice catching in that space between contentment and hesitation.

Neither of us moved right away. The world beyond the room could wait, and for now, the weight of his hand on my hip was enough to keep me anchored.

I wondered if he could feel the unspoken questions in the way I held myself—the quiet war between wanting more and fearing it.

He pressed a slow kiss to the back of my neck, as though answering without words.

Day Sixty-Eight: Some mornings don't need coffee to wake you—they just need the right person breathing beside you.

The morning came softly, sunlight slipping through the sheer curtains and casting golden lines across the sheets. I stirred, the distant crash of waves still threading through my dreams.

For a few blissful seconds, I didn't remember where I was—or that I wasn't alone.

Then his arm shifted around my waist, pulling me back against him, and the memory of the night before came rushing in, warm and steady as his breath against my shoulder.

"Morning," he murmured, voice thick with sleep.

"Morning," I echoed, my own voice catching in that space between contentment and hesitation.

Neither of us moved right away. The world beyond the room could wait, and for now, the weight of his hand on my hip was enough to keep me anchored.

I wondered if he could feel the unspoken questions in the way I held myself—the quiet war between wanting more and fearing it.

He pressed a slow kiss to the back of my neck, as though answering without words.

But the spell of the morning broke when my phone buzzed sharply on the nightstand. The screen lit up with a name I hadn't expected—and didn't want—to see.

I froze. He noticed.

"Who is it?" His tone was casual, but I felt the shift in the air.

"It's... complicated," I said, my fingers hesitating above the phone.

Day Sixty-Nine: Sometimes the outside world doesn't knock—it kicks the door open.

I didn't answer right away. The phone buzzed again, the sound sharper now, cutting through the quiet like a blade.

His gaze followed mine to the screen, and though he didn't say the name out loud, I saw the recognition in his eyes.

Mitch.

My stomach tightened. Even seeing the name felt like stepping back into a fire I'd only just managed to crawl out of.

"You gonna answer it?" His tone was even, but I could hear the current underneath.

"No." The word came out harder than I intended.

The phone finally fell silent, the glow fading until it was just us again. But the air had shifted, and the warmth of the morning felt like it had been pushed to the edges of the room.

"You don't owe me an explanation," he said quietly, "but I'm not blind either."

I closed my eyes, exhaling slowly. "It's not what you think."

"Then tell me what it is."

Day Seventy: The past doesn't always knock—it sometimes barges in and dares you to make a choice.

I sat up, pulling the sheet with me like it could shield me from the truth. My fingers twisted in the fabric, buying me seconds I didn't have.

"He's someone I used to be close to," I said slowly. "Someone I thought I'd left behind."

His eyes searched mine, steady, patient. "But you haven't."

I shook my head. "Not completely. Not in the way that matters."

The words hung there, heavy and unfinished. I didn't tell him about the nights I still woke up tangled in memories, or the way guilt could sneak in and choke me without warning. I didn't tell him that part of me still feared the hold Mitch had on my mind, even now.

"I'm not going back," I added, forcing strength into the words. "But I can't pretend I'm fully past it, either."

He nodded once, not in approval but in acknowledgment—like he understood that healing wasn't a finish line you crossed, but a road you kept walking.

"I can live with that," he said quietly. "As long as you keep walking."

Day Seventy-One: You can't heal in one breath, but you can choose, over and over, not to go back to the place that broke you.

I thought about giving him the neat version—the one without the jagged edges or the parts that would make him look at me differently. But when I met his eyes, I knew he'd see straight through it.

"It's a history I'm not proud of," I began. "One I've been trying to close the book on. But sometimes..." My voice trailed off.

"Sometimes the book doesn't stay closed," he finished for me.

I nodded, grateful he understood without me spelling it all out. "He's a part of my past that still thinks he has a claim on my present. And I don't always know how to stop him from trying."

He shifted closer, his hand finding mine, grounding me. "Then maybe you don't have to do it alone."

The simplicity of the offer cut deeper than any declaration could. I wanted to believe him. I wanted to believe I could hand over some of the weight without losing myself in the process.

"Maybe," I whispered.

Day Seventy-Two: Trust isn't built in grand gestures— it's built in the quiet moments when someone offers to stand in the fire with you.

We sat there in the muted light, the silence stretching between us—not uncomfortable, but fragile. I could feel the day pressing in at the edges, reality waiting just outside the door.

The phone buzzed again. This time, it was a text.

He didn't look at the screen, but I did. *We need to talk. – M.*

Three words that could unravel everything.

I locked the phone quickly, my pulse quickening. He caught the shift in my breathing.

"What did he say?"

"Nothing worth answering," I said, a little too fast.

His jaw tightened, but he let it go. "If you say so."

The distance in his tone cut more than I expected. I wanted to reach for him, to explain, but the words jammed in my throat.

Instead, I leaned back against the headboard, staring at the ceiling, feeling the weight of two men pulling me in opposite directions—one from my past, one from my present—and knowing I couldn't hold both for long.

Day Seventy-Three: Sometimes the battle isn't between right and wrong—it's between the life you've outgrown and the one you're afraid to step into.

The space between us grew tense, almost electric. His gaze was dark, fixed on me with a mix of frustration and desire that made my breath hitch.

Before I could say anything, he moved—closing the gap, his mouth on mine with a force that demanded surrender. There was no gentleness now, just raw, unfiltered need. His hands gripped my hips, pulling me beneath him, the mattress dipping under our combined weight.

I gasped against his lips, part shock, part anticipation, and he swallowed the sound like it belonged to him. Every kiss, every touch, carried an edge, a sharpness that bordered on too much but left me aching for more.

The world narrowed to heat and motion. Sheets tangled around us, his fingers pressing into my skin hard enough to leave marks. My body arched instinctively, matching him, meeting every rough thrust with my own urgency.

Somewhere in the blur of it, I realized this wasn't just about desire—it was about claiming, about proving something neither of us was ready to say out loud.

When we finally stilled, breathing ragged, he rested his forehead against mine. The air between us was thick, charged with everything we'd just poured into each other and everything we still hadn't said.

Day Seventy-Four: Sometimes passion is the language you use when words are too dangerous.

The room was quiet except for the sound of our breathing. My body was still humming, my pulse slow to settle, but underneath the heat was something else—something I didn't want to name.

He lay beside me, one arm draped loosely over my stomach, his fingertips tracing idle shapes on my skin. It should have felt grounding, but instead, it felt like the weight of unspoken truths pressed between us.

I turned my head to look at him. His eyes were closed, but I could see the faint crease in his brow, the tension that hadn't quite bled out with our bodies' release.

"That was…" I started, but the words caught.

"Yeah," he said, his voice low, almost unreadable.

I wanted to ask if it was anger, or fear, or something else entirely that had driven the roughness. I wanted to tell him that I'd welcomed it—that I'd needed it as much as he had—but the vulnerability in that truth kept me quiet.

Instead, I let my hand rest over his, holding it there like an anchor, even as the tide of my thoughts pulled me somewhere I didn't want to go.

Day Seventy-Five: Sometimes silence isn't safety—it's just the space where questions hide.

The silence stretched, thick enough to touch. I could feel the questions clawing their way up my throat, and for once, I didn't push them back down.

"Was that about me?" I asked quietly. "Or about him?"

His eyes opened, locking on mine, sharp and searching. "It was about us," he said, but there was hesitation in the way the words landed.

"Because it felt like you were trying to erase something. Or someone." My voice didn't waver, though my chest was tight.

He exhaled slowly, the air warm against my cheek. "Maybe I was. Maybe I needed to remind myself where we are... and where you are."

The truth of it hit harder than I expected. I didn't know if he meant where I was physically, emotionally, or in the messy in-between we kept finding ourselves.

"I'm here," I said, my hand finding his cheek. "But I'm still figuring out what 'here' means for me."

He nodded once, the tension in his jaw easing just a fraction. "Then I'll wait. But I'm not letting go."

Day Seventy-Six: Love can hold you close without loosening its grip—and sometimes, that's both comfort and cage.

Something in his eyes softened then, like my words had shifted something inside him. He slid closer, closing the gap between us until our foreheads touched.

"I don't want to be another wound you have to heal from," he murmured.

"You're not," I said, but my voice cracked on the last word. "You're the first thing in a long time that feels like it could last."

His hand cradled the back of my head, fingers tangling in my hair. "Then let me in all the way. Even to the places you're scared, I'll see."

The plea in his tone undid me. My chest ached with the weight of everything I hadn't shared—the late-night flashbacks, the panic that struck without warning, the way I still caught myself bracing for pain even in tenderness.

I didn't give him all of it. Not yet. But I gave him more than I had before.

"I'm still scared," I admitted. "Not of you. Just... of what happens if I lose you."

He kissed me then, slow and steady, like an answer. "Then we hold on. Together."

Day Seventy-Seven: Sometimes love isn't about fixing— it's about holding steady while the pieces find their place.

His name was Rafe.

I hadn't meant for him to become anything more than a distraction—a way to remember that I was still capable of feeling something good. But somewhere between the nights we spent tangled in sheets and the mornings where he poured my coffee just the way I liked it, he'd found a way under my skin.

And now, with his forehead pressed to mine, promising to hold on, I couldn't ignore the jagged truth pressing at the edges of my heart: I still loved Jake.

Jake, who had been my anchor when I was falling apart. Jake, whom I'd betrayed in ways I couldn't take back. Jake, who still haunted my dreams, was equal parts comfort and ache.

And then there was Mitch—the man who had broken me in ways I was only beginning to name, and who still lingered like a shadow in every corner of my life.

I was standing in the center of a triangle I hadn't asked for, pulled in three directions by love, regret, and unfinished war.

Before I could untangle my thoughts, there was a knock at the door. Sharp. Insistent.

Rafe's hand tightened on mine. "You expecting someone?"

I shook my head, but my stomach already knew the answer.

Day Seventy-Eight: Sometimes the past doesn't just knock—it arrives uninvited, wearing the face you've both longed for and feared.

I crossed the room slowly, each knock at the door echoing through me like a warning. Rafe stood just behind me, his presence steady but tense.

When I opened the door, the air seemed to drain from my lungs.

Jake.

He stood there in worn jeans and a weathered leather jacket, eyes locked on mine with a look I couldn't quite read—equal parts relief, accusation, and something else I didn't dare name.

"Hi, Emileigh," he said, his voice low, rough   like it had been a long time since he'd used it on me.

For a heartbeat, the world shrank to the space between us. The smell of him, the way his jaw tightened when he looked past me and saw Rafe.

Rafe didn't move. Neither did Jake.

And I was suddenly the fault line between two earthquakes.

Day Seventy-Nine: Sometimes the moment you've imagined a thousand times doesn't feel like a reunion—it feels like the start of a war.

Jake's gaze didn't waver, but his words landed like a stone in still water.

"So... this is what I walked into?"

Rafe stepped forward before I could answer, his voice low but edged. "You should ask her, not me."

The air between them thickened, two men sizing each other up—not strangers exactly, but not allies in any sense of the word.

"We were on a break," I blurted, instantly regretting it when Jake's expression shifted. His jaw flexed, his eyes narrowing just enough to cut.

"A break?" His voice was a mixture of disbelief and something sharp enough to wound. "Is that what we're calling it now?"

"I didn't think you were coming back," I said, the words tumbling out too fast. "You disappeared, Jake. No calls, no messages—nothing."

He shook his head slowly, like he was trying to make sense of a language he didn't speak. "So that makes this okay?"

Rafe crossed his arms but didn't speak. I could feel him at my back, solid and silent, a contrast to Jake's storm.

"It's not about okay," I said finally. "It's about surviving. And I did what I had to do."

Jake's laugh was short and humorless. "Yeah, well, congratulations. You survived. Now what?"

Day Eighty: Sometimes the fight isn't over what happened—it's over what it means.

Rafe shifted his stance, his voice low but firm. "Sounds to me like she owes you an explanation, not an apology."

Jake's eyes snapped to him. "And who the hell are you to decide that?"

"I'm the one who's been here," Rafe shot back. "When she needed someone, I showed up."

"That's because I wasn't given the chance!" Jake's voice rose, but it wasn't just anger—it was hurt, raw and unfiltered.

I stepped between them, palms out like I could hold back the weight of both their emotions. "Stop. Both of you."

Jake's gaze cut to me. "Did you tell him about us? About everything?"

My silence was answer enough.

Rafe's brow furrowed. "Everything?"

The air was heavy, full of words none of us were ready to say.

"Yes, everything," Jake said, his voice cold. "Every detail, every mistake, every night she swore she loved me."

My throat tightened. "Jake—"

He shook his head. "No. You made your choices. Just be sure you can live with them."

Day Eighty-One: Some truths feel like freedom. Others feel like standing in the wreckage you created.

Jake's eyes burned into mine, and I saw it—the exact moment he slipped back into the memory. The night everything had cracked wide open.

"I remember what it felt like," he said quietly, but there was no softness in his tone. "Hearing about you and Mitch. It was like someone reached inside and ripped me apart from the inside out. And the worst part? You didn't even fight for me to believe it wasn't true."

I swallowed hard, guilt pressing heavy in my chest.

Rafe glanced between us, his jaw tightening. "Mitch?"

Jake's gaze shifted to him. "Yeah. Mitch. The one she swore she'd never touch. The one she let in while she was still mine."

Rafe's shoulders stiffened, his expression unreadable.

Jake stepped closer to him, his voice low but sharp enough to cut. "You think you're different? That she won't do the same to you? Trust me—she will. Not because she's cruel, but because she's still broken. And broken people break people."

Rafe didn't flinch, but I saw the flicker of doubt in his eyes.

Jake turned back to me, shaking his head with a bitter laugh. "And God help me, I must be insane... because I still love you."

Day Eighty-Two: Sometimes love survives what it shouldn't. And sometimes, that's the most dangerous kind.

Rafe's jaw worked, but he didn't speak right away. I could see the calculation in his eyes, the way Jake's words wormed their way in despite his effort to block them. His fingers twitched like he wanted to reach for me, but the hesitation was telling.

"Is it true?" he finally asked, voice low. "Were you with Mitch while you were still with him?"

My mouth opened, but the answer wouldn't come out. Not in the neat, clean way he wanted to hear it. "It's... complicated."

Rafe's laugh was short and bitter. "That's not a no."

The space between us grew heavy. I felt the walls pressing in, the weight of both their stares, the unspoken demand to choose—not just between them, but between the versions of myself I had been with each of them.

Jake's eyes softened for just a fraction of a second before he masked it with anger. "I told you," he said to Rafe. "She'll hurt you. Maybe not today, maybe not next week. But it's coming."

Rafe didn't back down. "Maybe. Or maybe I'm willing to risk it."

And me? I was caught between wanting to scream at both of them and wanting to disappear entirely.

Day Eighty-Three: Sometimes the worst prison is the space between who you were and who you're trying to become.

The words clawed at my throat until I couldn't hold them back anymore.

"You want the truth?" I said, my voice shaking. "Here it is. I never believed I deserved love. Not real love. Not the kind that sees all of me and stays anyway. Jake—" I looked at him, my chest aching, "—you were the only man who ever loved me without conditions. And I didn't know what to do with that. I thought... I thought if I messed it up first, it would hurt less when you left."

My eyes burned, but I didn't blink the tears away. "Mitch... Mitch knew that about me. He knew the exact buttons to press, the exact words to say. He made me feel wanted in the most twisted way. And when he touched me..." My voice broke, shame flooding my veins. "I was weak. I hate it, but it's the truth. It wasn't about choosing him over you. It was about destroying myself before anyone else could."

Jake's jaw tightened, but I saw the flicker of pain in his eyes. Rafe stood still, processing, his expression caught somewhere between sympathy and wariness.

"I never wanted to hurt either of you," I whispered. "But I don't know how to turn off the part of me that thinks love isn't meant for me. And every time I get close to believing it... I find a way to break it."

Silence settled like dust after a collapse.

Day Eighty-Four: Confession isn't always about clearing your name—it's about showing the wounds you've been hiding, even if no one forgives you.

Jake stood there, every muscle tight, his breath coming slow and deliberate like he was trying to keep from shattering. His eyes searched my face as if he might find a different truth hiding behind my words, something easier to swallow. But there wasn't.

"Do you have any idea," he said finally, voice low but heavy with grief, "what it feels like to love someone who's already decided they're unlovable? It's like trying to keep water in your hands—you pour everything you've got into them, and it still slips away."

I couldn't answer. My throat was thick with the ache of knowing he was right.

Rafe shifted, running a hand over his jaw. "You know... I think I came into this thinking I could be some kind of hero in your story. But the truth is, Emileigh, we barely know each other. You don't owe me loyalty the way you owe it to him, and I don't have the history to fight for you against ghosts I can't see." His gaze softened, though, and he gave a small, sad smile. "But I do get it. More than you think. And I hope... I really hope you find a way to believe you're worth the kind of love he's still willing to give you."

He took a step back, letting the unspoken goodbye hang in the air.

Jake's eyes followed Rafe, then came back to me. "I'm so damn mad at you," he said, the words shaking. "But I hate how much I still want to hold you. How much I still want to believe we could be what we were before you let him in."

And in that moment, I knew the next words out of my mouth could either open the door to redemption—or slam it shut forever.

Day Eighty-Five: Sometimes the choice isn't between love and hate—it's between running from the fire or letting it burn you both alive.

I took a shaky breath, my heart pounding against my ribs like it was trying to break free. "Jake... I love you," I said, the words trembling but true. "You have to believe that. I've never stopped. Even when I was with Mitch, it wasn't love—it was... it was my thorn."

He frowned slightly, confusion and hurt mixing in his eyes.

"In the Bible," I whispered, "Paul said, 'When I try to do good, evil is always present.' My evil—my thorn—has a name. And it's Mitch. I can't explain why his shadow follows me, why his touch pulls me into places I swore I'd never go again. I hate that part of me. I hate that I've let it win more than once."

Jake's eyes softened, but his jaw stayed tense. "Then why should I believe it won't win again?"

"Because I'm still here," I said, my voice breaking. "Because no matter how far I've fallen, my heart always finds its way back to you. And maybe that's selfish. Maybe I don't deserve you. But I can't keep pretending that losing you wouldn't destroy me."

His hand twitched like he wanted to reach for me, then stopped midair. "You've got to want more than just not losing me, Emileigh. You've got to want to choose me, even when the thorn digs in."

"I do," I whispered, tears burning hot trails down my cheeks. "God help me, I do."

Day Eighty-Six: Love isn't just about who you run to— it's about who you refuse to run from, even when the shadows call your name.

Jake's eyes searched mine for a long moment, the silence stretching between us like a tightrope. "If you mean that, then there's only one way to prove it," he said finally. "You have to cut Mitch out. Completely. No contact. No excuses. No lingering what-ifs."

The air seemed to thicken, every beat of my heart echoing in my ears. "Jake—"

"No," he said sharply, then softened. "Don't tell me why you can't. Tell me why you will. Because if you can't, then everything you've just told me is just words. And I can't... I won't... go through this again."

The image of Mitch flashed in my mind—his smirk, the way he made my pulse race in ways I didn't want to admit. My thorn. My weakness. My sin.

"I won't pretend it's going to be easy," I whispered. "But if it means choosing you over the chaos, I'll do it. I'll block him, delete his number, shut every door he's ever slipped through."

Jake's gaze didn't waver. "Do it now."

My breath caught, but I reached for my phone, my hands trembling as I typed in the number I knew by heart and hit delete. Then I blocked it, my chest tightening like I'd just severed a vein.

When I looked back up, Jake's eyes held a mix of pain and hope. "That's the first step," he said. "But it's not the last."

Day Eighty-Seven: Sometimes choosing love means killing the thing that's been keeping you alive—because it's also the thing that's been killing you slowly.

The moment the block was done, a strange stillness settled over me. Like a door had slammed shut in a house I'd been living in for too long. Relief swirled with grief, because part of me—God help me—was already mourning the loss of something toxic.

Jake was watching me closely, his eyes searching for cracks. I gave him a small nod, but inside, my mind was a tangle.

I couldn't help but think about the city. The places Mitch might still haunt. The way I'd run into the streets once before, keeping my distance but feeling his presence like a magnet, I wasn't sure I could resist forever. Would Jake's love be enough to hold me steady the next time I saw that smirk, that easy swagger that had always, against my better judgment, pulled me in?

Because Mitch wasn't just temptation—he was the embodiment of every self-destructive impulse I'd ever had. And the ugly truth? His cocky charm and physical pull still lived somewhere in my veins. I could lie to Jake, to myself, but deep down, I knew the real battle hadn't even started yet.

I looked at Jake, memorizing the way he grounded me just by standing there. If I was going to win this fight, it would have to be for him, for us... and for the version of myself I wanted to believe in.

Day Eighty-Eight: Walking away is one thing. Staying away when the streets know your name—that's the real war.

It happened so fast I almost convinced myself it wasn't real.

I'd been cutting through a narrow side street downtown, my mind busy with errands and the hum of the city, when I heard it—his laugh. Low, cocky, unmistakable. My whole body went rigid before I even turned my head.

And there he was. Mitch.

Leaning against a brick wall like the street belonged to him, arms crossed, that same smug grin spreading across his face the second our eyes met. He looked me over slowly, like he was reading every thought I didn't want him to have access to.

"Well, well," he said, pushing off the wall. "Look what the wind blew in."

My heart pounded. I should've kept walking. I should've ignored him. But my feet betrayed me, halting like they needed permission to move again.

"I don't have time for you," I managed, though my voice didn't sound as steady as I wanted.

He smirked, taking a step closer. "You always had time for me, Emileigh. Even when you swore you didn't."

The truth was, I could feel that pull—the one I'd just promised Jake I'd fight. And here it was, testing me already, wrapping itself around my ribs and tugging.

I thought of Jake, of the way his eyes looked when I deleted Mitch's number. That was my lifeline, the thing keeping me from leaning into the very danger I'd sworn to escape.

"I'm not yours anymore," I said, forcing my feet to move. "Not now. Not ever again."

His chuckle followed me down the block, curling like smoke around my resolve.

Day Eighty-Nine: Some ghosts don't stay dead—they haunt the streets, daring you to break your own promises.

Chapter Seven

The news reached Jake before I could tell him myself.

I didn't know who saw us, or what version of the run-in they passed along, but when I walked into the café where he was waiting, I felt the tension hanging off him like a storm cloud. His jaw was tight, his hands curled into fists against the table.

"Who told you?" I asked quietly, sliding into the seat across from him.

"That doesn't matter," he said, his voice low but sharp. "What matters is whether it's true. Did you see him?"

I swallowed hard, knowing this was the moment. I could lie, dodge, or let the truth come out on my terms. And for once, I chose the truth.

"Yes," I said. "I saw Mitch. It wasn't planned. I was downtown, and he was just... there. We talked, but that's it. I walked away."

Jake's eyes searched mine, as if trying to catch a flicker of deceit. I forced myself to hold his gaze, even though the rest of the story—the part where Mitch caught up to me a block later, cornered me with his words and that damn smile, and kissed me until I shoved him off—burned at the back of my throat.

I wasn't ready to tell him that. Not yet. Maybe not ever.

"I'm telling you because I don't want you hearing it from anyone else," I said. "And because I'm trying to be different. To be better. For you."

His jaw worked as he processed that, the storm in his eyes not fully clearing. "We'll see," he said finally.

Before I could say more, a shadow fell across the table. That voice—smooth, arrogant—slid into the air.

"Mind if I join you two?" Mitch.

My stomach dropped. Jake's eyes flicked up, darkening instantly. Mitch pulled out a chair without waiting for an answer, leaning back like he owned the space. The smirk on his face told me everything—he knew exactly what he was doing.

I felt my pulse hammering. I hadn't told Jake the whole story, and Mitch's presence was gasoline on an open flame. Jake's hand tightened around his coffee cup, the muscles in his jaw ticking as he locked eyes with my past.

Day Ninety: Some storms you see coming. Others sit down across from you and dare you to survive them.

Mitch didn't just sit; he sprawled, legs stretched under the table like he was marking territory.

"Small world," he said, flashing that smug grin at Jake before letting his gaze slide lazily to me. "Guess I'm just lucky today."

Jake didn't answer right away. He just stared, the kind of stare that could strip a man down to nothing. I could see the tension building in his shoulders, the way his hand flexed against the coffee cup like it was the only thing keeping him from launching across the table.

I swallowed hard. "Mitch, what are you doing here?"

He chuckled, low and infuriating. "Just following where the day takes me. Looks like it led me to the two of you."

Jake's jaw tightened, his voice a dangerous calm. "You've had your fun. Now get up and walk away."

Mitch leaned forward, his elbows resting on the table. "See, here's the thing—I'm not here to talk to you, Jake. I'm here for her." His eyes pinned me in place, like he knew exactly which buttons to push. And he did.

I could feel the air between them thickening, the electricity of two men who hated each other on sight. But underneath that, my own guilt churned—because I hadn't told Jake everything. Not about the kiss. Not about how Mitch had caught up to me afterward.

Jake's eyes flicked to me, searching, suspicious. "Is there something I should know?"

My pulse hammered in my ears. I could keep dodging. Or I could tell him now, before Mitch used it like a weapon.

Chapter Eight

I leaned forward, my voice sharp enough to cut glass.

"You had no right to follow me, Mitch. None. Whatever game you're playing—it ends here."

He tilted his head, amused. "Game? You wound me."

I ignored him, the words tumbling out before I could stop them. "And while we're on the subject, Jake—this is the other part of the story I was trying to tell you before he barged in. He kissed me. Out of nowhere. I had to fight him off."

It wasn't the full truth, not exactly. The fight had been in my head as much as in my hands. But Jake didn't need to know that—not if I had any hope of keeping him.

Jake's eyes hardened instantly, his gaze swinging to Mitch like a blade. "You put your hands on her?"

Mitch leaned back, smirking. "If that was a fight, sweetheart, it must have been with our tongues. Because it sure wasn't with your hands."

The comment was a lit match to gasoline. Jake shot to his feet, his chair skidding back with a harsh scrape. His fists clenched, shoulders squared—every muscle coiled for the punch I knew was coming.

I braced for the explosion.

But then, a sharp crash from behind the counter—a tray hitting the floor, a barista yelping—cut through the tension. Jake's head turned toward the noise for just a second, enough for him to pull himself back from the edge.

When his gaze returned to Mitch, it was still molten with fury, but controlled. Barely.

"You should leave," he said, low and dangerous. "Now."

Mitch's smirk didn't falter, but he rose slowly, his eyes sliding over me one last time like a challenge.

Mitch adjusted his jacket, slow and deliberate, like he had all the time in the world.

"Fine," he said, glancing at Jake. "I'll go. But let's be honest—we both know she's not done with me yet."

The words hung in the air like   poison, his smirk daring Jake to swing. Jake didn't move, but I could feel the tension vibrating off him, like his rage had nowhere to go except deeper into his bones.

Mitch stepped back from the table, pausing just long enough to make sure his exit stung. "Take care of her, Jake. Or maybe... don't. Makes it easier for me."

Then he was gone, the bell over the café door chiming once before the silence rushed in to fill the space he'd left.

Jake's jaw was set like stone, his eyes still locked on the door. "He's trying to get under my skin," he said finally.

"He's trying to get under mine," I corrected, my voice soft but shaking. "And I'm not going to let him."

Jake looked at me then, really looked, like he was weighing my words against everything he knew about me—everything I'd done. Whatever he decided, it wasn't ready to be spoken. He just reached for his coffee again, though his hand trembled.

I knew the fight with Mitch wasn't over. Not for Jake. And maybe not for me, either.

We didn't speak much after Mitch left. Jake paid the bill without looking at me, and the walk back to his place was quiet—too quiet.

It wasn't until we were inside, the door shut behind us, that the dam finally broke.

"Do you have any idea what it's like," Jake began, his voice low and shaking, "to constantly feel like you're the only one choosing this? Choosing us?"

I opened my mouth, but he held up a hand. "No. Let me finish."

He paced, running a hand through his hair. "Every relationship I've ever had, I've put love first. Above my pride. Above my fear. Above every damn reason, I should have walked away. Because that's who I am. I fight for it. Even when it's messy. Even when it hurts."

His eyes locked onto mine then, raw and unguarded. "But I can't keep doing that if you won't meet me there, Em. I need to know—really know—that when it comes down to it, you'll choose me over... whatever the hell that was today. Over him."

The weight of his words settled heavy in the room.

"I am choosing you," I said, my voice breaking. "I just... I'm still learning how to not choose the things that destroy me."

He exhaled, his shoulders sagging, but his gaze never softened. "Then you'd better learn fast. Because I can't keep loving someone who's halfway out the door."

I took a deep breath, searching for words that didn't sound like excuses. "You're right," I said finally. "I can't undo what's been done, but I can promise you this—I'm done letting Mitch have any space in my life. I'm going to fight for you, Jake. For us."

It sounded good. It even felt good to say it. But deep down, I knew I was papering over cracks that went deeper than I wanted to admit.

Ninety-plus days of journaling my thoughts, bleeding my soul onto page after page, and still I wasn't cured. The same cracks kept showing up—different moments, different temptations, but always the same weakness waiting for the right trigger.

What was going to happen when the next test came? When Mitch, or someone like him, decided to slip past my defenses again? Would I really fight hard enough for Jake, or would I fall into the same familiar patterns that had wrecked every good thing in my life?

I didn't let my doubt show. Instead, I crossed the room and took his hand, squeezing it like the strength in my grip could somehow make up for the weakness in my heart.

"I'm not halfway out the door," I whispered. "I'm right here."

Jake looked at me for a long moment before nodding once. But the question lingered in his eyes, unspoken but loud—*for how long?*

We settled into a fragile quiet that night, each of us pretending the conversation had solved more than it really had. Jake's hand stayed in mine while we watched some mindless show on the couch, the flicker of the TV masking the fact that our thoughts were miles apart.

It was a truce—but one held together by threads, not steel.

For a little while, I managed to convince myself I could live up to my promise. I smiled more, touched him more, poured myself into the pieces of our life that still felt unbroken. To anyone looking in, we were fine.

But underneath, I was slipping.

The next test came fast. Too fast. A stranger at a work event with the same confident swagger, the same magnetic charm that Mitch had weaponized. I told myself I could handle it. That I'd smile politely, walk away, and come home to Jake with my promise still intact.

That's not what happened.

One drink became two. Two became the slow burn of a hand at the small of my back, the whisper of lips at my ear. And then it was happening again—my body betraying me, my knees weakening, the part of me I hated most steering the wheel.

It didn't go as far as Mitch. But it was far enough. Far enough that I knew the line between loyalty and betrayal wasn't as solid as I'd wanted Jake to believe.

When I came home, Jake was waiting on the couch. He smiled, kissed my cheek, and asked how my night was. I told him it was fine.

And just like that, the spiral tightened.

Chapter Nine

The days that followed looked normal from the outside. I woke up next to Jake, made coffee, went to work, and came home. We laughed sometimes. We fought sometimes. We had sex that was good enough to make me forget the cracks—for a while.

But inside, something was shifting.

It was in the way my eyes lingered a beat too long on strangers. The way my phone buzzed and I hesitated before answering, scanning for names that would pull me back into trouble. It was in the way I told Jake I was working late, when really I was just sitting in a bar nursing a drink and letting men look at me.

I wasn't actively seeking out Mitch—or anyone like him. But I wasn't slamming the door shut, either. And that was enough to make every day feel like walking a thin, fraying rope.

Jake didn't notice. Or maybe he chose not to. He was too busy planning his next big move at work, talking about taking us away for a weekend, about what we could be if we kept "choosing each other."

I nodded and smiled and kissed him when he said those things. But somewhere in the back of my mind, a question kept pulsing: *What happens when the next temptation knocks—and I'm too tired to pretend I don't want to open the door?*

It started small.

A man at the copy shop smiled at me—nothing unusual—but something about the way he held my gaze made my pulse stutter.

I should've looked away. I should've smiled politely and gone back to my errand. Instead, I let my eyes linger, just long enough for something unspoken to pass between us.

It wasn't an attraction, not exactly. More like recognition.

Like he could see the other person living inside me—the one who didn't care about promises, who wanted the rush more than the stability, who wanted to be wanted no matter the cost.

I told myself I was imagining it. But when he leaned slightly across the counter to hand me my receipt, his fingers brushing mine, the jolt I felt wasn't just from the contact.

It was from her.

That shadow-self who lived in the corners of my mind, waiting for cracks in the armor. She stirred now, stretching inside me like she'd just been woken from a nap.

Just one smile, she whispered. *Just a little more.*

I forced a polite thank you and walked out into the sun, clutching my bag like it could anchor me to the woman I wanted to be.

But my reflection in the shop window didn't look like her at all.

By the time I got home, the brush of his fingers still lingered in my mind. It wasn't even about *him*—it was about the way it made me feel. That flicker of adrenaline, the quickening of my pulse.

The shadow-self purred in satisfaction, curling back into the dark like she'd claimed a small victory.

Jake was in the kitchen when I walked in, sleeves rolled up, stirring something on the stove. He glanced over his shoulder and smiled, but there was a flicker of hesitation there.

"You okay?" he asked.

"Yeah," I said quickly, too quickly. "Just tired."

He studied me for a beat longer than necessary, then nodded and went back to cooking. But I could feel his eyes on me again when he thought I wasn't looking.

Later, while we ate, I laughed at something he said, the sound a little too loud, a little too bright. Overcompensating.

Jake's smile didn't reach his eyes. "You've been... different lately."

My fork paused halfway to my mouth. "Different how?"

He shrugged, but his gaze didn't waver. "Just feels like you're somewhere else sometimes. Even when you're sitting right in front of me."

I forced another smile and a shake of my head. "I'm fine."

But inside, I could feel her smirking—the other me—because she knew the truth. I *was* somewhere else. And Jake didn't even know he was losing me inch by inch.

It happened two days later.

I was running late for a client meeting, the kind where you skip breakfast and forget your umbrella even though the sky is promising rain. The elevator doors were about to close when I slipped inside, muttering a quick "thanks" to the man holding them.

He was tall, wearing a suit that fit like it had been made for him, and carried himself with the easy confidence of someone who knew he could have a room's attention if he wanted it.

I didn't think much of it—until the elevator jolted and stopped between floors.

"Great," I muttered under my breath.

He chuckled, the sound low and warm. "Guess we're stuck for a minute."

We stood there in the quiet hum of the emergency lights, the air between us charged in a way I didn't expect. He glanced at me, his eyes sliding over my face before settling on my mouth.

The look was fleeting, but it landed like a spark on dry kindling. My pulse quickened.

"I've seen you in the building before," he said. "You always rush past like you've got somewhere better to be."

I gave a small laugh. "Usually do."

The words weren't flirty, but my tone was. I heard it as soon as it left my mouth.

And that was all it took—her, the shadow-self, was suddenly wide awake. She pressed forward inside me, hungry for the attention, for the possibility.

The lights flickered, and the elevator lurched back into motion. I exhaled like I'd been holding my breath the whole time.

By the time the doors opened, I'd convinced myself it was nothing. But deep down, I knew it was *something*.

The second encounter came three days later.

I was at a wine tasting downtown, invited by a coworker who bailed at the last minute. I stayed anyway, telling myself it was just a few glasses and an early night.

That's when I felt it—that prickling on the back of my neck that meant someone was watching me.

He was leaning casually against the bar, not hiding the way his gaze moved over me. Not crude, but deliberate. When I glanced his way, he smiled like we already shared a secret.

I didn't go to him, but I didn't move away either. When he passed me a glass of deep red, his fingers grazed mine. It was the same jolt as the elevator. The same awakening of her—the woman inside me who had nothing to lose and nothing to hide.

We talked about the wine. About travel. About nothing that mattered but everything that made the air between us hum. When he finally walked away, I felt Soki's smirk from somewhere deep in my bones.

You see? You like the chase. You like the pull.

I didn't argue.

***

The storm came that night.

Mitch.

I wasn't expecting him, but the moment I saw him leaning against my car outside my apartment, every warning bell in my body went silent. Soki took the wheel without asking.

"You've been quiet," he said, his voice like silk dragged across skin.

"I've been busy," I replied, though we both knew that wasn't the truth.

He stepped closer, and before I could stop him, his hands were in my hair, his mouth on mine. It was fire—hungry, consuming. My back hit the car door, the cool metal a contrast to the heat rising between us.

I should have stopped it. I didn't.

We didn't make it inside. Clothes fell away in the shadows of the parking garage, my legs wrapped around him, his hands gripping me like he owned me. Every thrust was hard, unyielding, and yet I met him, matched him, wanted more.

It wasn't just sex—it was chaos turned into flesh. The kind of wild that left no room for thought, only sensation. The slap of skin, the taste of his sweat, the sharp edge of his teeth against my neck. I was drowning in it, in him, in *her*.

Because it wasn't really me there   , not the me Jake knew.

It was Soki Jealousy—answering every question I wouldn't admit out loud, feeding every desire I told myself I shouldn't have. She didn't care about love or loyalty. She cared about satisfaction, about that primal rush that Jake's steady devotion could never replicate.

When it was over, I leaned against the car, breathing hard, my body still humming.

And in that moment, I understood something that scared me more than getting caught:

Soki didn't just tempt me.
She completed me.

When Mitch was gone, the silence felt heavier than his presence.
I slid into the driver's seat, my hands still trembling, the scent of him clinging to my skin. Every nerve in my body screamed with the memory of him, and with it came the crash—the hollow ache that follows the high.

My head fell back against the seat. *What have I done?*

But even as the guilt began to seep in, Soki's voice was there.

What you needed. What you wanted. Don't pretend otherwise.

I hated her for being right. I hated myself for letting her win.

By the time I reached my apartment, I'd rehearsed the mask I would wear. Shower. Change. Erase every trace of Mitch from my skin.

Jake was on the couch when I walked in, one arm draped over the backrest, the TV casting soft light across his face. He smiled when he saw me—warm, open, trusting.

"Hey, you," he said. "I was starting to think you were avoiding me."

I set my bag down and kissed him lightly, the kind of kiss that said nothing and everything. "Just a long day," I lied, sliding into the seat beside him.

He pulled me close, his hand resting on my thigh, and I let myself melt into him. I laughed at his jokes. Asked about his day. Pretended the only thing   on my mind was *him*.

But in the quiet spaces between his words, I could still feel Mitch's hands on my body. I could still hear Soki's purr in my ear.

And Jake—sweet, steady Jake—had no idea that the woman in his arms was a battlefield he didn't even know he was standing on.

Chapter Ten

It was almost frightening how easily I could slip between them now.

With Jake, I was warmth, honesty, and stability—Emileigh, the woman who was learning from her mistakes, who looked at him like he was the answer to every prayer she'd ever whispered. I gave him soft touches, morning smiles, inside jokes that felt like they belonged only to us.

With Mitch, I was fire and hunger—Soki, the unapologetic creature who never denied herself. I gave him sharp wit, lingering looks, and the kind of raw passion that told him he still had a claim on me no one else could touch.

Neither man knew about the other's present hold on me. And neither could quite figure out the source of the unshakable confidence I carried lately.

The truth was, they were both getting exactly what they wanted.
And I was getting exactly what I shouldn't.

It should have made me feel powerful. Instead, it made me feel like I was standing in the middle of two tracks, each man barreling toward me from opposite directions.

Most days, I could ignore the sound of the approaching trains. But lately, it was getting louder. The weight of the lies. The way my hands shook when I thought too long about the truth.

I could see the cliff ahead—the moment when all of this would come crashing down—and still, I didn't move.

Because the ride, the rush, the control... it was intoxicating. And I wasn't sure how to get off without breaking into pieces.

The morning belonged to Jake.

We had coffee at the little café he loved, the one with mismatched mugs and creaky wooden floors. I listened to him talk about a new project at work, laughed at his dry humor, and reached across the table to squeeze his hand like he was the only man in my universe.

I meant it in that moment. I always meant it in that moment.

By the time we left, his eyes were softer, his guard down, his faith in *us* restored. He kissed my forehead and told me to have a good afternoon, not knowing where that afternoon would take me.

Because by two o'clock, I was Soki.

I slipped into Mitch's apartment without knocking, wearing the dress I knew would make his eyes darken in that instant, hungry way. His hands were on me before the door clicked shut, his mouth claiming mine like he had the right. I gave him what he wanted—sharp, urgent, messy kisses; my nails dragging across his skin; the kind of heat that left him leaning against the wall, catching his breath.

He grinned afterward, smug and satisfied, the look of a man convinced he still owned me. I let him believe it.

By six, I was back in my own apartment, barefoot in the kitchen, chopping vegetables for dinner with Jake like I'd spent the whole day running errands. I asked about his meeting. I teased him about the way he always over-salted pasta water.

No hesitation. No stutter in my voice.

The shift between women was seamless, terrifyingly so.

I caught my reflection in the microwave door at one point and almost didn't recognize her—the woman who could live two lives in one day and make both men feel like the center of hers.

Almost.

Sometimes, in the quiet between them, I think about what I'm doing.

The lies. The half-truths. The two sets of fingerprints on my skin.

And then I think about how I feel when I'm with Jake—safe, seen, loved in a way that feels steady enough to build a life on. I think about how I feel when I'm with Mitch—wild, reckless, alive in a way that makes my pulse race and my knees weak.

Yes, it's complicated. Yes, it's crazy. But I am the happiest I've ever been.

I know there's something deep-rooted in me that I've never dealt with—something tangled up in my past, my upbringing, my need for validation from men who could never fully have me. I know I'm not living the life a preacher's kid should live. But I stopped trying to live that life a long time ago.

The truth is, as long as Soki is happy, I'm happy. She fills in the cracks in my soul. She takes the edge off the ache I don't want to name.

And maybe that's twisted. Maybe that's wrong.

But it's mine.

It happened on a Thursday.

Jake had surprised me with lunch at the same bistro where Mitch and I sometimes met. I didn't think much of it—until I saw Mitch through the window. He was already inside, sitting at a corner table, scrolling his phone like he had all the time in the world.

My stomach dropped.

Jake followed my gaze, his brow furrowing. "You okay?"

"Yeah," I lied quickly, forcing my eyes back to him. "Just thought I saw someone I knew."

But Mitch had already looked up. His eyes found mine, and the slow smirk that spread across his face was all Soki.

I prayed he would stay put   . That he wouldn't make a scene. That the universe would let me have just one normal lunch.

Instead, he stood.

My breath caught as he started across the room, each step deliberate. Jake's head turned to follow my line of sight, and in that instant, I felt the world tilt.

Two men. Two lives. One truth barreling straight toward me.

Mitch's approach felt like slow motion.

I braced for impact—Jake's eyes narrowing, his jaw locking, the explosion I'd never be able to walk back from.

But just before he reached our table, a waitress stepped into his path with a tray of steaming plates. Mitch paused, sidestepped her, and glanced toward the door. His smirk deepened as if he'd just decided something.

Without a word, he pivoted and walked out.

Jake never looked back. By the time I turned my head, Mitch was gone—swallowed by the afternoon crowd.

"Em?" Jake's voice pulled me back. "You seem distracted."

I smiled, leaning forward like nothing had happened. "Just thinking about you."

He relaxed instantly, his hand covering mine. He had no idea he'd just been seconds away from shaking hands with the man who still had my body memorized.

Mitch, for his part, didn't care about lunches or long-term promises. He just liked knowing he could reach into my life whenever he wanted and pull me under. It wasn't love. It wasn't even a real connection. It was control—one I let him keep because part of me still craved it.

Jake, sweet, steady Jake, believed I was the wholesome woman he wanted to build a life with. And in some ways, I was. In other ways, I was Soki—the unapologetic voice inside me who always said *yes* when I should say *no*.

Poor Emileigh. She's the one holding all of this together, the one making sure both men feel exactly what they need to feel. And deep down, she knows if it came down to it, she would choose Jake over Mitch in a heartbeat.

But for reasons she doesn't want to look too closely at, she can't seem to give up the storm Mitch brings with him.

And Soki?
She's not giving him up for anyone.

That night, I stood in front of the bathroom mirror, wiping off my makeup.

The woman staring back at me looked calm. Composed. In control.

Jake was in the living room watching TV, completely unaware that my day had nearly imploded. Mitch was probably out somewhere with another woman, completely unaware that he'd almost shattered my other life.

And me?

I was in the middle, still standing.

Maybe I could really do this—keep my balance, keep the plates spinning, keep the men happy and the secrets intact. As long as I was careful, as long as Soki stayed in her lane, I could keep my two worlds from colliding.

I convinced myself of that as I turned off the bathroom light and slipped into bed beside Jake. His arm curled around me, warm and solid. For a moment, I let myself believe I belonged here and only here.

But the next test didn't wait.

Two days later, I was at the farmer's market picking up flowers for Jake's mom when I heard a voice behind me.

Not Mitch.

Not Jake.

A man I hadn't seen in years—one who knew me before Jake, before Mitch, before Soki had a name.

He leaned against the flower stand, smiling like he'd just found something he'd been searching for.

"Well, if it isn't Emileigh," he said. "Still as beautiful as I remember."

The way he looked at me stirred something I hadn't felt in a long time—something dangerous.

Soki woke up instantly.

I should have walked away. I should have smiled politely and kept moving.

Instead, I stood there, letting his eyes linger, letting his voice wrap around me.

Because some storms don't come from the people you expect.

His name was Adrian.

We'd met years ago, before Jake, before Mitch—before I had walls and before Soki had claws. Back then, we'd flirted without crossing lines, the kind of almost-romance that lives in looks and unfinished sentences. Seeing him now was like someone had pulled a thread I didn't know was still loose.

We got coffee.

One coffee became two.

Two became long text threads at night that I justified as *catching up*.

But Adrian didn't flirt like Mitch, all fire and dominance. And he wasn't like Jake, steady and grounding. He was soft but sharp, able to read between my words, to make me feel seen in a way neither of them did. That was its own kind of danger.

Soki welcomed him instantly—like she'd been waiting for him to take his place in the lineup.
Jake for stability.

Mitch for heat.

Adrian, for the emotional hit I didn't even realize I'd been craving.

It was a hoetation, and I was the center. The conductor. The woman with the power.

Except it wasn't really me running it.

It was Soki.

Emileigh was just the face—smiling, laughing, keeping the stories straight and the timelines separate. She was the one who remembered anniversaries with Jake, handled Mitch's texts in the middle of the night, and kept Adrian close enough to feel special but far enough not to suspect the others.

Some days, it was intoxicating.

Other days, it was suffocating.

Because while Soki thrived on the game, the thrill, the control—Emileigh felt herself splintering. She knew this wasn't sustainable. She knew there'd be a cost, one she wasn't sure she could pay.

Soki would be the death of her—naturally, emotionally, spiritually.

But right now?

Right now it was still... fun.

Soki wanted more.

Three men weren't just a thrill—they were a challenge. A puzzle she couldn't resist solving. How close could she get to the edge before someone noticed?

She started blurring the boundaries.

Answering Adrian's texts while lying in Jake's bed.

Letting Mitch leave marks she'd have to cover before brunch with Jake's family.

Sending Adrian pictures that were *just* innocent enough to explain away, but suggestive enough to keep his mind on her.

Each move was calculated.

Each risk made Soki stronger.

And then came the near miss.

Jake and I were out at a wine bar, our table tucked in the back, when I felt a familiar presence before I even saw him. Mitch—leaning against the bar, eyes locked on me like he'd been waiting for me to look up.

I forced my gaze back to Jake, but my body betrayed me—a shift, a breath, something small but sharp enough for Jake to notice.

"What?" he asked, his eyes narrowing just slightly.

"Nothing," I said quickly, reaching for my glass. But my hand shook just enough that a thin line of wine slid down the stem.

Jake's eyes lingered on me for a beat too long, and Soki stepped in with a soft laugh, a deflection, a story about something that happened at work. His attention slid back to me, the tension melting—at least on the surface.

When I dared glance toward the bar again, Mitch was gone.

But I knew better.

He wasn't gone. He was circling. Watching. Waiting for the perfect time to remind me that no matter how carefully I played this game, some pieces didn't belong to me.

And Soki?

She was daring him to make the next move.

Adrian's apartment smelled faintly of cedar and something darker—like the moment just before rain. He'd been texting me for days, painting pictures with his words until I couldn't resist.

I was Soki tonight. Entirely.

No hesitation. No apologies.

We barely made it to the couch before his hands were under my dress, his mouth claiming mine like he'd been starving. His kisses were softer than Mitch's, less disciplined than Jake's, but there was heat there. A hunger I hadn't tasted from him before.

And then the door opened.

A tall brunette in ripped jeans and a leather jacket stepped inside, her eyes locking on us instantly. Her mouth tightened, fists clenched at her sides.

"Oh," she said, voice cool but sharp. "So this is her."

I froze for a split second, waiting for the explosion. Instead, she dropped her bag, toed off her boots, and walked over like she was joining a conversation.

"You want me to stay?" she asked Adrian, her gaze never leaving mine.

His smirk was answer enough.

Minutes later, the tension had turned molten. Clothes hit the floor, breathless laughter mingled with low moans, and hands moved in places they shouldn't have. The air was thick with heat and something else—something reckless.

Her touch was different from theirs—curious, experimental, but surprisingly sure. Adrian kept his hands on both of us, pulling us closer, directing the rhythm until all three of us were moving as one.

When release came, it was messy and raw, a tangle of limbs and gasps. For a moment, no one spoke.

Then she turned to him, eyes sharp.
"Are you happy now?" she asked. "You finally got your threesome."

Adrian didn't even look at her when he answered. His eyes were on me.

"There's no *us*, Emileigh. There's only me and her."

Her.

The girlfriend he'd never really left.

Soki's satisfaction was shattered in an instant. It wasn't jealousy—it was rage. Pure, white-hot fury that someone had managed to write an ending she hadn't approved.

Because Soki was the author and finisher of relationships in her world.

And Adrian had just reminded her that in his, she was nothing more than a chapter.

Soki didn't rage out loud.

No screaming. No dramatics.

Her revenge was always quiet at first—measured, precise.

Adrian thought he could discard me like a casual fling? Fine. He'd learn exactly how costly that mistake could be. I didn't care about him the way I cared for Jake, and he'd never held the kind of dangerous power Mitch did, but this wasn't about love or lust. It was about control. And control was mine. Always.

By the time I left his apartment, Soki already had the blueprint: ruin him socially, shake him emotionally, and leave him wondering if he'd imagined my existence at all. Not because I wanted him back—because no one walked away from me without consequences.

But as the night air cooled my skin, my mind slipped back to Jake.

Jake, who believed I was still the woman he could trust.

Jake, who would never survive knowing how far Soki's web had spread.

And Mitch.

Mitch, whose hold on me was so deep that even Adrian's little game hadn't loosened it. In fact, it had tightened.

I realized something then—Adrian wasn't the threat. He was a distraction. The real storm was still Mitch. And the worst part? I wasn't sure I wanted that storm to end.

So I let the sting of Adrian's betrayal morph into something sharper, something I could wield. If Soki wanted Mitch, then Mitch would get all of her—enough to remind him why he couldn't quit me. Enough to risk everything Jake and I had built.

And the next move?

It was already in motion.

You said:

Both, but in order to keep her composure and her life's duality, Emileigh will have to have sex with Jake and Mitch   on the same day, just moments apart, because Jake's still choosing love has a surprise for Emileigh

ChatGPT said:

Perfect — here's Chapter Ten, Part 11, where Soki engineers back-to-back encounters with Jake and Mitch, all while holding her double life together because Jake's love comes with a surprise she can't ignore.

Soki thrived under pressure.

And today was the kind of pressure that could crush a normal woman.

Jake texted that morning—

Dinner tonight. Dress nice. I've got a surprise.
His tone was lighter than it had been in weeks, the edge of suspicion dulled but not gone.

I could have spent the day preparing for him, building the moment, but Mitch's name flashed on my phone before I could even reply.

Mitch: *Need to see you. Now.*

Soki didn't hesitate.

The pull was instant, magnetic, and reckless. Within the hour, I was in his apartment, pressed against the door as he kissed me like he'd been counting the minutes since the last time.

It was rough—nearly feral. He stripped me down without ceremony, his hands and mouth leaving trails of possession over every inch of me. The rhythm was urgent, the kind that didn't care about tomorrow, only the now. When the release came, it left me weak, trembling, and already calculating the time.

I was in Jake's driveway twenty-eight minutes later.

The contrast was whiplash.

Jake's hands were gentler, lingering on my face before sliding down my waist. His kisses tasted like the wine he'd opened early "just because." His lovemaking was slower, intentional—a reminder of how much he loved me, how much he wanted me to feel safe in him.

I let him believe it. I even leaned into it. Because when he rolled onto his side and pulled a small velvet box from the nightstand, my breath caught.

"I'm not asking yet," he said softly. "But I need you to know... I see us. Long-term. For real."

My throat tightened. Emileigh—the part of me that still remembered church pews and whispered prayers—wanted to cry. But Soki smiled, kissed him, and made love to him again, sealing the illusion that she belonged entirely to him.

Even as the scent of Mitch still clung faintly to my skin.

Mitch always knew when the stakes shifted.
He could smell it.

And Jake's little velvet box? That was blood in the water.

He didn't want to marry me. Hell, he didn't even want to date me in the conventional sense. What Mitch wanted was control—his brand of possession, the kind that left fingerprints on your soul long after the body healed.

So when he showed up outside my office two days later, leaning against his car like he had all the time in the world, I knew exactly what game he was playing.

"You gonna invite me in," he said, "or should we talk about how Jake's planning to chain you to him?"

I rolled my eyes. "It's called a commitment, Mitch. Not a chain."

He smirked. "Chains, rings... same thing if you're not ready."

Soki liked the way he said it. Emileigh hated that she did.

He leaned in closer, his voice dropping. "We both know you're not built for forever with one man. You like too much of *this*." His hand brushed my hip, slow and deliberate, sending a rush of heat I didn't want to acknowledge.

"I'm not trying to ruin you two," he continued, reading the protest in my eyes. "I'm just here to remind you of who you are. And when you're with me, you're exactly that."

It was subtle, calculated—just enough to plant the seed of doubt, not enough to make me run.

And the worst part? Jake could feel it.
Not in the specifics, but in the way he watched me now, like he was silently asking if he was still enough.

He believed he was. He loved me with all my isms and skisms, never flinching from the mess. Jake always chose love.

But Mitch? Mitch always chose manipulation.

And somewhere between the two of them, I was still choosing chaos.

It happened at the wine bar downtown—neutral territory, at least until Mitch walked in.

He didn't even look around. His eyes locked on me instantly, and that smirk told me the intrusion was no accident.

Jake stiffened beside me, his arm tightening around my waist.

Mitch didn't care. He strolled over like we'd been expecting him.

"Em," he said smoothly, ignoring Jake entirely. "You didn't text me back."

The alpha in Jake woke up in that moment. I saw it in the way his shoulders squared, in the heat that rolled off him before he even spoke.

"She doesn't owe you anything," Jake said, his voice low and dangerous.

Mitch chuckled, leaning just close enough to make it disrespectful. "She owes me more than you think."

And that's when Jake moved.

One second, he was sitting   ; the next, he was on his feet, towering over Mitch. The tension in the bar snapped like a wire—voices went quiet, eyes turned toward us.

"You don't talk to her. You don't look at her. You don't *breathe* in her direction unless she asks you to," Jake growled, his fists clenched.

For a heartbeat, I thought he'd throw the punch I knew he wanted to. But I stepped between them, my hands on Jake's chest, feeling the steady thump of his fury.

"Not here," I whispered. "He's not worth it."

Mitch smirked at me over Jake's shoulder, but Jake didn't bite again. He let me pull him toward the door, his hand gripping mine like he was claiming ownership in front of the whole city.

The air outside was sharp, cold , and charged.
Jake's mouth was on mine before we even reached the car. It wasn't gentle, wasn't patient. It was the kind of kiss that said *you're mine, and I'm done pretending otherwise.*

We stumbled into the alley beside the building, his hands pushing up my dress, my breath catching at the raw urgency in him.

"This is what you do to me," he rasped, and then there was no space left between us. The brick wall at my back, Jake's body pinning me in place, the night air biting at my skin while heat roared through me.

It was reckless. Public. And Soki loved every second of it.

When it was over, Jake's forehead rested against mine, his breathing ragged.

"I'm not losing you," he said.

And for that moment, I almost believed him.

Jake's alpha energy still buzzed in my veins hours later.

It wasn't just the sex—it was the way he claimed me without apology. For once, I wasn't holding him together. He was holding *me.*

But Soki... Soki wasn't satisfied.
She didn't just want to be claimed. She wanted to be fought over.

That's why, instead of going home like the good, reformed woman Jake thought I was, I found myself leaning against the hood of my car outside Mitch's building. The cold air bit at my skin, but inside, I was still burning.

He came out just after midnight, keys in hand, and froze when he saw me.

"Thought the boyfriend marked his territory tonight," Mitch said, smirk curling slow and lethal.

I shrugged. "Maybe I wanted to see if the other contender still had a shot."

His laugh was low, knowing. "You're playing with both matches and gasoline, Em."

"Maybe," I said, pushing off the car, closing the space between us. "Or maybe I just like watching you try."

He stepped closer, eyes narrowing with that predator's patience. "You think I'm going to fight him for you?"

"No," I whispered, letting Soki speak through me. "I think you'll fight him just enough to make him doubt. Just enough to keep me where you want me."

And the truth? Mitch didn't deny it. He didn't have to.

The way he kissed me said everything—that he knew exactly how to be the storm Jake feared and the drug I couldn't quit.

Somewhere deep down, Emileigh screamed at me to stop.
But Soki? She leaned in.

Mitch didn't rush me.

That was his power—making me wait, making me *want* before he even touched me.

"You smell like him," he murmured, brushing a strand of hair from my face.

"Maybe," I said, holding his gaze. "Or maybe he smells like me."

That earned me a slow, dangerous grin. "You're trouble."

"You've always liked trouble."

He stepped closer, his chest brushing mine. "You came here after being with him… why?"

I could've lied. Could've said I was here for closure or to end it once and for all. But Soki told the truth—the kind of truth that tasted like sin.

"Because you're the one I can't quit."

That was all it took. Mitch's hands were in my hair, his mouth crushing mine, the kiss all teeth and heat. He didn't ease me into it—he took. Every movement said he knew exactly where the soft spots were, the ones Jake hadn't touched tonight.

I found myself pressed against his door, his hand sliding up my thigh, pushing the hem of my dress higher until the cool air kissed bare skin.

"Upstairs," he ordered, and I didn't argue.

The moment the door shut behind us, the pace turned feral. Clothes hit the floor in careless trails. His hands roamed like he was mapping out old territory, memorizing every rise and curve.

When he pushed me onto the couch, my knees bent over the armrest, I didn't even pretend to resist. The first thrust knocked the air from my lungs, but I didn't want it back. His rhythm was brutal, relentless, a claiming all his own—but not like Jake's. Jake's was love; Mitch's was ownership.

Somewhere in the chaos, I realized I was letting Soki run this whole scene   because Emileigh would have said no. Emileigh would have chosen Jake.

But Soki? Soki wanted it all—the danger, the sin, the taste of destruction.

And when I came, it wasn't Jake's name that tore from my lips.

The morning light felt too clean for the night I'd had.

I stood in my bathroom, toothbrush in hand, scrubbing until my gums ached, as if mint and foam could erase the taste of Mitch from my mouth.

By the time Jake pulled up outside, I was wrapped in the version of me he knew—soft hair, soft smile, the kind of perfume he once said made him think of home.

"Morning, beautiful," he said when I slid into his car. His kiss was warm, familiar. Safe.

And God, I wanted that safety. I wanted him.

So I leaned into it. I asked about his day, laughed at the right moments, and touched his arm just enough to make him feel chosen. And in my own twisted way, I *was* choosing him—choosing to be here, to be the woman he believed in, at least for now.

But underneath, Soki purred.

Not smug. Not guilty. Just... satisfied. She knew she still had the reins, even if I was the one smiling at Jake over coffee.

Jake reached across the table, lacing his fingers through mine. "I'm glad we're okay," he said quietly. "I don't know what I'd do without you."

I squeezed his hand. "You won't have to find out."

It was the truth in the moment, the best way I knew how to give it.

Even if it wasn't the *whole* truth.

The days that followed felt almost like a honeymoon—minus the vows.
Jake and I found a rhythm that made me forget, for hours at a time, about storms with names like Mitch and Soki.

He'd text me in the middle of his shift just to say he missed me. I'd show up at his place with takeout, and we'd curl up on the couch, legs tangled, watching old movies we'd both seen a hundred times.

There were mornings we didn't leave the bed until noon, our bodies finding each other in that slow, unhurried way that wasn't about proving anything—just about being close. And each time, I felt the weight of his love settling deeper into me, heavy and steady like an anchor.

One night, lying in his arms after the kind of love-making that felt more like worship than sex, he pressed his lips to my temple and whispered, "I'm not going anywhere, Em. Not unless you push me away."

It should've been a comfort. And part of me believed him. But another part—Soki's part—shifted restlessly, almost irritated by the certainty.

Still, I tucked the words away   because the longer I stayed in this warmth, the harder it would be to leave.

And maybe, just maybe, I didn't want to leave at all.

Weeks passed in a blur of quiet mornings, late-night talks, and the kind of simple moments that sneak up on you and plant roots.

Jake started leaving more of his things at my place—a hoodie draped over my chair, his favorite mug tucked in my cabinet. I didn't ask him to, but I didn't move them either. Each item felt like a silent promise.

We took a weekend trip to the lake, just the two of us, no distractions. I caught him watching me when he thought I wasn't looking, that soft, unguarded gaze that made me feel like the only woman in the world.

And for the first time in a long time, I wasn't performing. I wasn't choosing between masks. I was just... me. Or maybe the me I wanted to be.

One night, as we sat on the porch, sharing a blanket against the crisp air, Jake's hand found mine. "You ever think about forever?" he asked.

I froze—not because I didn't want it, but because I wasn't sure I deserved it. "Sometimes," I said, careful to keep my voice steady.

His thumb traced lazy circles over my knuckles. "I do. A lot."

I didn't push for more. But later, when I caught him scrolling through a jeweler's website on his phone, something in my chest tightened.

He was getting ready to make a choice.
And I had to decide if I was ready to live with it—if I could keep Soki locked away long enough to say yes without lying through my teeth.

It happened on a Tuesday.

Jake said he had errands, but when he came back, there was a shift in his energy—lighter, almost boyish. He kissed me like he'd been carrying a secret all day, one he wasn't ready to spill but couldn't stop smiling about.

Later, while he was in the shower, his phone lit up on the nightstand. A text from a number I didn't recognize: *The ring will be ready for pickup on Friday.*

My stomach knotted. Not from fear of commitment, but from the jagged truth that I was still living in a glass house, and Soki was constantly throwing stones.

That night, I lay in bed, staring at the ceiling while Jake slept peacefully beside me. In my head, Soki's voice purred like velvet over steel.

Forever's a long time to play nice.

I tried to push her away, but the harder I resisted, the louder she became—reminding me of every thrill, every stolen touch, every fire I'd lit just to watch it burn.

Jake murmured my name in his sleep and pulled me closer, his arm draping over me like armor. I wanted to believe his love could protect me from myself.

But deep down, I knew the next test was coming.

And when it did, I wasn't sure who would answer— Emileigh... or Soki.

Friday came with a bite of autumn in the air. Jake left early, telling me he had to "handle something in the city" before we met up later. I didn't need a crystal ball to know what that something was—the ring.

I decided to clear my head with a walk, hoping the fresh air would quiet Soki's whispers. But halfway down the block, I saw him leaning against a black SUV, sunglasses low, smile sharp enough to cut glass.

Mitch.

My feet slowed before my brain could command them to move. He pushed off the car with that easy swagger, the kind that always looked like he owned the ground he walked on.

"Miss me?" he asked, voice dripping with the kind of confidence only a man who knew the answer could have.

"I thought we were done," I said, keeping my tone flat, my hands shoved in my coat pockets to keep them from trembling.

He stepped closer, close enough for his cologne to drag me back to nights I didn't want to remember but couldn't seem to forget. "You thought wrong."

Every part of me screamed to turn and walk away, to run straight back to Jake. But Soki leaned forward in my mind, grinning like she'd been waiting for this exact moment.

You didn't think it would be that easy, did you?

Mitch's eyes roamed over me like he was already undressing me in his head. "One drink. No strings. For old times' sake."

I should've said no.

Instead, I heard myself say, "One drink."

And just like that, I felt the first wind gust of a storm I knew I wouldn't be able to outrun.

The bar was dim, the kind of place where secrets could sit in the shadows and never be found. Mitch ordered my drink without asking, sliding it toward me with that smirk that always meant trouble.

"You look good," he said. "Too good for the life you're pretending to live."

I bristled. "I'm not pretending."

He leaned in, eyes locking on mine. "Then why are you here with me?"

Soki answered for me before I could. *Because I want to be.*

I felt my pulse spike, that dangerous mix of adrenaline and heat curling through me. Mitch knew it too—he always knew. His hand brushed mine on the bar, casual but deliberate, and I didn't pull away.

Miles away, Jake stepped into a quiet jeweler's shop. The clerk handed him a small black box, the kind that carried promises heavier than gold. He flipped it open, staring at the diamond that caught the light like it had been waiting for Emileigh all along.

Back at the bar, Mitch's hand slid to my thigh under the table, his touch sparking memories I swore I'd buried.

"This doesn't have to be complicated," he murmured. "It can just be what it's always been—us."

Jake signed the receipt with steady hands, his chest swelling with a hope he couldn't wait to bring home. He imagined my face when I saw the ring, the way my eyes might shine, the way my hands might shake when I said yes.

Mitch's lips brushed my ear. "Let's get out of here."

And Soki, without hesitation, smiled. "Lead the way."

Mitch's apartment was exactly as I remembered—low lights, leather, and the faint scent of whiskey and sin. The door clicked shut behind us, sealing me in with every bad decision I'd ever made in his presence.

He didn't waste time. His mouth crashed into mine, hands gripping my hips with that same urgency that had always made my resolve melt. I told myself to stop, to remember Jake's face, Jake's love.

But Soki had already shoved me into the backseat of my own mind.
This is ours, she purred. *Not his.*

Clothes fell away in pieces, and soon there was nothing between us but heat and history. Mitch moved like he knew every inch of me—because he did. Every kiss was a claim, every thrust a reminder of the pull I'd never fully escaped.

It was wild, almost reckless, the kind of sex that blurred the line between pleasure and surrender. My nails raked his back, his teeth grazed my skin, and the sound of our breathing filled the room like a storm tearing through the night.

When it was over, I lay there catching my breath, skin slick, heart racing. Mitch smirked, pulling me against him like he'd just won something.

But in that haze, I knew the truth—this wasn't love. It was Soki feeding on chaos, on temptation, on the dangerous satisfaction of getting exactly what she wanted.

And somewhere, probably sitting in his truck with that ring in his pocket, Jake was still choosing me. Still believing in the version of me that I wanted to be but couldn't seem to hold onto.

My chest tightened. Because no matter how many times Soki took over, deep down, I still loved Jake.

I just didn't know if love would be enough to survive me.

The morning light felt different. Not soft or forgiving— just bright enough to expose everything I wanted to hide.

I showered longer than usual, scrubbing my skin until it tingled, hoping the water could wash away what had happened. But no matter how hard I tried, Soki's voice stayed close.

We had fun. Don't ruin it with guilt.

By the time I reached Jake's place, I had my smile ready, my story straight, and my heart aching in that way it always did when I saw him. He opened the door, and there he was— my safe place, my steady ground.

"Morning, beautiful," he said, kissing my forehead like I was made of something worth protecting.

I melted into his arms, inhaling the scent of coffee and him. This was the life I wanted to choose. This was the man I wanted to fight for.

We spent the day like nothing had shifted. He made breakfast; I laughed at his terrible pancake-flipping skills.

We took a walk, fingers laced, and he pointed out houses he thought we'd like "someday."

The ring in his pocket was still a secret, but I could feel it in the way he looked at me—like he was already building a life in his head with my name on it.

And I let him. Because choosing Jake—at least in the daylight—felt right.

But later, when he stepped into the kitchen to grab more coffee, Soki's reflection caught mine in the darkened window. Her smile was slow, satisfied.

You can play the good girl all you want, she whispered. *But we both know who's really running this show.*

I blinked, forcing the thought away before Jake came back, slipping my hand into his like it belonged there.

Because for now, it did.

The weeks that followed were deceptively calm. Almost peaceful.

Jake and I fell into an easy rhythm—morning coffee together, his hand brushing mine when he left for work, his texts throughout the day that made me smile even when I didn't want to.

We cooked dinner at home more. We talked about music and road trips and the kind of house that had a porch big enough for a swing. And the more we talked, the more I felt him weaving me into his future like it was already written.

I caught him staring at me one evening while I was curled up on his couch, reading. His expression was so full of something—love, maybe even awe—that it made my chest tighten.

"What?" I asked, smiling despite myself.

"Just... you," he said softly. "Sometimes I think about how lucky I am. How lucky I could be."

It was the kind of moment that should've made me feel secure, but instead it made me restless. Because I could feel Soki shifting inside me, scratching at the walls like she was waiting for her turn to speak.

One night, Jake reached across the dinner table and took my hand.

"Em... I've been thinking. There's something I want to ask you soon. Not tonight. Not like this. But soon."

The look in his eyes left no room for guessing—he was moving toward forever.

And part of me wanted to run straight into it, to lock the door behind us and shut out every storm.

But the other part—the darker, hungrier part—was already wondering how long it would take before I blew it all apart.

I should've known the calm wouldn't last.

It never did with Mitch.

I was leaving the grocery store when I saw him leaning against his car like he'd been waiting for me all day. Hands in his pockets, that crooked grin that had been both a curse and a lifeline once upon a time.

"You look... domestic," he said, eyes flicking to the paper bags in my hands. "Playing house with lover boy?"

I didn't answer. The smart move would've been to keep walking, get in my car, and drive away. But I didn't.

He fell into step beside me. "Word on the street is Jake's about to lock you down. That true?"

The weight in my chest was instant. "You've been asking around about me?"

"Don't have to ask," he said with a shrug. "People talk. And I don't like what I'm hearing. You and me—" he leaned in closer, voice dropping "—we're not done."

I scoffed, but it came out shaky. "We were done a long time ago."

"Funny," he said, his gaze pinning mine, "you never look at me like you look at him. With me, you're alive. I see it. And you feel it, even if you won't admit it."

His words burrowed under my skin, the way they always did, finding the cracks I didn't want him to see.

He stepped back, smirking. "I'm not here to break you two up. I just want to make sure you don't forget where the fire started."

As he walked away, I stood frozen in the parking lot, my pulse pounding. I could feel Soki leaning in close, smiling in that way that made me nervous.
He's not wrong, she whispered.

I shoved the thought down and drove home, rehearsing a smile for Jake. But the truth followed me into the house, curling up beside me like it planned to stay awhile.

Atlanta is big.

Too big for this.

That's what Jake said later, but in the moment, I could feel the air shift before I even saw Mitch. We were at a midtown street festival, music pumping, food trucks lining the block, Jake's arm slung comfortably over my shoulders. It felt... safe.

Until Mitch's voice cut through the crowd.

"Well, if it isn't my favorite couple."

I stiffened. Jake's hand tensed against my shoulder, his eyes narrowing before he even turned. Mitch was standing there in a dark tee and jeans, looking like trouble disguised as casual charm.

"Twice in two weeks," Jake said evenly. "What are the odds?"

Mitch smirked. "Guess the universe likes putting us in the same orbit."

Jake didn't respond right away. He just studied Mitch—too calmly, like he was measuring the space between a laugh and a punch. Then his gaze slid to me. Not accusing, not doubting... but questioning.

"You two know each other from before, right?"

"Yeah," Mitch said before I could answer, his tone slick. "Old friends. Real old."

Jake's jaw flexed, but he smiled, that sharp, alpha kind of smile I'd never seen from him before. "Good to know who's who. Always nice to put a face to a name."

They shook hands, and for a second, I thought Jake might crush his bones. Mitch didn't flinch, but I caught the way his mouth tightened.

When Mitch finally walked away, Jake didn't speak. He just scanned the crowd for a long moment before pulling me closer.

"This city's too big for all these chance encounters," he said quietly in my ear. "I don't know what's going on... but I'm here for it."

It wasn't a threat. It was a promise. And something in me—Soki, maybe—thrilled at the sound of it.

We barely made it through the door.

Jake had been quiet all the way home, but his hand stayed on my thigh like it belonged there. When the door clicked shut behind us, he turned, caging me against it.

"That guy..." His voice was low, vibrating through me. "I don't like the way he looks at you. I don't like the way he talks to you. And I damn sure don't like that he keeps showing up."

My breath caught. "Jake—"

"No." His mouth was at my ear now, his grip firm on my hip. "I've been patient. I've given you space. But I'm done letting someone else think they have a claim on what's mine."

The words lit something in me I didn't expect—something Soki recognized instantly. Alpha. Possessive. Unyielding.

Before I could answer, he kissed me hard, the kind of kiss that demanded, not asked. His hands were everywhere—pulling, gripping, owning. My back hit the wall, and his mouth claimed my neck, teeth grazing until I gasped.

If he could stay like this—commanding, unapologetic—Mitch wouldn't stand a chance. Soki wouldn't need him. And maybe, just maybe, I could let her sleep forever.

But Jake didn't know that. He didn't know he was already part of a triangle that would shatter him if the truth ever surfaced.

As his hands slid under my shirt and his mouth crushed mine again, I made a silent decision: I had to marry him. Before he found out. Before Mitch figured out how deep he still ran in my veins.

Because if Jake ever learned the truth, it wouldn't just ruin us—it would ruin him. And I couldn't live with that.

Jake didn't give me a chance to catch my breath. He scooped me up, carrying me to the bedroom like I weighed nothing. The air between us was charged—feral, hungry.

He set me down on the edge of the bed, his eyes locked on mine. "Strip," he ordered, voice rough.

Something in me—Soki—answered before Emileigh could even think. I peeled my clothes off slowly, letting them fall in a careless heap on the floor.

Jake stood at the foot of the bed, watching, jaw tight. When I was bare before him, he moved, his hands gripping my thighs to drag me to the edge.

"You're mine," he said again, lower this time, as if staking a claim in the marrow of my bones.

His mouth was on me before I could speak, tongue and lips working with unrelenting precision until my fingers knotted in his hair. He didn't let up—not when I gasped, not when my hips jerked—until I was shaking, toes curling in the sheets.

Then he was over me, pinning me down with his weight, his mouth crashing onto mine as he pushed inside. Deep. Hard.

Every thrust was a declaration, every groan a promise. He kept his hand at my throat, his eyes locked on mine as if daring me to look away. I didn't. I couldn't.

When I came again, it was with his name on my lips—not Mitch's, not anyone's.

Soki was purring, satisfied in a way Mitch had never managed. And in that moment, I knew—if Jake could keep this side of himself alive, I could keep her quiet forever.

By the time we collapsed together, slick with sweat and breathless, my mind was already spinning. I'd marry him. Soon. Before the truth burned us to the ground.

Chapter Eleven

The morning light was soft, spilling across Jake's bare chest as he slept. I lay beside him, studying the man who'd just unknowingly shifted the entire balance of my world.

If he stayed this Jake—the Alpha, the protector, the man who made both me and Soki feel claimed—there would be no need for Mitch.

But I knew storms didn't just vanish. Hurricane Mitch still lurked somewhere out there, and Tornado Soki… she never stayed quiet for long.

For now, though, I curled into Jake's side, breathing him in, letting myself believe in a happily ever after that might actually be within reach.

Because today, I was choosing love. And for once, it felt like love might be choosing me back.

For the next few days, the city seemed to slow down just for us.

No interruptions. No chance encounters. No Mitch.

Jake worked his shifts and came straight home. I cooked—or at least tried—and we ate together at the little kitchen table that had seen more takeout containers than homemade meals. He'd tease me about my "culinary experiments," and I'd roll my eyes, but inside, it warmed me.

Evenings were our time. We'd curl up on the couch, me tucked under his arm while he absentmindedly ran his hand along my thigh, tracing circles in a way that felt almost absentminded until it didn't. The touches that turned into kisses. The kisses that turned into heat.

We weren't making love to fill a void or patch a wound—it was different now. Slower sometimes. Deeper. The kind of intimacy that didn't just happen in the bedroom.

Jake was choosing me, over and over again. And I was letting him.

Because if I could keep us here—this space where I didn't crave Mitch's chaos—maybe we'd make it.

Soki hated it. I could feel her pacing inside me like a caged animal. No drama. No temptation. No raw, reckless highs. Just Jake. And me.

One night, as we lay in bed after hours of talking and laughing, he pressed a kiss to my forehead. "You know," he murmured, "I've never wanted something to work as badly as I want this to work."

I swallowed, my throat tight. "Me too."

And for the first time, I almost meant it with all of me—not just the part that could play perfect for him.

Mornings started to feel... normal.
Jake would make coffee before I even got out of bed, and I'd hear the clink of the mug against the counter before his footsteps padded back to the bedroom. He'd hand it to me with that sleepy half-smile that made me want to stay under the covers all day.

We'd talk about nothing—whether it was supposed to rain, a new place to try for lunch, the neighbor's ridiculous lawn decorations—and I liked it. No edge. No performance. Just… us.

Jake trusted me more every day. I could see it in the way his shoulders relaxed when I was late getting home, the way his questions shifted from *Where were you?* to *How was your day?*

Soki was restless, sure, but I kept her on a leash. For now, she could simmer in the background. She could watch as I let Jake be the anchor instead of the storm.

One afternoon, we drove out past the city limits just because. We ended up at a little roadside diner that looked like it hadn't changed since the '70s. We ate greasy burgers, shared a slice of pie, and Jake laughed so hard at one of my stories that the waitress brought over more coffee just to keep us talking.

For the first time in a long time, I didn't feel like I was lying to him just by being in the same room.

Nights with Jake were easy.

We'd watch old movies, the kind he'd seen a hundred times but still quoted word-for-word. He'd make popcorn, toss in extra butter just because he knew I liked it that way, and I'd let my head rest on his chest, listening to the steady rhythm of his breathing.

He wasn't trying to impress me. He wasn't angling for control.

He just *was*. And that was enough.

Every so often, his hand would find mine, our fingers locking together without a word. That small gesture—the quiet certainty of it—was more grounding than any speech he could've given me.

Soki didn't understand it. She whispered in the back of my mind about excitement, about the thrill of being wanted by more than one man, about the heat that came from danger. But for now, I ignored her. I wanted to stay here in this quiet place, where my biggest choice was between Netflix and old VHS tapes.

On Sunday morning, he made breakfast. Real breakfast. Eggs, bacon, toast, the works.

I sat on the counter in one of his shirts, sipping coffee and watching him move around the kitchen like he owned it. Like he owned *this*.

"Why are you looking at me like that?" he asked, catching me mid-smile.

"Like what?"

"Like I'm the only man in the world," he said, sliding a plate in front of me.

I bit my lip. "Because right now, you are."

And I meant it—at least in that moment.

We ate in comfortable silence, the kind that comes when you don't have to fill the air to feel connected.

Later, we went for a walk through Piedmont Park, the city buzzing quietly in the background. He held my hand the whole time, and I let him. I didn't look over my shoulder. I didn't check my phone.

For the first time in months, I wasn't chasing anything or anyone. I was exactly where I wanted to be.

The next evening, Jake showed up at my door with a bottle of wine and that smile that always made my knees weak.

"No special occasion?" I asked, letting him in.

"Every day with you is a special occasion," he said without missing a beat. Cheesy? Absolutely. But the way he said it—soft, steady, eyes locked on mine—made it land.

We cooked dinner together, though "cooked" might be generous. It was more like Jake doing all the actual work while I stole bites of pasta and distracted him with kisses. He caught me once, arms wrapping around my waist from behind, his mouth brushing against my ear.

"You know you're trouble, right?" he murmured.

"Maybe," I said, turning in his arms. "But I'm your trouble."

After dinner, we stayed in the kitchen. We didn't make it to the couch, or the bedroom, or anywhere else. His hands were in my hair, mine were tangled in his shirt, and somewhere between his laugh and my gasp, the wine bottle was forgotten.

We made love slow that night, like neither of us wanted to get to the end too quickly. Every kiss felt deliberate, every touch memorized. He held me after, his hand tracing slow circles on my back, and I thought—maybe Soki could stay quiet forever if it always felt like this.

Jake kissed the top of my head. "You're it for me, Em. You know that, right?"

I nodded, not trusting my voice. Because if I spoke, I'd have to admit that I wanted to be "it" for him, too.

Chapter Twelve

The days started to bleed together in the best way. Coffee in the morning with Jake before work. A text from him at lunch—*Just thinking about you*. Dinner together at least three nights a week. Weekends spent doing nothing important but somehow making everything feel important.

It was dangerous, this peace.

Because peace has a way of making you believe the war is over.

Even Soki was quiet, tucked away in some back corner of my mind, like she'd been lulled into hibernation. I wasn't looking for trouble. I wasn't chasing danger. I was... happy.

Jake was happy, too. He stopped watching my eyes for secrets. He stopped asking where I'd been when we weren't together. He stopped holding his breath when my phone buzzed.

It wasn't perfect—we still had moments where the air got tight between us—but for the first time in months, we both believed we could do this. That maybe love was enough.

The first whisper of trouble didn't even come from Mitch.

It was a man I barely knew, a passing acquaintance from years ago, stopping me outside a bookstore on a Tuesday afternoon. His smile lingered too long. His hand brushed mine when he didn't need to. I walked away without giving him my number, but the hum in my chest—the spark I hadn't felt since Mitch—was enough to make me uneasy.

I didn't tell Jake.

Not because I wanted the man, but because I didn't want to admit that part of me still craved the attention.

It's strange how something so small can plant itself in your mind and grow roots.

I kept replaying the bookstore encounter, not because it mattered, but because it reminded me that I could still turn heads. That maybe I hadn't lost all of me in this new version of my life with Jake.

And that's where the danger was—because with Jake, I didn't *want* to be anyone else. But with Soki, I wanted *everything*.

That night, I curled up next to Jake on the couch, his arm slung lazily around me. He was telling me about some ridiculous thing that happened at work, his voice easy, his laugh warm, and yet... my mind drifted. Not to the man from the bookstore, exactly, but to the feeling he stirred in me.

I hated it.

I wanted to live in this bubble with Jake, wanted to believe I could. But Soki had woken up enough to stretch her legs, and she was watching. Waiting.

Jake didn't notice. Or maybe he chose not to. He kissed my forehead, asked me if I wanted dessert, and for a moment, I convinced myself it was fine.

But deep down, I knew the truth.

This wasn't the kind of temptation that knocked down your door. This was the kind that slid through the cracks in your walls, unnoticed, until it was already inside.

It happened in the most ordinary way.

I was running late, juggling a paper coffee cup and my phone, when I nearly collided with someone rounding the corner outside the parking garage.

"Careful," a voice said, low and amused.

The coffee almost slipped from my hands before I even looked up.

Mitch.

He was dressed like he'd stepped straight out of a magazine—dark jeans, a fitted black shirt, jacket slung casually over his shoulder. That smirk I knew too well curled at the edge of his mouth.

"Small city," he said, like it was a joke only we were in on.

"It's not that small," I replied, my voice sharper than I meant it to be.

His eyes tracked me like they always did—lazy, knowing. "Guess we just have a knack for finding each other."

It was nothing. A three-minute exchange at most. No lingering touches, no stolen kisses, no whispered invitations. But the weight of his gaze stayed with me the rest of the day.

Jake called that night, voice warm and unguarded, telling me he missed me. I said it back, meaning every word.

But lying in bed, I could still hear Mitch's voice in my head.

And that's when I realized it—these weren't chance encounters. Mitch wasn't letting go.

Mitch had never been one for patience.

But this—this was a game worth playing slow.

He leaned against the hood of his car after I walked away, watching me disappear into the glass-and-steel building. He didn't follow. Not today.

Because Mitch knew the rules , you didn't break the bubble all at once—you poked it. Just enough to make her think about you when she shouldn't. Just enough to keep your presence humming under her skin.

Jake thought he had her wrapped up on Sunday mornings and safe choices. But Mitch knew better.

He'd *felt* it in the way her pulse jumped when she saw him. The way her eyes lingered half a second too long. That wasn't love. That was instinct.

And instincts always won.

He lit a cigarette, letting the smoke curl into the cool evening air, and smiled to himself. He wouldn't take her from Jake. Not yet. No—he'd give her enough rope to tangle herself in.

Because when she came back—and Mitch had no doubt she would—it would be on her knees, desperate, and on *his* terms.

Mitch never lied to himself—he didn't want Emileigh in the way Jake did.

He didn't want Sunday mornings or shared bills or "our song" moments.

What he wanted was simpler.

Control.

Emileigh had been his once, body and mind. And somewhere deep in that dark part of him, Mitch believed she always would be. Not because of love—he didn't believe in that. Because he knew her flaws, the cracks she tried to hide from the world. He knew the parts of her that were too raw, too restless to be content for long.

And if Mitch couldn't keep her, he damn sure wasn't going to let her be happy without him.

It wasn't even about her anymore—it was about the power. The thrill of knowing that no matter how far she ran or who she tried to be with, one look, one touch from him could pull her back into the undertow.

Mitch didn't call it cruelty. In his mind, it was just the truth. He thought Jake was living a fantasy, building a future with a woman who couldn't outrun herself.

And Mitch was more than willing to prove it.

Jake's world didn't have storm clouds tonight.

He stood in the kitchen barefoot, sleeves rolled, humming low to himself while he stirred something on the stove. The scent of garlic and rosemary wrapped around the room like a blanket.

When I padded in, hair damp from my shower, he looked up and grinned—like I was the only thing he'd been waiting on all day.

"Dinner's almost ready," he said, wiping his hands and pulling me in for a kiss. It was soft, unhurried, the kind of kiss that said *you're home* even if we were standing in a one-bedroom apartment.

I let myself sink into it, into him, into the dangerous warmth of believing this could last. The laughter, the way he made space for me without asking for anything in return, the steady way his hand rested at the small of my back like I belonged there.

If Mitch was fire, Jake was water—cooling, cleansing, necessary. And yet... water couldn't stop me from craving the burn.

Jake ladled pasta onto two plates, poured me a glass of wine, and slid into the chair across from me. His eyes searched mine—not suspicious, just curious—like he wanted to memorize this version of me, the one who wasn't guarded or distracted.

"I like nights like this," he said. "No plans. Just us."

I smiled, meaning it more than I wanted to admit. "Me too."

And for the length of that meal, I believed my own lie.

Jake had a way of looking at me like he was already seeing the rest of our lives.

It made my chest ache in a way I couldn't name—half longing, half guilt.

We'd been curled up on the couch after dinner, a blanket over us, some old movie playing in the background. My head rested against his chest, listening to the steady beat of his heart. It was the kind of night where time blurred, where you could almost believe the rest of the world didn't exist.

His fingers traced lazy circles on my arm, a quiet rhythm that made my eyes heavy. But then his voice shifted, deepening just enough to make me glance up.

"I've been thinking," he said.

That tone—careful, deliberate—meant it was something big.

"About us," he continued. "About what we're building here. And… where I want it to go."

A flicker of panic sparked inside me, quick and sharp. I pushed it down before it could reach my face. "Where do you want it to go?"

His smile was soft but sure. "Forward. Permanently forward."

My breath caught, but I didn't let it show. Instead, I brushed my lips against his jaw. "I like the sound of that."

He kissed the top of my head, as if my answer had sealed something for him. I didn't know it yet, but Jake was already making plans—ring-sized plans.

I let my eyes drift shut, burying myself in his scent, his warmth. If I could just stay here, in this moment, maybe I wouldn't have to think about the truth—that no matter how much I wanted to be the woman Jake believed I was, Soki was always somewhere in the shadows… waiting for her turn.

Mitch's contempt for love didn't start with Emileigh — she's just the one who triggers it the most.

His Backstory.

Years before Emileigh, Mitch was in love with a woman named Tahlia. She was the first person he ever let see all of him—his flaws, his insecurities, the things he hid behind that easy smirk. He believed she'd stand by him no matter what. But when Mitch's life hit turbulence—bad investments, legal trouble, and a scandal that cost him his career—Tahlia didn't just leave. She humiliated him.

She ran straight into the arms of one of his closest friends and later married him. Mitch told himself he'd never be vulnerable again, never let love put him on his knees. That betrayal hardened him, and ever since, he's treated relationships like games—something to control, manipulate, and discard before they can discard him.

Why Emileigh?

Emileigh wasn't the cause of his bitterness, but she's the perfect storm for it. She's beautiful, complicated, and—most importantly—she's loved him *and* left him before. That combination feeds his obsession. Mitch doesn't want her in the forever sense; he wants to prove to himself that he can still own her, still be the one who pulls her strings, no matter who she's with.

Every time she chooses Jake, it's not just about her—it's a challenge to Mitch's ego, a reminder of the one time in his life a woman truly slipped away. And Mitch doesn't forgive slipping.

Later that night, after Emileigh had fallen asleep, Jake slipped quietly out of bed. He padded across the room to the small drawer on his dresser, pulling it open with the same careful reverence you'd give a sacred thing.

Inside, wrapped in the corner of an old flannel shirt, was the ring. Simple. Elegant. Timeless. Just like her.

He held it in his palm, feeling the cool weight against his skin. It wasn't just gold and stone—it was a promise. One he was ready to keep, even with all the storms they'd weathered.

Jake closed his eyes, whispering almost to himself, "I choose you, Em. Always you."

What he didn't see—what he couldn't see—was the storm already forming beyond their door. Mitch wasn't done. Not even close. And in his world, love wasn't something you nurtured. It was something you bent until it broke.

And Mitch? He was a master at breaking things.

Chapter Thirteen

Mitch never moved without a plan.

The city skyline stretched out before him from the balcony of his condo, the glass of bourbon in his hand catching the last streaks of sunset. From here, Atlanta looked almost peaceful. Almost.

He wasn't thinking about peace.

He was thinking about Emileigh—about the way her lips had trembled when she told Jake she'd walked away from him. She'd left out the kiss, but Mitch didn't mind. That omission was the hook. He didn't need to burn her whole world down at once. No, the trick was to apply just enough heat to keep her off balance... and to keep Jake wondering.

That was the art.

He set his glass down, pulling his phone from his pocket. One text could shift the energy in a room before he even stepped inside. And Mitch had no problem stepping inside their world when he pleased.

Mitch: "Running into you again was... unfinished business. Let's not keep it that way."

He smirked, picturing her seeing the message with Jake in the room. She'd feel the pull. She always did.

This wasn't love. Mitch didn't believe in love. But the game? The control? The knowing that he could have her— physically, mentally, emotionally—whenever he wanted? That was the high he couldn't give up.

He took a slow drink of bourbon, letting the burn settle in his chest. "Enjoy your peace, Jake," he muttered to the night air. "It won't last."

Somewhere across the city, the woman they both wanted was curled against the man she claimed to love. But in Mitch's mind, that just made the victory sweeter when he took her back, if only for a night.

Because with Mitch, it was never about keeping her.

It was about proving he could.

Mitch wasn't used to looking over his shoulder.

But Tahlia had that effect.

She didn't so much *walk* into the restaurant as *arrive* — heels clicking, hair falling in waves over one bare shoulder, eyes that could peel a man's pride off him in one look. She didn't even have to see Mitch yet for him to feel it — that shift in the air that told him he was no longer the alpha in the room.

When her gaze finally landed on him, it was like she was appraising something she already owned.

"Mitch," she purred, sliding into the seat across from him without invitation. "You've been busy."

He sat back, forcing a smirk that didn't quite stick. "Always am."

Her lips curved, but it wasn't a smile. "Don't play with me. Atlanta's smaller than you think."

The pause was deliberate.

So was the way she leaned in. "Emileigh."

The name hit harder than the wine she'd just ordered. Mitch didn't flinch, but something in his jaw ticked.

"I don't know what you think you know," he said, voice low.

"Oh, baby," Tahlia said softly, tilting her head, "I *always* know. And so does her man. Or he will."

She sat back like she'd just set fire to the table and was waiting to see if he'd run. "You were always too predictable when it came to women. That's why you're so easy to break."

Her phone buzzed. She didn't look at it. Didn't need to. She'd already said what she came to say.

"Enjoy your... games," she added, standing. "But remember—when they blow up, it won't be on my hands. I just gave you the match."

She left him there — the great Mitch, leaning back in a chair that suddenly didn't feel like it fit him.

For a long moment, he didn't move. Tahlia's words rang in his ears, not because she'd caught him off guard, but because she'd reminded him of something he'd almost forgotten — what it felt like to be on the wrong side of power.

And Mitch hated being powerless.

By the time he walked out of the restaurant, the smirk was back. But it was sharper now, dangerous. Tahlia thought she'd rattled him? She had   just enough to make him focus.

If Emileigh thought she could drift closer to Jake without him...   If Jake thought he could have her without feeling the shadow of Mitch's hands still on her...

Mitch thumbed through his phone until he found the number he wanted.

The smile deepened.

The match had been struck. Now it was time for the fire.

Jake found the envelope tucked under his windshield wiper.

No name. No return address.

Inside — a photo. Blurry, grainy, clearly taken from a distance.

Emileigh.

Downtown.

A man's hand on her arm.

Her face turned toward him, half-shadowed, unreadable.

On the back, in black ink: *Thought you should know.*

Jake sat in the driver's seat, photo on the passenger side, engine idling. The whole world seemed to go quiet except for the pounding in his ears.

He wanted to dismiss it. Wanted to tell himself it was nothing.

But the city of Atlanta was starting to feel too small. And Mitch's smug smirk — the one from that café — kept replaying in his mind.

***

Across town, Emileigh leaned against the counter in a dimly lit loft, heart hammering.

She hadn't meant to end up here.

Hadn't meant to be this close.

The man — tall, broad, smelling like cedar and trouble — had been leaning in, his thumb brushing her lower lip like he owned it.

"Tell me to stop," he'd said.

And for three long seconds, she hadn't.

Her body remembered the ache, the rush, the craving Soki thrived on. It would've been easy. Too easy. A few more inches and she'd be on the other side of a line she couldn't uncross.

But then Jake's laugh — that warm, unguarded sound — flashed in her memory.

And she pulled back.

"I can't," she whispered, shoving past him, grabbing her purse. "I have someone."

Out on the street, the cool night air slapped her cheeks. She hated herself for wanting it. For knowing, if the moment came again, she might not walk away.

Something was wrong with her.
Something deep enough that even love couldn't cauterize it.

But for tonight, she'd chosen Jake. And she prayed to God that it wouldn't be the last time she could say that.

Jake didn't call first.

Didn't text.

He just showed up at Emileigh's door, photo in hand.

She opened it with that soft, surprised smile that usually dissolved his tension. But not tonight.

"What's wrong?" she asked, stepping back to let him in.

He held out the picture. "You tell me."

Her brow furrowed as she took it, flipping it over to see the scrawled words. Her pulse spiked instantly.

"Where did you get this?"

"Does it matter?" His voice was low, controlled, but there was an edge beneath it that cut into her. "Is it real?"

She stared at the image — blurry, yes, but still her. Still, the moment earlier tonight when she'd been too close to the edge. But the hand on her arm wasn't *that*. It hadn't been sex. It hadn't been a betrayal. Not all the way.

"It's not what it looks like," she said, forcing herself to meet his eyes. "I was... in a bad conversation, that's all. I walked away."

Jake searched her face the way he always did when he needed to know if he was standing on solid ground or quicksand.

"Why didn't you tell me?"

"I didn't think it was worth telling," she lied smoothly, the way Soki had taught her to. "Because I handled it. It was nothing."

He wanted to believe her. God, he wanted to.

But something inside him twisted. Atlanta was too big for all these "chance encounters," and this one had found its way into his hands in a way that felt... deliberate.

"Nothing," he repeated slowly, as if testing the word for weight.

"Yes," she said firmly, reaching for his hand. "Nothing. You're everything."

Jake let her fingers curl around his, but the picture still lay on the coffee table between them — a silent witness neither of them could unsee.

And somewhere across the city, Mitch poured himself a drink, smiling at the thought of that photograph doing exactly what he intended.

Mitch wasn't in a hurry.

That was the thing people never understood about him — he could wait.

Patience wasn't a virtue; it was a weapon.

He leaned back in his chair at the corner table of the low-lit bar, whiskey glass in hand, watching the guy across the room slide an envelope to the courier. That envelope would end up on Jake's doorstep before the night was over, and Mitch didn't even have to lift a finger.

Let the city do the work for you, he thought, swirling the ice in his drink.

The photo wasn't explicit. That was the genius of it. It was suggestive — a captured moment where Emileigh leaned just close enough to another man that the line between conversation and something more blurred. Anyone could make their own story from it. And Jake? He'd make the one Mitch wanted him to.

This wasn't about taking Emileigh back. Mitch didn't even want her.
Not in the way Jake did, anyway.

What Mitch wanted was control — the satisfaction of knowing that no matter how far she ran toward "happily ever after," he could yank her back into the mess with one well-placed tug.

It was petty. Cruel. And it thrilled him.

The bartender passed by and topped off his glass without asking. Mitch tossed a bill onto the counter, rising with that slow, unhurried swagger that was part intimidation, part invitation.

By morning, Jake would be staring at that photo, questioning everything.

By next week, he'd be wondering why these little cracks kept showing up in the perfect life he thought he was building.

And Mitch? Mitch would be right here, watching. Always close enough to disrupt.

Never close enough to get caught.

It happened on a Tuesday.

The kind of Tuesday where the sky was the color of wet cement and the city smelled like rain.

I was just running errands — at least that's what I told myself. But somewhere between the dry cleaner and the coffee shop, I walked into temptation.

His name was Roman.

Tall, broad shoulders, eyes like dark chocolate that had been melted just enough to pour over something sinful. He held the door for me, and I swear the way his gaze lingered felt like a touch.

We talked. Just casual, harmless chatter. Except there was nothing harmless about the way my pulse was beating in my ears or the way I leaned into the scent of his cologne.

When his hand brushed mine as he passed me my drink, the air between us thickened. And when he stepped closer, the smallest smirk tugging at his mouth, I didn't step back.

I let him stand there, too close.

I let him ask if I wanted to get out of here.

And God help me — I wanted to say yes.

The images came fast — his hands, my skin, the heat of something reckless and unplanned. The thrill Soki lived for.

But somewhere underneath the rush, a quieter voice cut through.
Jake's voice.

"I just need to know you'll choose me."

I stepped back like the ground was on fire. "I can't," I said quickly, my breath unsteady. "I have someone."

Roman studied me for a beat, then nodded like he'd seen this movie before. "Your loss." He turned and walked away.

The moment he was gone, I felt it — that gnawing truth.

There was something wrong with me.

Something that would risk *everything* for an orgasm or two.

And yet... I didn't.

Not this time.

I chose love.

I chose Jake.

But as I walked out into the rain, I knew this wasn't over.

The next storm was coming — and I wasn't sure I'd survive it.

By the time I got home, my phone was buzzing. A message from an unknown number.

No text. Just a picture.

Roman and I — standing too close in the coffee shop. His hand   brushes mine. That smirk on his face. My eyes locked on his like I was starving.

My chest tightened. Whoever took it had been close. Too close.

I read the image again and again, like I could will it to disappear, like the angle didn't make it look as bad as it did.

But the truth was, it *looked* exactly like something it wasn't.

A second message came through:

"How long until Jake sees this?"

I dropped the phone like it burned me.

My mind started working in overdrive, sifting through faces, moments, anyone who could have been watching me. But only one name made sense.

Mitch.

Of course, it was Mitch. Who else would work this hard to sabotage my shot at a happily ever after? Who else had both the motive and the nerve?

But I had no proof. Nothing to take to Jake that wouldn't sound like a deflection.

And what scared me more than Mitch's games was the fact that... if Jake *did* see this, I wasn't sure my explanation would be enough.

Because pictures have a way of telling their own stories.

Jake didn't notice my hands shaking when I slid into his passenger seat that night.

He just smiled — that warm, easy smile that made me forget, for a second, that my phone held the power to end us.

"Long day?" he asked, starting the engine.

"You have no idea," I said, leaning my head back and forcing my voice to sound light.

He reached over and threaded his fingers through mine like it was the most natural thing in the world. "Well, it's over now. I've got you."

And he meant it. I could feel it in the steady squeeze of his hand, in the way his eyes softened every time he looked at me.

Jake had no idea about the picture. No idea that somewhere out there, someone was trying to plant seeds in his mind. He was blissfully unaware — and completely certain that I was his.

I hated myself for keeping it from him.

But I loved him too much to hand Mitch a weapon that deadly.

So instead, I let him take me to that little rooftop place he knew I loved, let him order the wine I couldn't resist, let myself melt into the sound of his laugh.

For a few hours, I forgot. I forgot about Mitch. I forgot about the photo. I forgot about the gnawing truth that I was living in a house built on sand.

When Jake walked me to my door later, he kissed me like I was his forever — slow, deliberate, leaving no space between us.

And somewhere deep inside, I wished I could find the version of me that would never let him down.

Jake's thumb traced lazy circles over the back of my hand as we sat in his living room, the TV flickering with some old movie neither of us was really watching.

"You've been downtown a lot lately," he said casually, eyes still on the screen.

My heart stuttered, but I forced a shrug. "Just errands. A couple of meetings. You know... life."

He nodded slowly, too slowly. "Yeah. Just... funny how big Atlanta is, and yet you always seem to run into the same people."

It wasn't an accusation — not yet. But I heard the question in it, the unspoken thread he was pulling on.

I leaned in, kissing his jaw, letting my lips linger just long enough to redirect his attention. "Maybe I'm just lucky," I whispered.

He smiled at that, but it didn't quite reach his eyes. "Maybe."

And that was it. The conversation shifted, his arms wrapped tighter around me, and we went back to pretending nothing was there.

But I felt it.

The seed had been planted.

And if Mitch was the gardener, it wouldn't be long before something ugly bloomed.

I see him even when he's not there.

In the reflection of a shop window.

In the slow roll of a black sedan behind me.

In the tilt of a stranger's smile that's just a little too familiar.

I don't have proof. Not the kind I could hand Jake and say, *See? It's him. He's the one following me.*

But I know.

Who else would spend this much time, this much energy, on destroying something he doesn't even want?

Who else would take every chance encounter and turn it into a question mark hanging over Jake's trust?

Who else knows my weaknesses like muscle memory?

Mitch doesn't have to be in the room to get to me.

Sometimes, I think that's his favorite way to play — just close enough to rattle the glass, but never enough to shatter it completely.

Because shattering me would mean the game was over. And Mitch loves the game.

The worst part?
A piece of me still answers when he calls.

Not because I want him — God, I don't — but because Soki wants the thrill. The chase. The danger.

And I can't decide which scares me more:

That Mitch won't stop…

Or that I won't, either.

Jake's hands were shaking, but his eyes never left mine.

"I don't have everything figured out," he said. "And maybe I never will. But there's one thing I know — I want you. The good. The bad. All of it. I choose you, Emileigh."

The little velvet box was in his palm before I could breathe.
Inside, the ring caught the café light, a perfect circle I didn't feel worthy of.

"Marry me," he said simply.

For a heartbeat, the whole world went still. No Mitch. No Soki. Just Jake.

"Yes," I whispered, because despite every lie I'd told, every line I'd blurred, Jake had always chosen love… and I wanted so badly to choose him back.

He kissed me like the decision was already binding, like the ring on my finger sealed more than just a promise — it sealed my future.

But futures have shadows.

And mine walked into the café not twenty minutes later. A courier in a black jacket dropped an unmarked envelope on our table.

"No signature required," he said before disappearing out the door.

Jake opened it before I could reach for it. Inside was a single photograph.

Me.

In the parking garage downtown.

Pressed against a concrete wall.

Mitch's mouth on mine.

The timestamp in the corner mocked me.

I felt Jake's whole body stiffen beside me. His jaw worked once, twice, like he was holding back every word, trying to claw its way out.

He placed the photo face down on the table, his eyes meeting mine — not accusing yet, but close.

"We'll talk later," he said quietly.

And in that moment, I knew Mitch was almost out of time... but not before he could light the match that might burn everything to the ground.

The silence in the car was worse than shouting.

Jake didn't turn on the radio. He didn't reach for my hand.

He just drove.

When we pulled into his driveway, he killed the engine but didn't move.

"Inside," he said, his voice low, clipped.

I followed him in, the weight of that photograph between us heavier than any door we closed behind us.

He paced the living room once, twice, then stopped and faced me.
"I need you to tell me exactly what happened."

"Jake—"

"No," he cut in, sharper this time. "I don't want the version you think I can handle. I don't want the safe story. I want the truth. All of it."

The demand in his voice hit somewhere deep, and for the first time, I realized just how much restraint he'd been showing with me all these months.

"He showed up out of nowhere," I said. "I tried to walk away, but he followed me. He—"

"Kissed you," Jake finished for me, his jaw tight.

"Yes. But I pushed him off."
It wasn't the whole truth, but it was the one I clung to.

Jake's fists clenched at his sides. "Do you know what that picture did to me? I have spent months choosing you over every doubt, every rumor, every gut punch… and then I see that."

He stepped closer, close enough that I could feel the heat of his anger. "I always choose love, Emileigh. Always. But I need to know you'll do the same. Because I can't keep carrying this for both of us."

His voice broke, just slightly, and that did more damage than the anger.

"I'm here," I whispered. "I'm choosing you."

He searched my face for a long moment, then exhaled hard and pulled me into him, crushing me against his chest. But the grip wasn't soft — it was possessive, almost desperate, like he was staking a claim.

And deep down, I knew — if I couldn't keep Mitch away, this side of Jake was going to be the one to meet him next.

I spotted him before Jake did.
Mitch.

He was leaning against the bar like the whole damn room was his, eyes locked on me the second we walked in. That smirk—confident, predatory—sent a cold rush down my spine.

Jake didn't notice until Mitch straightened and started toward us.

"Evening," Mitch drawled, like we were all old friends catching up.

Jake's jaw set instantly. "Turn around and walk away."

Mitch ignored him, his attention fixed on me. "We keep running into each other, Em. Starting to think it's fate."

Jake stepped in front of me, chest to chest with Mitch now. "You've had your fun. It ends here."

"Fun?" Mitch's smirk sharpened. "That's not what she called it when—"

Jake moved so fast the crowd gasped. His fist was halfway up before I grabbed his arm, shouting his name. People turned, phones came out, and for a split second, I thought he'd hit him anyway.

Something in Jake's eyes shifted—rage barely reined in. He shoved Mitch back instead, his voice low but deadly. "Stay away from her."

And just like that, Mitch backed off, grinning like he'd already won something.

I stood frozen, my pulse pounding, my mind somewhere else entirely.

Because in that moment, watching Jake defend me like his life depended on it, I remembered the story from Sunday school—the one about Hosea and Gomer.

I remembered how Gomer kept running back to the very places that broke her, how she couldn't seem to stay in the arms of the man who loved her most. And yet, Hosea kept going after her. Again and again. Pulling her out of every brothel, every alley, every bad decision, because his love wasn't conditional.

And for the first time, I wondered—at what point did Gomer realize that she would choose Hosea for real? Did she ever stop running?

I had to believe she did.

I had to believe she looked at him one day and decided, once and for all, to stay.

Because this is my story.

My life.

And I'm choosing Jake.

The morning light filtered in soft and gold, spilling over the sheets tangled around us. Jake's arm was draped heavy across my waist, his hand resting where my heartbeat was steady beneath his palm.

We hadn't said much when we got home last night.

We didn't need to.

Some things weren't meant to be talked to death—some things were meant to be felt, to be lived in, to be absorbed without overthinking. Last night was one of those things.

He stirred first, tightening his hold like even in sleep, he was afraid I'd slip away. When his eyes opened, they were still clouded with sleep, but softer than they'd been in weeks.

"Morning," I whispered.

His lips curved faintly. "Morning."

There was no interrogation in his gaze, no demand for more answers about Mitch. Just Jake, as he's always been—steady, choosing love even when it would be easier to walk away.

He kissed my shoulder, slow and lingering, and I felt something loosen in my chest. This was the man who kept coming for me. My Hosea. My anchor.

And for a moment, lying there wrapped in him, I let myself imagine the life we could have without the storms—without Mitch, without Soki, without the parts of me that kept sabotaging my own happiness.

I let myself imagine that choosing Jake wasn't just a choice I made in the moment… but the choice I would keep making.

Even when it got hard.

Even when temptation came knocking.

Even when Soki whispered otherwise.

Because deep down, I wanted to believe that I could be the woman who didn't run.

And Jake… Jake still looked at me like I already was.

Across town, Mitch sat at the bar nursing a whiskey he didn't even like. The amber liquid caught the dim light, but he wasn't looking at it. His eyes were locked on the photo glowing from his phone screen—one of Emileigh, laughing at something Jake had said.

It wasn't a recent shot. He'd taken it weeks ago from across the street, hidden in plain sight. He didn't delete it. Couldn't.

The thing about Jake was that he didn't even realize how fragile his hold was. Mitch knew where the cracks were, where to wedge himself in just enough to rattle them without shattering the whole thing. Not yet.

He smirked, swirling the glass in his hand. This wasn't about love. It never had been. He didn't want Emileigh forever—he wanted her *because* Jake thought she was his forever. And because she'd never be fully free of what they'd had, no matter how many times she tried to shove it into the past.

He took out his phone and typed a quick message to someone whose number he kept under a fake name. *She'll be there tomorrow. Make it look like nothing. I just need him to wonder.*

Sliding the phone back into his pocket, Mitch leaned back, satisfied.

He didn't need to break them apart completely. Not yet.

Just a seed of doubt—that was all it took.

Because the truth was, he could be patient.

The storm didn't have to hit all at once.

It could build, slow and quiet, until it felt like it came out of nowhere.

And when it did, he'd be the one holding the match.

The boutique was quiet except for the faint hum of jazz drifting through hidden ceiling speakers. Emileigh had ducked in to kill time before meeting Jake—she told herself she was just browsing.

She was flipping through a rack of dresses when she felt it. That inexplicable *charge* in the air. It made the hairs on her arms rise before she even turned around.

"Those would look good on you," a low, smooth voice said behind her.

She turned—and froze.

The woman standing there was tall, broad-shouldered, with a fade cut tight on the sides and a single silver hoop in her left ear. Her eyes—dark, deliberate—looked at Emileigh like they already knew her secrets. Like they'd been let in without an invitation.

Emileigh's throat went dry. She'd never been attracted to women. Not once. But this was different. There was something magnetic, almost dangerous, about the way this stranger's smile curved slow, deliberate.

"I'm Ayla," she said, offering her hand but holding Emileigh's gaze the entire time.

Her touch was warm—too warm. It lingered a beat too long.

"I'm—" Emileigh started, but her voice caught. "I'm just looking."

"I hope not," Ayla murmured. "Because I'd love to help you find something that… fits."

The air between them thickened. And for the first time in a long time, Emileigh's temptation didn't have a man's face.

Ayla took a step closer, lowering her voice so only Emileigh could hear. "You have that look about you. Like you're caught between who you are… and who you *really* want to be."

The words slid under Emileigh's skin, unsettling in their accuracy. She told herself it was harmless—just a conversation—but her pulse told a different story.

She pulled herself away, laughing softly as if brushing it off. "I have to go."

Ayla didn't stop her. Just gave a knowing smile, like she'd already won something.

And as Emileigh walked out, she didn't see Mitch's car parked a block away. Or the subtle nod he gave to Ayla as she passed him on the sidewalk.

Mitch leaned back in the driver's seat, one arm draped casually over the wheel, watching Emileigh's retreating figure through the tinted glass. She didn't even glance around. Didn't realize she'd just stepped into the newest play in his game.

Ayla slid into the passenger seat, still smiling.

"She's even prettier up close," Ayla said. "And she's curious. You can see it in her eyes."

Mitch's mouth curved in satisfaction. "Good. I don't need her to do anything... not yet. Just get in her head. Make her wonder about herself."

Ayla chuckled, shaking her head. "You're twisted, you know that?"

"Yeah," Mitch said without shame. "But it works. Jake's walking around thinking he's got himself a reformed woman. I'm just making sure the cracks stay open."

He lit a cigarette, taking a slow drag as his eyes stayed on the sidewalk where Emileigh had disappeared.
"She's not built for happily ever after," he murmured, more to himself than to Ayla. "I'm just reminding her of that. One temptation at a time."

Ayla studied him. "Why do you even care? You don't want her. You've told me that."

Mitch's jaw tightened. "I don't want her happy. Not with him. Not in some white-picket-fence fantasy. He's not better than me. He's just... safe. And safe doesn't win."

He flicked ash out the window, his smirk returning.

"She'll break herself before she ever makes it to that altar. I'll make sure of it."

Jake stood at the counter of the little jewelry shop tucked away on Peachtree Street, running his thumb over the velvet box in his palm. The diamond wasn't the biggest in the case, but it was the one that felt right. Elegant. Strong. Like her—at least the version of her he believed in.

The saleswoman smiled warmly. "She's going to love it."

"I hope so," Jake said, his voice quieter than he intended.

He'd been replaying the last few weeks in his mind—her laugh over coffee, the way she curled into him at night, the rare moments when her walls came down and she looked at him like he was the only safe place she had left. It was those moments that anchored him. That made him believe they could survive anything.

Still, there was a faint itch in the back of his mind, something he couldn't quite shake. The chance encounters. The interruptions. The way Mitch's name seemed to hang in the air longer than it should.

He shook it off, slipping the box into his jacket pocket.

Love meant trusting. Love meant choosing—over and over again—and he'd decided long ago he would always choose her.

Jake stepped out into the cool evening air, pulling out his phone to text her.

Dinner tomorrow? Just you and me. I have something to ask.

He smiled as he hit send, completely unaware of the storm Mitch was preparing.

The café was warm and dimly lit, the kind of place Emileigh might've passed by a hundred times without noticing. Tonight, she couldn't remember why she came inside—only that something pulled her in.

That's when she saw her.

Ayla was seated at the far end of the counter, one leg crossed over the other, her eyes the kind of deep brown that dared you to get lost. She looked up from her drink, and Emileigh felt that jolt—sharp, unexpected. She'd never been drawn to a woman before, not like this.

Ayla smiled, slow and knowing, and gestured to the empty stool beside her. "Looks like you could use company."

Emileigh hesitated, then slid onto the stool. "Rough day."

"Or rough month?" Ayla's voice was low, sultry, the kind that could slip into dreams and stay there. "You've got that look."

They talked   about nothing and everything—and with each passing minute, Emileigh felt herself leaning in, caught in the orbit of someone who made the room fade. Ayla's laugh was warm, her hand brushing against Emileigh's as if by accident, her questions just personal enough to feel intimate.

And somewhere, two tables away, Mitch nursed a whiskey, his gaze fixed on them. He watched Emileigh's posture soften, watched that little smile creep across her lips, and felt satisfaction curl through him.

By the time Emileigh left, she was rattled. She told herself it was nothing—just conversation. But in the back of her mind, Soki purred.

Two days later, Emileigh was cutting through the park, coffee in hand, her thoughts tangled between Jake's proposal and the strange current Ayla had stirred in her.

She almost didn't notice the figure on the bench until she heard, "Well, if it isn't my favorite stranger."

Ayla.

She was in a soft sweater and ripped jeans, hair loose around her face, the kind of casual perfection that looked like it had taken no effort at all.

Emileigh stopped, blinking. "You hang out here?"

"Only when I'm hoping to run into someone worth my time," Ayla said, patting the bench beside her. "Guess today's my lucky day."

The pull was still there, stronger now. Emileigh sat, telling herself it was harmless. Just conversation. But the way Ayla's eyes lingered, the way her fingertips brushed Emileigh's wrist when she handed over her coffee to "try a sip," made her pulse pick up.

"I was hoping I'd see you again," Ayla said softly. "You've been on my mind."

Emileigh swallowed, caught between flattered and unsettled. "That's... unexpected."

"Maybe," Ayla murmured, leaning in just enough that Emileigh caught the faint scent of her perfume, "but I don't think it's a bad thing."

Across the park, behind the cover of a tree, Mitch watched again. A faint smirk tugged at his mouth. Ayla was playing her part perfectly—smooth enough to make Emileigh question herself, bold enough to leave a mark.

Ayla's hand lingered on Emileigh's thigh longer than necessary as they sat side by side on the park bench. Her voice was low, her words deliberate. "You've got this... energy about you. Like you don't even know how dangerous you are."

Emileigh opened her mouth to deflect, but something shifted inside her.

Soki.

The warmth in her chest hardened into something sharper, hungrier. Without fully deciding to, she turned toward Ayla, closed the gap between them, and caught her mouth in a kiss that was not hesitant, not experimental—it was possession.

Ayla gasped against her lips, but Soki didn't give her room to retreat. She deepened the kiss, letting it roll over into something slow and devastating. Fingers tangled in Ayla's hair, pulling just enough to make her breath hitch.

When they finally broke apart, Ayla's pupils were blown wide. "What… was that?" she whispered, clearly rattled.

Soki smiled through Emileigh's lips. "That's me."

It wasn't part of the plan, not exactly. Mitch had wanted a little teasing, some blurred lines—enough to stir the pot for Jake. But the way Ayla looked at her now wasn't about a game anymore.

"I want to see you again," Ayla said, her tone vulnerable in a way that didn't match the casual confidence she'd worn before. "Not for him. Not for anyone else."

Soki's smirk deepened. "Careful, Ayla. You don't even know me."

"Maybe I want to," Ayla murmured.

Across the park, Mitch saw the exchange, and something in his smirk faltered. Ayla's body language was all wrong— soft where it should be sly, leaning in where she should be pulling back.

This wasn't a script anymore.

For the first time, Mitch realized the weapon he'd aimed at Emileigh might be angling itself back toward him.

Mitch caught up to Ayla before she even made it to her car.

"What the hell was that back there?" he hissed, grabbing her wrist hard enough to make her stop.

Ayla yanked her arm back, eyes narrowing. "That was me doing what you asked. Just… maybe better than you thought I could."

His jaw clenched. "It wasn't supposed to be *better*. It was supposed to rattle her—make Jake wonder, make Emileigh question herself. Not..." He exhaled sharply, his voice lowering, "not make you look like you caught feelings."

Ayla crossed her arms, leaning against her car. "And what if I did?"

Mitch froze for a beat. "Then you'd better lose them. Fast."

She studied him with an infuriating calm. "You don't own me, Mitch. You set up the board, sure. But you forget— pieces have minds of their own. You might have underestimated her... and me."

For the first time in a long time, Mitch's mask cracked. He stepped closer, so close she could smell the mix of whiskey and his cologne. "Don't get cute, Ayla. You play your part, or I will end it. And you."

From across the street, Emileigh watched, Soki fully in control, leaning casually against a lamppost like she'd been waiting for this exact moment. Her smile was small but razor sharp. She knew the look in Ayla's eyes—half-defiance, half-need—and she knew what it would do to Mitch.

This wasn't just about Jake anymore. This was about watching Mitch scramble to keep his carefully crafted chaos from spinning out of his hands.

And Soki loved nothing more than watching a man like him lose control.

Jake sat at his kitchen table, laptop open, coffee steaming beside him. He should've been working, but instead, the search bar on his screen read: *unique proposal ideas.*

It was ridiculous, he told himself. They'd been through hell—maybe more than two people should survive—and yet here he was, dreaming about forever with her. With Emileigh.

No, he corrected, with *the woman he loved.*

He clicked through articles about intimate getaways, public declarations, and small, candlelit dinners. He didn't care about the setting so much as the feeling. He wanted her to look at him and know she was chosen—not just once, but every day after.

For Jake, love wasn't a gamble. It was a commitment. And Emileigh... she was the one thing he'd bet everything on.

He closed his laptop, leaned back, and smiled faintly. He'd surprise her soon. He just needed the right moment.

Across town, Mitch was pacing his apartment, Ayla's words echoing in his head. She had feelings? For Emileigh? That wasn't part of the deal. He needed Ayla to *shake* her, not get tangled in the same web he was spinning.

But now there was a new risk—Ayla going rogue, Emileigh getting wise, Jake stepping up as the "forever guy" before Mitch had the satisfaction of breaking them.

Mitch poured himself another drink, staring out at the city lights. He'd underestimated Emileigh's ability to pull people in, even without trying.

That was about to change.

The knock on my apartment door was gentle, almost shy. When I opened it, Jake stood there holding a bouquet of lilies—my favorite, though I'd never told him.

"How did you know?" I asked, taking them from his hands and pressing my face into their soft fragrance.

He shrugged, the corner of his mouth curling. "I pay attention."

Inside, he set a small white box on my coffee table. No ring—my stomach checked for that instantly—but when I opened it, I found a simple silver bracelet, delicate and understated. Dangling from the chain was a tiny charm in the shape of a key.

"It's to remind you," he said, "that no matter what's going on, you already have the key to my heart. You don't need to earn it, or fight for it, or... prove anything."

Something in me broke a little. The way he looked at me—like all the chaos didn't matter—made Soki go quiet. No biting remarks, no sideways smirk, no whisper about Mitch or temptation. Just silence.

"Thank you," I said, meaning it. "I... I needed this."

He stayed for dinner. We talked about nothing and everything, laughter spilling over wine. For a few hours, the past didn't matter, and the future didn't scare me. It was just us.

When he left that night, kissing me slow at the door, I leaned against the frame and watched him go. For the first time in weeks, I felt steady.

But across the street, parked in the shadow of an oak tree, Mitch sat in his car, watching.

Mitch didn't move when Jake's taillights disappeared. He just leaned back, a slow smile cutting across his face.

Patience. That was the game now.

The next morning, a plain manila envelope showed up at Jake's office. No return address. Inside—three glossy photos.

In each one, Emileigh stood too close to another man. In one, she was laughing with her head tilted back. In another, his hand brushed her arm. In the third... it was the same moment Jake had walked into weeks ago—her and Mitch in the café—but cropped to show only her smiling and Mitch leaning in, their faces closer than truth would allow.

There were no explanations, no captions. Just an implication.

Jake sat at his desk for a long time, the photos spread in front of him. He wasn't a fool—he knew the city was big, the chances of all these "coincidences" too strange to ignore.

But still... he loved her. And love was stubborn.

That night, when he came to see her, he didn't mention the envelope. Instead, he kissed her like he was trying to remind himself who she really was. She kissed him back, harder than usual, like she was trying to answer a question she didn't know he'd asked.

Somewhere across town, Mitch poured himself a drink, satisfied. The seed had been planted.

He wasn't Mitch.

He wasn't Jake.

He was someone new—someone she'd met by accident when she ducked into a wine bar to escape the rain. A smile, an offer to buy her a drink, a casual "you look like you could use company" that landed in all the wrong places.

They talked. He was charming in that easy, effortless way. His knee brushed hers, and instead of moving away, she stayed put. Soki leaned forward in her mind, ready to take over, ready to let the evening slide into another story Emileigh couldn't tell Jake.

And then... it hit her.

Not lust. Not adrenaline.

Fatigue.

It washed over her so suddenly she almost swayed in her chair. Not the kind that comes from lack of sleep, but the kind that seeps into the marrow—the kind that whispers, *You're tired of running. Tired of lying. Tired of proving you can't stop.*

Her hands wrapped around her glass, and she realized she didn't want this. Not him. Not tonight.

She wanted Jake.

She wanted the man who had chosen her, over and over, even when she made it damn near impossible. The man who, like Hosea, loved her past the point of reason. The man who might be the only one capable of saving her from herself.

"I should go," she said, sliding off the stool before his hand could rest on her thigh.

He smirked, like he thought she was playing coy. "You sure?"

She didn't answer—just walked out into the rain, letting it soak her hair, her clothes, everything. Each drop felt like it was washing something off her.

By the time she reached her car, she knew.

She had to marry Jake. Not someday. Not eventually.

Soon.

Because she was finally—*finally*—tired.

Jake opened the door before she even knocked twice.

His face softened instantly, but his eyes scanned her—drenched hair clinging to her cheeks, clothes plastered to her skin, makeup smudged from the rain.

"Em—what happened?" he asked, stepping aside so she could come in.

She shook her head. "Nothing happened. That's… the point."

He closed the door, confusion flickering across his features. "Okay… you're gonna have to explain that."

"I walked away tonight." Her voice trembled—not from the cold, but from the truth pressing against her chest. "I could've gone down a path I've gone down too many times before. But I didn't. I left. And all I could think about was you. I'm so tired, Jake. Tired of being torn. Tired of living in two worlds. I just… I want you."

Something shifted in his face, like he was weighing whether to believe her. But then he pulled her into his arms, wet clothes and all, holding her like she might disappear.

"You have me," he said against her hair. "You've always had me."

She pulled back just enough to meet his eyes. "Then keep me. For good. Marry me."

The words hung between them, reckless and raw.

Jake blinked, stunned. "You're asking me?"

"I'm telling you," she whispered. "Before I lose the nerve. Before life tries to pull me in another direction. You are it, Jake. My beginning, my end. My... Hosea."

Emotion flickered in his eyes—love, relief, maybe even a bit of that alpha rage she'd seen when he'd stood up to Mitch. He cupped her face, his thumbs brushing away the rain.

"You want forever?" he asked.

"Yes."

He kissed her, deep and certain, like the answer had been yes all along.

What neither of them saw, what neither of them could have guessed, was that a dark sedan sat parked across the street. Inside, a camera clicked quietly. Mitch's smirk stretched wider with each photo.

Because while Emileigh had finally chosen Jake... Mitch wasn't done.

Chapter Fourteen

The sedan was warm, engine idling low, but Mitch barely noticed. His eyes locked on the café's glass door like a sniper sighting a target.

They walked out together—hand in hand, bodies leaning close like they had something sacred between them. Emileigh's smile wasn't just polite; it was soft, unguarded. He hadn't seen her wear that look since the beginning. And it wasn't for him.

Mitch's grip tightened on the steering wheel.

That's what Jake had now—*her*. The part she never gave freely to Mitch, the part she hid like a treasure. And the bastard didn't even know how fragile it was.

He could break it.

Not crush it completely—that would be too easy. No, Mitch wanted cracks. Fractures. Tension she'd carry into every kiss, every whispered "I love you." He wanted Jake to feel what Mitch felt: always second-guessing, always waiting for the floor to give way.

And he knew exactly how to start.

His gaze shifted to the passenger seat where a phone rested—unlocked, bait loaded and ready. All it would take was the right push in the right moment, and Jake's world would tilt.

Timing, that's all this game needed.

Mitch smirked, shifting the car into gear.

"Enjoy it while you can, sweetheart," he murmured, eyes on Emileigh's retreating figure. "We both know forever isn't in you."

The evening air was cool, carrying the faint scent of roasted coffee and rain-soaked pavement. Jake's hand was warm in mine, grounding me in a way that made the noise in my head go quiet.

For the first time in months, I wasn't calculating, covering, or deflecting. I wasn't slipping into Soki's skin. I was just *me*—walking beside the man who had just asked me to marry him.

The ring was still new on my finger, and every time it caught the light, my heart clenched. Not from guilt—at least not tonight—but from this aching sense that maybe, just maybe, I could actually be the woman he thought I was.

Jake looked at me like I was his entire world, and the weight of that trust made my chest ache.

"I can't stop smiling," he admitted, brushing his thumb over my knuckles.

I laughed, leaning into him. "Good. I like you like this."

He kissed my temple, his voice low. "I like *us* like this."

We spent the walk home wrapped in easy conversation—talking about dinner plans, about nothing at all—our bodies finding that quiet rhythm people only fall into when they're safe. And in that moment, I believed I could keep us safe.

Even if part of me knew storms never ask for permission before they roll in.

Chapter Fifteen
Back-to-Back Temptations

It started with a voice I knew too well.

"Em?"

I turned, and there he was — Marcus. Same lazy smile, same magnetic pull, same trouble. We hadn't seen each other in over a year, but history has a way of jumping out of the shadows when you least expect it.

"Marcus," I said, keeping my voice flat. "Didn't think you were still in Atlanta."

"Couldn't stay away," he said, stepping closer. "You look... damn." His eyes dragged over me like he was remembering everything he'd ever done to me in bed — and I remembered too.

I told myself to keep walking. I didn't.

We made small talk, but every word felt like a slow rewind to the past. Then his hand brushed my arm, just light enough to make my skin remember his touch. And before I could talk myself out of it, his mouth was on mine.

It wasn't soft. It was urgent, hungry. And my body betrayed me, answering with equal force. Marcus always knew how to kiss like he owned the moment. I kissed him back until the edge of reason came into view. Then I shoved him away, breathless.

"This is not happening," I snapped.

He smirked like I'd just promised to call him later. "You'll be back."

"No," I said, walking off with my heart pounding. "Not this time."

***

I told myself that was the end of it. I told myself I'd won. But temptation never knocks once.

Two hours later, I was in a bookstore, browsing the travel section, when a stranger's voice said, "Let me help you with that."

He reached over me, grabbing the book I'd been stretching for. Tall. Broad shoulders. The kind of eyes that made you want to tell secrets.

"Thanks," I said, and for some reason, I kept talking. His name was Evan. We joked about the places we'd travel if money   weren't an issue. It was harmless... until I saw him again in the parking lot, leaning against his car like he'd been waiting.

"Guess we're on the same schedule," he said.

I should've gotten in my car and driven away. Instead, I smiled. That was all the invitation he needed.

One step closer. Another. His hand slid to the back of my neck, and then we were kissing. Slow. Deep. The kind of kiss that made my knees soft and my brain useless.

My fingers tangled in his hair, my body leaning into his like I was already his. And then —

God, help me.

It wasn't a shout. It wasn't even out loud. But it was urgent. *If   you don't help me, I'm not going to stop.*

I pulled away, breathless. "I... can't."

He looked confused. "Why not?"

"Because I'd regret it," I said, backing away.

I got in my car before I could change my mind, gripping the steering wheel until my knuckles hurt. My body was still humming. My heart was still racing. And in that quiet moment, I realized the truth: I was tired.

Not the kind of tired that sleep could fix. Soul-tired. Spirit-tired. Tired of living at the edge of a cliff and calling it love.

If I was ever going to have my happily ever after with Jake, I needed God's help to walk away — not just today, but from every temptation that would follow.

By the time I pulled into the driveway, the sun was already dipping low, spilling soft orange light over the porch. My hands still gripped the steering wheel like I was afraid to let go.

I could feel it — that heaviness in my chest. Not guilt exactly, but something deeper. A mix of shame, relief, and the kind of exhaustion that seeps into your bones when you've been fighting battles no one else knows about.

I wasn't ready to face Jake. But he was my safe place. My choice. The man I kept promising myself I'd choose, even when my actions painted a different picture.

He opened the door before I could knock, smiling that slow, warm smile that always made me forget how chaotic my world could be.

"Hey, beautiful," he said, leaning down to kiss my forehead. "Rough day?"

I forced a light laugh. "You could say that."

He took my bag, setting it on the chair, then guided me into the living room. The lamp was on, music low, and the scent of something rich and savory drifted in from the kitchen.

"I made dinner," he said, like it was nothing. "Thought you might like a night in."

Something about the way he said it — the simplicity, the steadiness — made my throat tight. He didn't know the war I'd been fighting in parking lots and bookstores. He didn't know how close I'd come to losing myself today.

Jake sat beside me on the couch, resting his hand over mine. "You've been carrying something lately," he said quietly. "I don't know what it is, but...   You don't have to carry it alone."

For a second, I almost told him. Not everything, but enough. But then Soki stirred — that self-preserving, smooth-talking part of me that always convinced me to protect the fantasy at all costs.

"I'm just tired," I said, which wasn't a lie, but wasn't the truth either.

Jake studied me like he could see the layers I was trying to hide behind. Then he nodded, pulling me against his chest. "Then rest here. I've got you."

And in that moment, I wanted so badly to believe that was enough. That choosing him in this quiet, safe space could undo the storm brewing inside me.

But I knew better.

Because storms don't stop just because you're holding someone's hand.

The smell of coffee woke me before the sunlight did. I rolled over to find Jake already up, the space beside me still warm but empty.

For a moment, I just lay there, listening to the faint clink of dishes in the kitchen. It was such a rare kind of peace — no phone buzzing, no rush, no reason to put my armor on. Just him.

When I padded into the kitchen, he was standing at the stove barefoot, flipping pancakes, wearing nothing but gray sweatpants and a look of quiet focus.

"Morning," he said without turning around, as if he knew exactly when I'd appear. "Your timing's perfect. Breakfast is almost ready."

I slid onto one of the stools at the counter, wrapping my hands around the mug of coffee he'd already poured for me. "You're spoiling me," I murmured.

"Not spoiling," he said, setting a plate in front of me, "investing."

I laughed softly. "In what?"

"In us," he replied simply, meeting my eyes before sliding onto the stool beside me. "I want you to know that no matter what's out there—whatever storms try to pull you away—my choice will always be you."

Something in me ached at his words. They weren't dramatic or flashy. Just steady. Honest. And it made me want to scream at myself for the secrets I was keeping, for the double life I couldn't seem to walk away from completely.

We ate in comfortable silence for a while, Jake occasionally brushing his fingers over mine. Every little gesture felt like he was pouring something into me — trust, security, love.

By the time breakfast was done, I was leaning into him on the couch, my head against his shoulder. "You're making it really hard for me not to fall completely in love with you," I teased.

His lips brushed my temple. "That's the idea."

And just like that, I knew — this was the headspace I needed him to stay in. If he could stay here, if I could keep him here, maybe Soki would fade. Maybe the storms would pass before they destroyed everything.

But in the back of my mind, I could already feel the shift — that subtle tightening in the air that meant Mitch was getting ready to move again.

It started with a text.

Unknown number.

You look happy.

I stared at the screen, my pulse skipping. The number wasn't saved, but I didn't need it to be. The cadence of those three words, the smugness I could almost hear — it was Mitch.

I deleted it without replying, but the ghost of the message stayed lodged under my skin.

That evening, Jake and I were out walking through the Saturday market. The air was thick with the smell of kettle corn and grilled corn on the cob, the hum of vendors calling out their deals. I had just reached for Jake's hand when I caught a glimpse of him — Mitch — leaning against a vendor's booth across the street.

He wasn't looking at me. Not directly. He was sipping a bottle of water, talking casually with the vendor, but every now and then, his eyes slid over, just enough to let me know he'd seen me.

Jake followed my gaze. "Do you know him?" he asked.

My stomach tightened. "Not really," I said, too quickly.

We kept walking, but I could feel Mitch's presence like static electricity against my back. Even when I didn't look, I knew he was behind us, keeping just enough distance to avoid confrontation.

When Jake stopped to sample some honey, I risked a glance. Mitch was gone.

It should have eased me, but it didn't. It only confirmed what I already knew — he wasn't finished. He was just letting me know he could still reach me whenever he wanted.

Hurricane Mitch was circling again.

Jake didn't say much as we moved to the next row of vendors. He kept my hand in his, but I could feel the shift — the subtle way his thumb stopped tracing lazy circles against my skin, the way his eyes scanned the crowd more than the booths.

"You've been quiet," he said finally, his voice steady but probing.

"Just tired," I replied, forcing a small smile. "It's been a long week."

He nodded, but his gaze lingered on me longer than usual, like he was trying to read the truth underneath my words.

We stopped at a stall selling fresh flowers. While I looked over a bunch of sunflowers, I caught movement out of the corner of my eye. Mitch again — this time on the far side of the street, leaning casually against a lamppost, pretending to scroll through his phone.

I turned away quickly, pressing the flowers to my nose like they could block the sight of him. But my pulse had already given me away.

Jake's hand came to rest on my back. "Hey," he said softly. "You okay?"

"Yeah. Fine."

He didn't push. That was Jake — he loved without cornering, but it didn't mean he wasn't cataloging every detail.

When we walked away from the booth, Mitch was gone again. No goodbye, no confrontation, just the quiet confirmation that he was close enough to watch, close enough to wait.

By the time we got back to Jake's truck, I could feel the question hanging in the air between us. He hadn't asked it yet, but I knew he would eventually: *Who is he to you?*

And when that moment came, I wasn't sure which version of the truth I'd be ready to tell.

Jake sat at the kitchen table long after I'd gone to bed. The house was quiet except for the low hum of the refrigerator, but his mind wouldn't rest.

He replayed the day like a crime scene — the way my smile never quite reached my eyes, the tiny hitch in my breath when I thought he wasn't looking, and that man's silhouette in the background.

It wasn't the first time.

Atlanta was too big for these "chance" encounters to keep happening. Jake wasn't naive enough to think it was all a coincidence, but he wasn't ready to believe I was orchestrating it either.

He loved me too much for that.

Still, something about the man — the way he stood, the subtle arrogance, the half-smile he'd caught once from across the street — told Jake this wasn't a stranger. This was someone who knew me. Knew me well enough to provoke a reaction I couldn't hide.

Jake leaned back in the chair, rubbing the back of his neck. He'd always chosen love first. In every relationship, in every fight, in every uncertainty. And I'd always been the one he was willing to gamble his heart on, no matter the odds.

But love, he knew, could be blind. And blindness could get you hurt.

His phone buzzed with a text from one of his friends. Just a simple: *You good? Thought I saw Em downtown with someone.*

Jake didn't answer. He turned the phone over, screen down, and stared into the darkened window.

If he let himself dwell on it, he'd start imagining things — and that was a dangerous game. But he also knew something was coming.

Mitch, or whatever his name was, wasn't just passing through.

He was circling.

And Jake would be ready.

Mitch leaned against the hood of his black sedan, parked just far enough from the café to be invisible but close enough to watch the door.
Patience wasn't his thing, but when the payoff was this sweet, he could wait all day.

He'd been tracking Emileigh's patterns for weeks now — the places she liked to grab coffee, the boutiques she wandered through when she thought no one was watching, even the grocery store aisles she lingered in.

It wasn't hard. She was predictable when she was comfortable, and lately, she'd been far too comfortable.

Jake was part of that problem.

The guy walked around with the kind of quiet confidence Mitch hated — the "good man" routine that made women trust him, made them feel safe.

It disgusted Mitch.

Not because he wanted her in any real sense. He didn't love. Not anymore. Not since Tahlia.

She'd taken whatever tenderness he had left, shredded it, and made him crawl back for more like a dog that didn't know any better.

And he had crawled back.

He'd hated himself for it, but he couldn't stay away. She'd owned him in a way no one ever should, and the worst part? She still could.

That was why he understood Emileigh better than Jake ever would.

He could see the weakness under her polished surface — the part of her that responded to chaos, that craved danger even when it was bad for her.

It was the same part of himself that kept answering Tahlia's calls.

The difference was, Mitch knew how to weaponize it.

Tonight wasn't about stealing her. Not exactly.

It was about reminding her of who she really was.

And reminding Jake that no matter how much he loved her, no matter how many rings he put on her finger, there would always be a part of her that didn't belong to him.

Mitch watched the door swing open.

There she was.

Same jacket she'd been wearing when he kissed her last — and the way she glanced over her shoulder, just once, told him she felt it too.

That pull. That itch.

He smiled, sliding into the driver's seat.

The game wasn't over.

It was just getting fun.

She saw him before he saw her.

Tall, broad shoulders cutting through the crowd, that same swagger in his walk that always made her pulse quicken before she could think.

She froze for a heartbeat. Her mind screamed *turn around* — but her body remembered the taste of him.

He spotted her. That slow smile spread across his face like a warning and a promise all at once.

"Mornin', beautiful," Mitch drawled, stepping closer.

Her feet wouldn't move. Every nerve ending in her body was firing. She could feel the heat radiating off him before he even reached her.

"Don't," she whispered, though her voice lacked the force she wished it had.

"Don't what?" He closed the space between them. "You and I both know—"

"I said *don't*." Louder this time, but her chest was tight. The memory of every stolen moment they'd had pressed in on her like a tide trying to pull her under.

And then his hand brushed her arm. Just that small contact sent a shock straight through her, and she knew if she stood here one more second, she'd be gone.

So she ran.

Not a fast jog or some casual retreat — she *ran*. Heart pounding, lungs burning, she didn't stop until she ducked into a corner store two blocks away. She pressed her back against the cold metal shelf, hands shaking.

And then, the strangest thing happened.

Relief.

Not the kind that comes from escaping danger, but the kind that fills your soul when you realize you've just walked — no, *run* — out of the lion's den without being devoured.

She closed her eyes. *Thank You, God.*
After all these years, all the prayers she thought had gone unheard, here was her proof. He still listened. He still answered.

But that joy was threaded with something colder — the awareness that this had never happened before. She had never turned Mitch down. Never left him standing there wanting and angry.

And Mitch didn't take *no* well.

Somewhere out there, he was rethinking his entire playbook. And that scared her more than anything.

Day One-Hundred-Twelve: Sometimes victory doesn't look like triumph. Sometimes it looks like running for your life... and knowing the war isn't over.

Chapter Sixteen

Mitch stood in the middle of the sidewalk, people streaming around him, staring at the spot where she'd just been.

She ran. Not walked off in a huff. Not tossed him some coy parting shot over her shoulder.
She flat-out ran.

And that had *never* happened before.

For a second, he just stood there, jaw tightening, trying to wrap his head around it. He'd always been her weakness. The button he could press whenever he wanted. The tether that yanked her back, no matter how far she drifted toward someone else.

Jake. His lip curled at the name.

He started walking — slow, deliberate, each step feeding the slow burn that was catching fire in his chest.
It wasn't about wanting her anymore. Not really.
He didn't want her in the "happily ever after" sense. He wanted her in the *you'll-never-get-away-from-me* sense.

And now she was starting to think she could.

That couldn't happen.

Because it wasn't just about her, it was about the fact that *he* was the one she could never say no to. That was his power. That was his edge. And now… she'd chipped it.

His pride wasn't just bruised — it was bleeding.

"Alright, Em," he muttered to himself, the corner of his mouth lifting in a dangerous half-smile. "You want to play hardball? You think Jake makes you strong? Let's see how strong you are when I take him apart piece by piece."

And just like that, the plan shifted.

It wasn't about seducing her anymore.
It was about dismantling the life she thought she could build without him — starting with the man who thought he could save her.

Because Mitch knew one thing: if Jake fell, Emileigh would fall with him.

And when she hit the ground, Mitch planned to be there waiting.

Jake was in the shop, polishing a table he'd built for a client, when his phone buzzed.

It was nothing urgent—just a text from Emileigh telling him she'd be over later—but something in the way she worded it caught him. No emojis. No drawn-out pet name. Just *see you tonight.*

He told himself it was fine. Not every message had to be dripping with affection. Still, there was a subtle shift he felt in his gut, the same way you feel the air change before a storm.

He brushed it off and went back to work, but his thoughts kept circling the same question: *What would it take for her to choose me, every single time, no hesitation?*

The truth was, Jake had no real proof she'd been unfaithful—no smoking gun, no undeniable lie—but the coincidences were stacking up. Too many "chance" encounters with Mitch. Too many times, he'd seen that guarded look in her eyes when his name came up.

He loved her. God, he loved her in a way that didn't make sense to anyone else. And he'd made peace with the fact that she wasn't perfect—that neither of them was. But love like his came with risk, and right now, that risk felt heavier than usual.

Jake leaned on the table, closing his eyes. He thought about all the times he'd chosen love over pride, over suspicion, over the easy way out. He thought about the way she fit against him when she finally let herself breathe. He thought about proposing—not someday, but soon—before doubt could ruin what they had.

But what he didn't know, couldn't know, was that Mitch had already set his sights on him. That somewhere out there, a man with a vendetta was building the kind of storm you didn't see until it was on top of you.

Jake wiped his hands on a rag, glanced at the door, and smiled faintly at the thought of Emileigh walking through it. He had no idea he was already standing in the path of the hurricane.

Mitch sat in his car, parked two blocks from Emileigh's apartment, replaying the moment she pulled away from him.

It wasn't the first time she'd said *no*, but it was the first time she meant it. Her eyes had been sharp—focused—not that foggy haze he was used to seeing when he touched her. It had shaken him.

For years, he'd been the one thing she couldn't resist. The ace in her deck. The itch she couldn't stop scratching. And just like that, she'd broken the pattern.

That couldn't stand.

Mitch lit a cigarette, watching the tip burn, feeling the heat in his lungs. He could still taste her defiance, and it left a bitter edge on his tongue. Tahlia had been right—he had a weakness for women who thought they could walk away from him. But this wasn't just about Emileigh anymore.

If she was strong enough to resist him, she was strong enough to commit to Jake. And if she committed to Jake, Mitch lost his favorite game.

No, he wouldn't try to tear them apart outright—that was too obvious. He'd feed Jake just enough poison to keep him second-guessing. A stray photo here. A vague "I saw her with someone" there. Never enough to be proof, but always enough to leave a crack.

Mitch flicked his cigarette out the window and started the car.

The first move was already in play. He'd called in a favor from someone who owed him—someone who happened to know exactly where Jake would be next week. A setup, subtle and clean. Jake would see something that would make him wonder if he knew Emileigh at all.

And the best part? Mitch wouldn't have to touch her to make it work.

But he'd still be there, in the shadows, knowing she was thinking about him. That even if her body was with Jake, a part of her mind would be occupied with the storm she couldn't quite shake.

Mitch smirked. "You can't outrun me, Em," he muttered. "You never could."

Jake wasn't the type to snoop. He hated games, hated drama. But when Marcus from work slid into the booth across from him at lunch with a half-smirk and a "Man, you might want to see this," he couldn't ignore it.

On Marcus's phone was a blurry photo, taken from a distance, the angle just enough to make the context impossible to read.

Emileigh.

She was laughing, head tilted back, hair falling over her shoulder like it used to when they first started dating. But she wasn't alone. A man—tall, broad-shouldered—was leaning in just a little too close, his hand brushing her arm. The shot caught it mid-moment, enough to make it look intimate.

"She's probably just talking to someone," Jake said, his voice steady, though his stomach had tightened.

Marcus shrugged. "Hey, man, I'm just saying. My cousin was downtown Saturday night and saw her like this for a while. Didn't look like small talk."

Jake slid the phone back across the table. "Thanks."

The rest of the lunch tasted like cardboard. He drove back to work replaying the image in his mind, telling himself it meant nothing—but also wondering why she hadn't mentioned being downtown that night at all.

By the time he got home, the quiet of his apartment felt like a test. His phone sat on the counter, buzzing with a text from Emileigh: *Can't wait to see you tomorrow. Miss you.*

He stared at the words, his thumb hovering over the keyboard.

Just ask her. No—don't make it a thing unless it is one.

Still, that photo had planted itself in his chest like a splinter.

Across town, Mitch poured himself a drink, knowing the seed was already in the soil. All it needed was time.

Marcus leaned against the doorway like he owned the place, that same half-smile he'd worn the night he almost got her to cross the line.
"Jake," he greeted casually, like they were old friends. "Thought you'd want to see this."

He slid his phone across the counter. The photo was grainy but unmistakable—Emileigh on the sidewalk, Mitch's hand cupping her cheek.

Jake's stomach knotted. "Where did you get this?"

Marcus shrugged, voice low and unbothered. "Atlanta's a small city when you know where to look. Ran into a buddy who snapped it. Figured you'd want to know."

Jake knew exactly what Marcus was doing. This wasn't kindness—it was calculated. Marcus had once been a temptation Emileigh almost gave in to, and he'd never forgotten it.

"Why are you showing me this?" Jake asked, his voice sharp.

"Because," Marcus said, his smirk widening, "I know what it's like to think you've got someone all to yourself, only to find out maybe you don't."

Jake's grip tightened on the phone until his knuckles whitened. His mind was a storm—rage, doubt, love—all colliding at once. He didn't want to believe it. God, he *couldn't* believe it.

And somewhere, far from the café, Mitch was probably smiling. Whether Jake realized it or not, Mitch had just planted another crack in the foundation.

Jake set the phone back on the counter with deliberate calm, his jaw tight.

"Marcus," he said evenly, "you've got a history. So does Mitch. Neither of you has ever wanted to see me and Emileigh together. So, unless you're showing me a video where I can hear her voice and see her lips move, I'm not taking this as fact."

Marcus smirked, like he'd expected that answer. "Suit yourself. Just remember—I tried to help."

Jake didn't respond. He watched Marcus leave, the door swinging shut behind him, then exhaled slowly. The image still burned in his mind, but so did the knowledge of who it came from. Mitch and Marcus weren't allies—they were vultures, circling for the smallest sign of weakness.

In Jake's mind, this wasn't about truth—it was about sabotage. Somebody was working hard to plant doubt in his head. He didn't know if it was Mitch, Marcus, or both, but he wasn't giving them the satisfaction of watching him crumble.

Not without proof, he could see with his own eyes. Proof that was undeniable.

So he decided to move carefully, to watch, to wait. Proceed with caution. Keep loving her, but stay alert.

What Jake couldn't know—what no one could know—was that Emileigh had already started to change. She had resisted Mitch for the first time in her life. She had stared down temptation after temptation and walked away, trembling but victorious.

The irony was cruel: Jake was searching for evidence of betrayal that no longer existed. Emileigh's storms were beginning to pass, but the shadow of her past still lingered like the smell of rain in the air.

And in the quiet, doubt began its slow, patient work inside him.

Chapter Seventeen

Emileigh couldn't stop smiling. It wasn't the kind of smile you wear for a camera or to be polite. It was the slow, warm kind that blooms when you know you've just conquered something that used to own you.

She replayed the moment in her head — Mitch's hands reaching for her, his voice dripping with that old confidence, the one that had always made her knees weaken. But this time, she didn't crumble. She didn't negotiate with herself. She didn't even stall. She walked away. No—she ran. And the further she got from him, the lighter she felt, like each step peeled another layer of chains from her spirit.

God still answers prayers. That truth sat heavy and sweet in her chest. For years, she had begged for the strength to resist Mitch, and for years, the answer had been silence. Or so she thought. Maybe it wasn't silence. Maybe God had been building this moment brick by brick, waiting until she was ready to see herself as He saw her—capable, worthy, and free.

She poured herself a glass of wine when she got home, letting the hum of the refrigerator and the soft tick of the wall clock fill the room. No music, no phone, no distraction. Just her and this quiet, rare joy.

Across town, Jake sat in his car, engine idling, staring at her building. He hadn't gone up yet. Something about today didn't sit right. Emileigh seemed lighter lately, yes. Happier, even. But in the same breath, something in her eyes told him there was more to the story. And until he knew what it was, he couldn't relax.

She thought she was celebrating in peace. He was silently taking notes.

Chapter Eighteen

Jake lay awake that night, eyes tracing the faint shadows dancing across the ceiling. Emileigh slept beside him, her breath slow and even, her hand resting lightly on his chest as if nothing in the world could disturb her peace.

But Jake's mind was restless.

The scent was still there—subtle, lingering in the sheets like a question that wouldn't leave. Sandalwood. Not strong enough to accuse, but just enough to remember. He told himself it could have been anything: a hug from someone at work, a brush past a stranger in a store. Still, the thought worked its way into the cracks of his certainty, curling around every tender place he had for her.

He watched her in the soft blue wash of the moonlight. She looked... different lately. Not just happier—lighter. And while part of him loved that, another part hated it, because he didn't know what had changed. And not knowing felt dangerous.

In the morning, he rose before she did, lingering in the doorway as he pulled on his jacket. She stirred, smiling sleepily at him, completely unaware that he was studying her the way a man studies a map before entering unknown territory.

"Breakfast?" she asked, voice still thick with sleep.

"Maybe later," he said with a half-smile, though his eyes were already elsewhere—cataloging, comparing, storing away every detail for some unspoken reckoning he wasn't ready to have.

By the time he left the apartment, the question had only grown louder in his head. And no matter how much he loved her, he knew—love alone wouldn't quiet suspicion.

Chapter Eighteen

Emileigh

The hum of the fridge, the soft tick of the wall clock, the weightless hush after a hard-won victory—she let it all settle into her bones. She'd run. She'd *resisted.* The word itself felt like a silk ribbon tightening into a bow around a gift she hadn't known she could give herself.

She rinsed her glass, smiled at nothing, whispered, "Thank You," to the God who had not been silent after all— just patient. When the knock came, she opened the door still glowing.

Jake

He kissed her cheek and breathed in—sandalwood. Not her usual floral. It wasn't loud, just a ghost of something that didn't belong. He tucked it away with a practiced smile and a longer-than-usual hug, the kind that said *I'm here* while his mind quietly took notes.

That night, he lay awake, her hand warm on his chest, the question still faint and insistent as dawn pressed pale light through the blinds.

Mitch

Across town, Mitch stared at the inside of his windshield until the streetlights doubled. She had run from him. Not a flirty retreat. A *flea.* The unfamiliar sting in his chest surprised him.

"Okay," he said to the empty cab. "New play."

He could be patient. Patience wasn't surrender; it was a strategy.

Mitch flicked his lighter open and shut, watching the flame bloom and vanish, over and over. His knee bounced, his jaw worked, but his mind was still. He wasn't going to call her. Not yet. Not after the way she'd looked at him—like he was a threat instead of a memory.

That was fine. He'd learned a long time ago that the moments people thought they were safe were the moments they loosened their guard.

She'd left him standing there with nothing but the echo of her refusal, but he knew her rhythms. The quiet days. The restless nights. The way she pretended to fill her time but left just enough empty space for old habits to slip in.

And when they did, she always came back.

Mitch smirked, killing the lighter one last time. The trick wasn't forcing the door. It was waiting for her to crack it herself.

Chapter Nineteen

Jake

Her call came ten minutes after he'd missed her: bright, breathless, easy.

"Sorry, babe—I was in the shower," she said, voice lilting like the excuse was casual, not calculated.

Later, when he dropped by, her hair was perfectly dry and perfectly styled, each curl deliberate. He kissed her, smiled in all the right places, and asked about nothing.

He had learned not to interrogate a moment; some things revealed themselves in time. Still, he tucked the mismatch away, like a carpenter sliding a spare nail behind his ear.

Emileigh

She hadn't been in the shower. She'd been sitting at the kitchen table, palms pressed together, talking to God like He was leaning on the other side of a screen door.

"I'm not the same," she whispered. "Help me to keep it that way."

She didn't want to bring Mitch into this new light, didn't want his name—or his shadow—clouding what God had cleared. Some truths were too raw to be spoken yet, even to Jake.

So she kept it simple. *I'm okay. I'm choosing You. I'm choosing Jake. I'm choosing me.*

Mitch

He let her ignore two calls. Then, nothing. No follow-up text, no "where are you," no hook to pull on. The silence itself was the bait.

Mitch knew from experience—withdrawal breeds hunger. She might think she was past it, but the longer she went without him, the sharper she'd feel his absence when he finally appeared.

He took mental inventory: the coffee shop she loved, the grocery store where she always parked two spaces from the cart corral, the bench in the park that faced the church.

He didn't need to be everywhere. He just needed to be somewhere when she wasn't expecting him.

Jake

He noticed she was lighter lately, but it wasn't the kind of light that came from shared joy. It felt... separate. Like she'd found a secret spring to drink from when he wasn't looking.

Part of him wanted to be happy for her. Another part wanted to know who—or what—was holding the cup.

He brushed the thought aside, telling himself not to be paranoid. But the thought didn't leave.

Emileigh

She brewed tea instead of wine that night, curling on the couch with a blanket and the kind of peace she'd stopped trusting long ago.

If she kept choosing right, maybe Jake would feel it. Maybe that would be enough to steady them.

She had no idea he was already feeling it—just not the way she hoped.

Mitch

He leaned against the hood of his truck, a cigarette burning low between his fingers, watching the entrance to the grocery store.

He wasn't looking for her tonight. Not exactly. But if she appeared... well. He'd smile. Maybe nod. Maybe hold the door.

Not to push her back inside his world—Just to remind her it was still open.

Chapter Twenty

Emileigh

The bell above the café door jingled, and her stomach dropped before her mind caught up. Mitch. Hat low, smile careful, hands empty.

"Just coffee," he said, as if the words weren't loaded. "I'm not staying."

She nodded, throat tight, feet rooted. He kept a soft distance, ordered, and left. The whole thing was nothing. And yet, her pulse thudded like she'd sprinted.

When a friend asked later how her morning went, she said she'd been home. Easier. Cleaner. Safer.

Jake

At dinner with friends, she offhandedly mentioned "running into an old acquaintance at the coffee shop." Two days earlier? She'd told someone she was home all morning that day.

Jake didn't call her on it. He just smiled, topped off her water, and made a joke that everyone laughed at.

But in the back of his mind, the carpenter's nail found its place, resting where he could reach for it later.

Mitch

He'd "accidentally" run into her at the coffee shop, kept the conversation light, and kept his hands to himself. She looked nervous—good. That meant the door wasn't locked, just cracked. He could work with that.

He left before she could tell him to. Let her think she'd been in control. Let her walk away believing she'd won something.

Emileigh

Back home, she replayed the encounter, her body alternating between relief and unease. Relief that he hadn't pushed. Unease because part of her feared the push would come later—when she wasn't ready.

She tried to pray but found herself just breathing in and out, telling herself she'd done the right thing.

Jake

She was quiet that night, distracted in a way that didn't feel like tiredness. He offered to rub her shoulders, and she said yes, but her muscles stayed taut beneath his hands.

He didn't ask why. Sometimes silence told him more than an answer.

Mitch

He sat in his truck a block away from her place, sipping bad coffee and thinking about the way she'd held her mug at the café—both hands, fingers curled tight like she was bracing against something.

He smirked. He didn't need to force the tension. He just needed to be the relief.

Chapter Twenty-One

Jake

Mitch's name skimmed the edge of a conversation like a shadow on water. Someone mentioned him in passing—just a harmless anecdote—and before Jake could react, Emileigh had already steered them somewhere else.

Her smile didn't falter, but Jake saw it: the ripple in her shoulders, the flicker of something in her eyes before she smoothed it over.

He didn't push. He just let the silence afterward stretch out, thin and fragile as spun sugar. Easy to crack.

Emileigh

She hated that saying Mitch's name still pulled the air wrong in her lungs. She wasn't protecting Mitch; she was protecting herself. Protecting the part of her that was finally learning how to stand without him.

Some stories, once opened, swallowed entire rooms. And she wasn't ready to watch Jake get swallowed in hers.

So she turned the conversation. Not tonight. Not when she was finally breathing right.

Mitch

He spotted her at the grocery store, two aisles over, the curve of her hip turning the corner before she did. She didn't see him. That was fine.

He watched her run her finger under the shelf labels, like she was reading between the lines. She smiled at the cashier without flirting, left with exactly what she came for.

Discipline looked good on her. But discipline got tired.

Jake

That night, she curled against him, her head on his shoulder. He wanted to ask, *What is it about him that still gets to you?* But the words stayed trapped in the cage of his chest.

If she told him, it would be because she wanted to—Not because he pulled it out.

Emileigh

She felt his stillness beneath her cheek, the way his breathing stayed steady, but his body didn't soften. She knew he was thinking. She just didn't know if it was about her—or about him.

Either way, she was too tired to go chasing the answer.

Mitch

He walked past her car on the way back to his truck. Not close enough to look suspicious, not far enough to look accidental. Just enough that if she glanced up, she'd see him in her periphery.

She didn't. But he saw her. And sometimes, that was enough.

Jake

Her phone lit up on the table—just an M and a single line of text before the screen went dark.
She didn't notice him noticing.

Later, curled into his side, she traced lazy shapes over his chest—circles, lines, a slow cross that felt like a prayer she couldn't say out loud.

He kept his arm around her, eyes open in the dark. That single letter weighed more than her whole embrace.

Emileigh

She saw the notification too late. M.
A message so small and sharp it could cut through the seams of the life she was trying to stitch together.

Delete. Block. Breathe.

She did all three, but the ghost sting stayed. She pressed her lips to Jake's shoulder and whispered into his skin, "I'm not that woman anymore."
She needed him to hear it—even if he never knew why she'd said it.

Mitch

He sent the single letter on purpose. A knock, not a battering ram. She'd feel it—that subtle reminder that he was still in her orbit.

He wanted her to delete it. Wanted her to think she'd won some moral victory. Because victories took energy, and energy ran out.

When it did, he'd be there.

Jake

The next morning, she was extra affectionate—coffee already made, her lips warm and lingering on his neck. Most men would take it at face value.

Jake took it as a sign. Not that she'd done anything, but that she was working hard to prove she hadn't.

Emileigh

She hated that every time she fought the old temptation, she still felt guilty—like resisting wasn't enough unless she could erase the temptation itself.

But she couldn't. Not yet. Maybe not ever.

All she could do was keep saying no, one day at a time.

Mitch

He drove past her street that night with no plan to stop. Just to remind himself where she was. Just to remind himself, she still was.

Because people could resist for months... until they didn't.

Chapter Twenty-Three

Jake

The ring had lived in his nightstand so long it felt like part of the furniture. Twice he'd carried it out, ready to ask. Twice the moment had slipped—once because she seemed distracted, another because *he* did.

Now, he wanted the third time to be the one that silenced all the questions in his head. Not just hers saying *yes*, but her eyes saying *only you*.

Until that moment came, the box would stay closed.

Emileigh

She found the ring while digging for a charger, the velvet brushing against her fingers like an unspoken promise. She closed the drawer with a smile that felt equal parts hope and ache.

Twice he'd asked. Twice, life had swayed beneath them like an old bridge.

"God," she murmured, hand on the wood, "if You're healing us, let it be whole."

She set her phone face-up on the counter, a small rebellion against secrets, and made tea that smelled like citrus and rest.

Mitch

He stopped thinking in words and started thinking in interruptions. Not grand gestures—those got noticed. No, he wanted *moments*.

A bouquet with no card. A song from their past drifted out of a bar she liked. A mutual friend "accidentally" mentioned him when she least expected it.

The point wasn't to pull her back. The point was to make *forward* feel crowded.

Jake

He started mapping out a day that wasn't a performance—just them. The farmer's market where she'd haggle gently and he'd carry peaches. Coffee on the library steps. The park bench that faced the church she loved.

He wouldn't propose until the air between them was clean. Until there was no flicker in her eyes to read into.

Emileigh

She imagined that day, too, but hers ended without the question. She didn't want another almost. If they were going to step forward, she wanted it to be on solid ground.

She had no idea they were both waiting for the same thing.

Mitch

He pictured Jake planning something sweet and small. Cute. Predictable. Easy to disrupt.

He didn't have to ruin the day. He just had to bend it slightly.

Because bent things rarely stand straight again.

Chapter Twenty-Four

The morning was warm enough for short sleeves, the sun bright but not overbearing. Jake had planned the day exactly how he wanted it—no fanfare, no crowd, no staged perfection. Just them.

They strolled through the farmer's market, the smell of peaches and fresh bread curling through the air. Emileigh haggled gently with a vendor over a basket of strawberries, her laughter soft and easy. Jake stood beside her, holding the peaches she'd chosen, watching the way sunlight caught in her hair.

From there, they wandered to the library steps, coffees in hand, sitting shoulder to shoulder as people passed by in lazy waves. They didn't talk much—didn't need to. It was the kind of quiet that felt earned.

The park was their last stop, the one bench that faced the old brick church, sitting under the gentle shade of an oak tree. Jake set the peaches beside him, shifted so he could see her clearly.

"I've been holding onto something," he said, voice low but steady.

Her eyes softened. "I know."

He reached into his jacket and pulled out the velvet box. He didn't open it right away, just let it rest in his palm. "I've asked before. Twice. And maybe I didn't ask right. Maybe we weren't ready."

Her fingers touched the box lightly, like she was afraid it might vanish.

"But I love you," he went on. "And I want to spend the rest of my life making sure you know it. So... Emileigh." He opened the box, the ring catching a ray of sunlight that made her blink. "Will you marry me?"

Her breath caught, tears gathering quick and unashamed. "Yes," she said, her voice breaking. Then again, firmer: "Yes."

Jake slid the ring onto her finger, his hands trembling just enough for her to notice. She smiled through her tears, and he leaned in, kissing her in the quiet shade while the world carried on around them.

For a moment, everything was perfect.

Mitch

From across the street, Mitch leaned against the hood of his truck, arms crossed, sunglasses hiding the exact shape of his glare.

Predictable. He'd known Jake wouldn't wait much longer. Known he'd go for the sweet, quiet proposal that made him look like the safe choice.

Mitch didn't mind. Safe didn't keep a woman's blood warm at night.

He flicked his lighter open and shut, the soft metallic click a promise to himself. This wasn't over. Not even close.

The rest of the day felt like a dream wrapped in sunlight.

Jake kept her hand in his as they wove through the farmer's market again, the stalls winding down for the afternoon. Every few minutes, Emileigh would touch her ring—lightly, almost absently—like her fingers were checking it hadn't slipped away. Every time she looked down at it, her lips would curve into a smile that seemed meant just for her, like she was letting herself believe in forever.

They stopped at a bakery, the scent of warm bread spilling into the street. Jake bought a loaf, tore it in half right there, and handed her the bigger piece. They walked and ate, her laughter floating between them when the crust cracked too loud.

It felt... normal. Peaceful.

But now and then, Jake's eyes caught on little things. The way her phone stayed buried in her bag the whole afternoon. How she'd glance over her shoulder when they crossed certain streets. Once, when he told her he loved her and brushed his thumb over her ring, her smile faltered—not much, just a ripple—before she caught it again.

It was nothing. It was everything.

***

By the time they made it back to her apartment, the sky was painted in shades of copper and deep blue. She curled into him on the couch, her legs tucked under her, talking about the wedding.

"I don't want a big show," she said. "I want it to feel like... family. Like home."

He smiled and kissed her temple. "Then that's what we'll do."

But in the back of his mind, the day kept playing over like a film reel. He'd replay the glances, the pauses, the little catches in her voice. None of them added up to anything. Yet.

***

Across town

Mitch stubbed out his cigarette and tossed the butt into the gutter. He'd let them have their pretty little day. Jake was easy to read—safe, steady, the kind of man who thought love was enough if you just held it still.

That was fine. Mitch didn't need to knock the whole thing down. He just needed to shift the foundation.

He already had his first move in mind—subtle, quiet. Something that wouldn't touch her directly, but would make Jake's gut twist in just the right way. A rumor here, a "chance" sighting there. A reminder that history never really stays in the past.

***

Over the next week, the glow of the proposal settled over them like soft light. Emileigh was freer with her affection, lingering in his arms in the mornings, surprising him with takeout when he worked late. They talked about venues, colors, and guest lists.

But Jake noticed other things too.

A missed call, she said, was "just a wrong number."

An uncharacteristic hesitation when he asked about her afternoon.

Her phone lit up while she was in the shower, a notification disappearing before he could read it.

None of it was proof. But it was weight—light at first, then heavier with each day.

***

One Friday evening, as they walked to their car after dinner, Jake's arm around her, a voice called from across the street.

"Emileigh?"

She froze before turning. A man he didn't recognize—tall, dark jacket, a smirk just sharp enough to notice—lifted his hand in greeting.

"Hey. Been a while."

She gave a polite smile, said, "Yeah, it has," and kept walking.

Jake didn't press. But he filed it away.

***

Mitch

From the shadowed mouth of an alley, Mitch watched them pass. He didn't wave. Didn't need to. The guy he'd sent over had done his job—plant the seed, walk away.

It wasn't about being seen. It was about being remembered.

***

Back at Emileigh's place, Jake sat on the couch while she made tea in the kitchen. He could hear the clink of the spoon against the mug, the whistle of the kettle, the hum of her voice as she hummed a tune he didn't recognize.

For the first time in days, the ring on her finger didn't reassure him. It reminded him that even promises could be broken.

They settled into a rhythm that felt new and tender. Mornings, she'd text him pictures of her ring catching the sun on the dashboard, captions like *still feels unreal* and *don't wake me up*. Evenings, he'd bring groceries, and they'd cook side by side—music low, shoulders bumping, kisses stolen between simmer and stir.

But the small things kept finding him.

A Sunday, soft and bright

Church was steadying for both of them. Emileigh lifted her hands during the last song, that clear, unguarded look on her face Jake loved most—like she'd slipped all her armor and walked out into a field.

On the final chord, he glanced toward the aisle and caught a man in a dark jacket slipping out the side door. Not Mitch—wrong build. But when Jake walked them to the car, a scrap of paper waited under the wiper.

Congratulations. No name.

"Probably someone from church," Emileigh said, folding it into her pocket. Her voice was even. Her fingers were not.

Jake nodded, smiled, and opened her door. Later, when she wasn't looking, he checked the handwriting again. Careful letters. Confident stroke. He had the odd feeling it wasn't meant for *both* of them.

Venue hunting

They toured a small garden space midweek—brick walkways, climbing roses, strings of Edison bulbs under a canopy of trees. It felt like them. The manager, cheerful and harried, flipped through a ledger.

"Such a sweet story," she said. "And your friend called earlier about dates—Mitch, was it? Wanted to be sure he had the same information."

Emileigh's smile cooled so fast the temperature seemed to drop with it. "He isn't... he's not part of the planning."

"Oh! My mistake." The manager kept talking, but the air shifted. Jake felt it hit the base of his skull—the ache of a question he didn't want to ask.

They finished the tour. They thanked her. They walked to the car in a silence that sounded like distant thunder.

In the driver's seat, Jake's hands rested on the wheel. "You told me you blocked him."

"I did." Her jaw worked once before she found the rest. "I don't know how he knew."

He believed her. He also hated that it was getting harder to separate what he believed from what he feared.

A song in the wrong place

Two nights later, they stopped by a quiet bar after dinner. A cover band eased through old R&B staples. Midway through their second drink, a new song slid in—*their* song, the one she once told him Mitch used to play at the start of every apology. Emileigh's spine stiffened before she smoothed it out.

Jake watched the bandleader glance toward the door, as if hitting a cue.

"Wanna go?" he asked softly.

She nodded, eyes shining with a frustration that wasn't for him. On the sidewalk, she looped her arm through his and pressed her cheek to his shoulder. "I'm not going back," she said, almost fierce. "I'm not."

"I know," he said. He did. And yet the song kept playing in his head long after the street noise swallowed it.

The bouquet

The flowers arrived at her office in a heavy, gracious spill—peonies and ranunculus and a single, bright gardenia that scented the whole room. No card in the envelope. Just *For the bride.*

"My aunt," Emileigh said when Jake picked her up that evening. "She does this. Big gestures. No notes."

He lifted the bouquet to the light, admiring because admiring was what you did, and his eye caught the florist's sticker on the wrap. A shop across town. The same block as the café where Mitch "accidentally" bumped into her.

"Beautiful," he said. It was true. So was the way his stomach dropped and didn't climb back.

The almost-message

Her phone chimed while she showered. On the counter: a preview he wasn't trying to see. A single letter—M—from a number with no name. The text itself blinked away before it rendered.

He stepped back like it had burned him. When she came out, hair damp, eyes hopeful, he kissed her and said nothing. That felt like love. It also felt like cowardice.

That night, he prayed in the dark for wisdom and for a softness that wouldn't make him stupid. He asked for the kind of courage that told the truth without breaking the person he loved.

***

Mitch

He didn't need to show up to watch it work. A nudge here, a whisper there. Call a venue, ask a bar for a song, send flowers that look like a relative's kindness. If you set the table right, people feed themselves the doubt.

From the driver's seat, he traced the edge of his lighter with his thumb, thinking about timing. Jake would start asking questions soon. Good. Pressure made people pick faster. And fast choices were rarely clean.

"Steady, steady," he murmured, as if he were teaching a child to balance. "We're almost there."

***

The change in her eyes

The next morning, Jake watched Emileigh rummage for keys. She was humming. Light. But there was a new alertness to the way she checked locks, scanned the street, kept her phone on silent but within reach.

He pressed the ring finger to his lips. "You good?"

"I'm good," she said. Then, softer, "I'm trying to be."

He understood that more than she knew.

The missed turn

On the way to dinner, Jake drove right past their exit. She laughed and touched his arm. "Baby, did you forget where we're going?"

He didn't answer right away. He was thinking about a florist's sticker and a bar's setlist, and a venue manager who said the wrong name out loud.

"Sorry," he said finally, signaling for a U-turn. "Got lost for a second."

"You and me both," she said, barely above a whisper, like she hadn't meant to let it out. Then she squeezed his hand and turned the radio up just enough to make talking optional.

Marcus, again

They ran into Marcus on a Saturday afternoon at the home store—pots and throws and a debate about which lamp looked less like a waiting room. He was polite, distant, and a little too eager to leave.

After he walked away, Emileigh was quiet. Jake remembered a story she'd told half-finished months ago and the way it had ended in ellipses.

"You okay?" he asked.

"Yeah," she said, and reached for a lamp that wasn't either of the ones they'd been discussing. "Let's just get this one."

He watched the lamp in the cart like it might explain something.

That night, the city hummed below her window. Jake stood in the kitchen drying a plate that had been dry for a full minute, listening to Emileigh brush her teeth, then rinse, then pause like she did when she was rehearsing what not to say.

When she came out, she leaned on the counter, elbows wide, chin down. "I'm telling you the truth," she said. "I'm not talking to him. I'm not... I'm not *with* him."

"I know," he said, and hated the way the words sounded like a promise he couldn't cash.

She nodded, eyes glistening. "I just want the past to leave me alone."

He put the plate down and pulled her in. "Me too."

Neither of them said *Please make it stop* but the plea hung in the air like steam.

Mitch

He circled her block with the radio off, the city's noise a distant throb. He wasn't pep-talking himself. He didn't need it. This wasn't about winning a heart. It was about proving he could still touch it.

He parked two streets over and cut the engine. For a few minutes, he just sat, picturing the look on Jake's face—careful, patient, cracking at the edges. He smiled without teeth.

"Predictable," he said, and flicked the lighter open and shut, open and shut, until the tiny metal sound felt like a metronome counting down.

By the end of the week, nothing had happened, and everything had shifted. The ring on Emileigh's finger flashed when she laughed. The bouquet still sweetened the apartment air. The venue held their date. The bar was just a bar again.

And still, Jake felt it—the slow, quiet lean of a building whose foundation had been shaved by a degree you couldn't see yet.

He kissed her forehead. He promised an easy weekend. He meant it.

He also drove home with both hands tight on the wheel, noticing how easy it would be, if a man wasn't paying attention, to miss a curve he'd taken a hundred times.

Chapter Twenty-Five

The weekend was supposed to be theirs. No errands. No obligations. Just two days to breathe, to be together without the shadow of a to-do list.

Jake picked her up Saturday morning with a thermos of coffee and a surprise destination. Emileigh guessed the whole way—antique markets, the lake, some tiny diner two towns over—but he kept smiling and shaking his head.

When they finally pulled up to a quiet vineyard on the outskirts of the city, she laughed. "You really *are* getting romantic in your old age."

"I'm younger than you," he teased.

"By six months," she shot back, but her hand lingered on his cheek before they walked toward the tasting room.

The vineyard air was crisp, the rows of vines stretching into soft hills. They took their time, sipping wine and stealing glances, leaning close when the wind caught her hair. Jake felt himself relax for the first time in weeks.

They were halfway through a cheese plate when a server came to refill their glasses.

"Compliments of the gentleman at the bar," she said, nodding toward the tasting room.

Jake turned, expecting to see someone from work or church. Instead, there was only a man in a ballcap, leaning on the counter, looking down at his phone. No glance toward them. No acknowledgement.

"Probably a mistake," Emileigh said quickly, but her eyes didn't follow her voice.

The server apologized and retreated. Jake let it go—but part of him knew she'd recognized something she didn't want to name.

They took the long way back, winding through neighborhoods with houses that leaned in on tree-lined streets. Emileigh reached for the radio and landed on an old soul track, singing softly under her breath. Jake joined in, off-key enough to make her laugh.

For a moment, it was easy again.

Until they stopped at a light, and a dark pickup eased up beside them. The driver didn't look over. Just idled there.

When the light changed, the truck turned left. Emileigh's gaze followed it in the side mirror a beat too long.

"You okay?" Jake asked.

"Yeah," she said, and reached for his hand. "I'm fine."

Mitch

From two blocks away, Mitch watched them drive past, the pickup just a piece of the set. He didn't even know the driver. Didn't have to. People saw what they feared. He just made sure the angles were right.

They woke to the smell of cinnamon. Jake had started breakfast—sticky buns from a recipe his grandmother swore by. Emileigh padded into the kitchen barefoot, hair tousled, smiling like she wanted to remember this moment forever.

"Perfect," she said, wrapping her arms around his waist.

It wasn't until her phone buzzed on the counter.

Jake didn't look. He told himself it was respect. He told himself it was trust. But when she picked it up and her thumb hovered just a second too long before unlocking, something in his chest tightened.

They ate on the balcony, the city stretching out below them. She talked about guest lists and favors and whether they should write their own vows. He nodded, made suggestions, and laughed when she made jokes about him crying at the altar.

But he was already picturing her phone screen, the way her hand had shielded it from the light.

Mitch

He didn't send a message that morning. He didn't need to. The absence was just as loud. When people expected a strike, not striking became its own kind of pressure.

That night, Jake lay awake while Emileigh slept curled into him. Her breathing was steady. He was not.

He looked at the ring on her finger and felt the weight of every unanswered question pressing against it.

Chapter Twenty-Six

Monday arrived with a bright, indifferent sky. Emileigh told herself she was fine. She put on the pearl studs her mother gave her, tied her hair back, and walked into work ready to be the woman she'd promised God—and herself— she'd be.

The envelope was waiting on her desk.

No return address. No postage. Just her name in block letters that tried too hard to look anonymous.

She stood a moment, keycard lanyard twisting around her fingers, then slid a letter opener along the seam. Inside: a single photograph. Years old. Her head tipped against Mitch's shoulder, laughter caught midflight. His hand at her waist like it had a right to be there.

Her throat clicked dry. She turned the photo over— blank. No message to answer, no number to block. Just proof of a past she was already paying to leave behind.

She dropped it into the shredder, watched the machine chew until the image became thin confetti. Then she emptied the bin into the trash herself, walked it down the hall, and kept walking until she hit daylight.

On the sidewalk, she called Jake.

"Lunch?" he asked immediately, hearing everything she hadn't said.

"Please."

They met at the tiny place on the corner with the chalkboard menus and too few tables. She tried to tell him about the envelope without giving the picture more power than it deserved. He tried to ask questions without sounding like a detective.

"So there's... nothing to trace?" he asked finally.

"Nothing." She took his hand, squeezed. "I'm not contacting him. I'm not responding to anything. I just... I'm tired of feeling hunted by what I already left."

"I know." He thumbed her knuckles, the gesture tender and taut. "We'll figure this out."

He meant it. He also heard the word *we* and wondered how much of this fight belonged to him and how much might break them if he carried it wrong.

Mitch

He didn't have to see the photo land to feel its weight. Old moments had a way of arriving like fresh ones if you sent them in the right envelope.

From his truck, he watched the lunch rush swell and thin. He saw Jake and Emileigh step out into the light—closer, yes. Also quieter.

Good. Quiet people thought more. Thought people reached conclusions.

He turned the lighter over in his palm and smiled without amusement.

That evening, Emileigh insisted on driving. "You've been carting me around everywhere," she said, jingling her keys. "Let me." The sky teased rain and changed its mind, leaving the streets in a film of almost.

Halfway home, a text flashed across her phone on the console: Unknown: Miss you. No initial. No name. Just two words.

She didn't touch it. Didn't even glance down long enough to unlock. Her shoulders squared. "I'm not that woman anymore," she said, to the windshield, to God, to herself.

Jake stared straight ahead and swallowed. "I know."

He did know. He also knew that not touching a flame didn't make the smell of smoke leave a room.

When they got to her place, he offered what he could hold without resenting: "Let me set up call filters. New number, two-factor everything. We can talk to someone about a restraining order."

"I don't want him to feel important," she said, voice steady. "I just want him to be gone."

"Sometimes you have to name a thing to make it leave," he said softly.

She looked at him—a long, searching look—and then nodded. "Okay. Tomorrow."

Tuesday, a rumor found him first.

Jake was grabbing coffee when a friend from church, well-meaning and under-informed, said, "Hey—small world. A buddy swears he saw Emileigh near the Riverfront on Sunday. Said she looked... distracted. Was she okay?"

"We were at the vineyard," Jake said, level.

"Oh, then he's probably mixing up days." The friend grinned, oblivious. "You know how it is. Congrats again, man."

Jake carried the coffee out into the air that suddenly felt too thin. He didn't confront her with it. He just set the rumor beside the bouquet with no card, the venue manager's slip, the song in the wrong place, and the envelope with the photo that no longer existed.

The pile didn't accuse her. It accused *him* of not being able to let go.

That night, he told her the truth anyway. "A guy said he saw you by the Riverfront Sunday."

She didn't flinch. "He didn't."

"I know." He exhaled. "I'm telling you so there's nothing I'm holding on to that you can't see."

Her eyes softened, then shone. "Thank you." She stepped into him, pressed her forehead to his. "I'm not going to lose us because of a man I already left."

He held her like the decision had already been made. Maybe it had.

Mitch

He didn't bother with Sunday sightings. People loved handing out the shape of a story. All you had to do was frame it.

He made a different call instead—this one to the garden venue. He never said his name. He didn't even use a voice that could be remembered. He just asked whether the deposit had cleared for Jake and Emileigh's date, sounded disappointed when they said yes, and then requested the runner-up hold be released on the other spring Saturday "so the couple can keep their options open."

He hung up smiling. Options were where certainty went to die.

By Wednesday, Emileigh was done being polite with her past. She spent an hour with a technician locking everything down: new number, new passwords, authentication that forced a pause long enough to make impulse feel like a choice.

When she came out into the afternoon, lighter, she found Jake waiting across the street with two lemon ices, the kind that made your tongue sting and your cheeks pucker. She crossed to him, took the cup, and the world felt briefly, blessedly small.

They walked to the park bench facing the church. A woman pushed a stroller by; a jogger pounded past. Ordinary life moved around them like traffic in a roundabout: constant, dizzying, survivable.

"I want to tell Pastor," she said suddenly. "Not details. Just… ask for covering. For us."

Jake nodded. "Okay."

He didn't say how relieved he was to have a thing they could do that wasn't just watching a door and waiting for the knob to turn.

The first real argument came that night, small and sharp.

"I don't want to change my route home," she said, untying her shoes by the door. "That's my street."

"And I don't want to pretend there isn't a man who knows that street," he said, trying to keep his voice level. "We can choose inconvenience for a while. It's not surrender. It's stewardship."

She looked up, eyes tired. "You think I don't know what he's like?"

"I think you're brave," he said. "And I think bravery without strategy is just bait."

The word hovered between them. She flinched like it had grazed something tender. "So I'm bait now?"

"No." He reached and stopped, hand in the air. "No. I'm saying I can't lose you because we didn't take a turn five minutes sooner."

Silence stretched. Then, softer: "Okay. We'll take the long way." She swallowed. "Just... don't talk to me like I'm the problem. I already left."

"I won't," he said, and meant it, and still hated that sometimes love and fear wore the same voice.

Mitch

He tried the front door once—called from a new number, let it ring twice, hung up. The point wasn't contact. The point was the echo it left.

Then he did something bolder: left a small jewelry box in the lobby mail table downstairs, no unit number, lid cracked just enough to show the bracelet he'd once bought her after a fight. Anyone could have picked it up. Anyone could have claimed it. He didn't care who delivered the message.

He walked out into the evening, hands in his pockets, lighter unlit.

They found the box on their way up from groceries.

Emileigh saw it first. The bracelet shone like a memory she'd outgrown and now had to touch again. She didn't. She closed the lid and slid the box toward the building manager's "lost & found" tray like it was hot.

Jake watched her face more than the bracelet. Relief and grief and something like fury crossed in quick succession.

"I'm not taking it," she said.

"I know," he answered.

But upstairs, he couldn't stop seeing it in the mirror of his mind, a loop that made it hard to hear anything else.

Rain finally came—late, sudden, loud. It hammered the windows, softened the city edges, turned brake lights into smeared rubies on the slick streets below.

Jake stood at the glass, phone in his hand, thumb hovering over a number he didn't plan to dial. He was tired of reacting. He wanted to move first. Tell someone. Do something.

"Come sit," Emileigh called from the couch, tucked under a blanket, a movie paused at a wide shot of a field. "Please."

He set the phone down, walked to her, and let the sound of rain fill the spaces neither of them could.

"Tomorrow," she said into his shirt. "We'll talk to the pastor. And maybe… the police."

"Okay," he said, and kissed the crown of her head, tasting lemon and rain and resolve.

He told himself it would be enough.

Mitch

He sat in his truck a block away, wipers thudding, watching the glow of their window blur and sharpen, blur and sharpen.

He had learned the rhythm of storms. They lull. They drum. They distract.

"Almost there," he murmured, and flicked the lighter open once, then tucked it away like a secret you don't need to show to believe.

Chapter Twenty-Seven

Morning came with a clean blue sky like the city had scrubbed itself overnight. Emileigh woke lighter and didn't question the gift. She brewed coffee, sent Jake a good-morning photo of her ring laid against a folded napkin, and whispered a simple prayer over the day: *Let it hold.*

They met at the church just before ten. The sanctuary was empty except for the muffled sound of a vacuum somewhere far off, and Pastor's door stood open like an invitation.

He didn't ask for details. He asked for the truth.

They gave him enough to cover them without peeling old wounds raw. He listened, hands folded, eyes kind, and when he prayed, it felt like someone had thrown a heavy blanket over a fire—not to smother, but to contain.

"Protection and peace," he said softly. "Wisdom, too. Not the kind that looks brave, the kind that *keeps you.* And unity—so what comes at you from outside doesn't find a crack inside."

When they stepped back into the sun, they both breathed like they hadn't in days.

"Thank you," she said, not entirely sure whether she meant him or God or Jake. Maybe all three.

"Lunch?" Jake asked.

"Let's."

They chose a little place with potted herbs in the windows and menus on clipboards. For forty minutes, life behaved. They ate. They laughed. They made a list of wedding things that could be decided without drama—save-the-date style, cake flavors, and whether they wanted a receiving line (no).

Then the afternoon went practical. At the precinct, a clerk walked them through the process: documentation, timeline, and what "no contact" meant in actual steps. Paper, signatures, a stack of pamphlets that made the threat feel both smaller and more official.

"Thank you," Emileigh said.

The clerk nodded like she did this a hundred times a week and still cared about every single one. "You're doing the right thing."

Outside, the sun had slid to a sweeter angle. They decided to take the long way to her place, windows down, a light song on the radio that made the city look softer than it usually did.

They hit the turnpike just before traffic thickened. Jake felt loose in the shoulders for the first time in a while. He talked about a weekend picnic, about learning the first dance even though they both had two left feet, about how he wanted vows that sounded like *them*, not like something off a greeting card.

Emileigh turned her face into the breeze and closed her eyes. "We're gonna be okay," she said, like she was testing the words in her mouth.

"Yeah," he said, believing it for a full, whole second.

That was when her phone buzzed in the cup holder.

Jake didn't look. He had learned not to. The buzz came again, a second later, sharp enough to snag the edge of his attention.

Ahead, a delivery van shifted two lanes without signaling, and the sedan in front of them braked hard.

"Jake!" she shouted.

He saw the red blink too late. His foot slammed down, tires chirped, the nose of the car dove, and for a breath the world narrowed to the rectangle of brake lights filling his windshield. He jerked right. The shoulder shuddered under them. Gravel spat. A horn behind them smeared into an angry ribbon of sound.

They stopped crooked, chest to dashboard, hearts sprinting.

"You okay?" he asked, breathing like he'd run.

She nodded so fast it was almost a tremor. "You?"

He nodded back, hands still at ten and two like he might need to will the car into being steady.

For a long beat, they just listened to the engine tick.

A tow truck blasted by and shook the air. Jake eased them back into traffic when the gap came. No one honked this time. No one knew how close they'd come to being a headline that started with *Authorities say…*

Emileigh put her hand on his thigh. "It wasn't your fault."

He swallowed. "I know."

He did. And also knew that he'd felt the phone buzz and half thought of *what if* tug the corner of his vision at exactly the worst second.

They drove in quiet the rest of the way, the kind that didn't accuse anyone, just left a mark.

At her building, the lobby smelled like lemon cleaner and wet umbrellas. A cardboard sign on the manager's desk said NO SOLICITING in a marker that had started to die.

On the elevator, Jake stared at the brushed steel doors and saw brake lights. Emileigh stared at the ceiling camera and saw an envelope.

Inside her apartment, she set her bag down and leaned both palms on the counter. "We're okay," she said, because saying it out loud sometimes made the room obey.

"We are," Jake answered. He meant it, even with his heart still tapping a nervous code against his ribs.

He made tea. She changed into soft clothes and wiped off her makeup like she was erasing the part of the day that tried to write itself over her.

The kettle clicked. The apartment exhaled.

Then her phone—with its new number, new settings, new walls—buzzed once more. A voicemail icon appeared without a ring. Unknown number. Transcription unavailable.

She put the phone face down. "Not tonight."

Jake slid the mug toward her. "Not tonight," he agreed.

They sat on the couch and watched a show where the worst thing that ever happened was someone forgetting an anniversary. It helped until it didn't.

Across town, at a gas station that smelled like antifreeze and fried chicken, Mitch bought a pack of gum and leaned on the counter long enough to watch the screens behind the cashier cycle through security feeds—four angles of a parking lot, nothing happening in any of them.

He wasn't thinking about the near crash. He hadn't planned the van. He didn't need to. Life did the work if you let it. A nudge here, a buzz there. People carried their own kindling. He just supplied the matchbook with half the matches missing.

The clerk cleared his throat. "You good, man?"

Mitch smiled a little too wide. "Perfect."

He walked out into the early evening with the gum in his pocket and the day's map in his head. Routes. Exits. Intersections that pinched without looking like they did. Practice runs were valuable. Not for him—for them. Teach a body to flinch now; it would flinch bigger later.

He flicked the lighter but didn't strike it. Click. Close. Click. Close.

At dusk, the heat broke and the sky went lavender. Jake stood on the balcony while Emileigh answered emails inside, and watched the city lights dot on like someone was taking attendance.

His phone buzzed with a message from an unknown group thread—some scatterbrained mass text a mutual friend had added him to. He almost ignored it. Then he saw the image.

A photo of Emileigh and a friend in front of the café, months old and clearly daytime, captioned: *Look who I ran into today!*

He felt the drop before he could talk himself back onto the ground. Today? No. He knew it wasn't. Knew it was lazy captioning. Knew, knew, knew.

Still, he clicked through to the original post and checked the timestamp. Three months ago. He breathed out, shame stinging. He knew better. He'd still looked.

Inside, the microwave beeped. Emileigh poked her head out. "Popcorn or ice cream?"

"Both," he said, smiling for real this time. He held up his phone. "Also, random group text etiquette should be a crime."

She rolled her eyes, laughing. "Capital offense."

They ate on the couch, fingers dusted with salt, mouths sweet, pretending the day had been simpler than it was. It worked. For a while.

Before bed, she put the pamphlets from the precinct in a neat stack on the nightstand, then set the ring on top of the way people set paperweights on stacks they don't want blown apart. Jake watched her do it and didn't know whether to feel comforted or warned.

"Tomorrow," she said, sliding under the sheet. "We'll start the restraining order. We'll send Pastor the dates for counseling. We'll—"

He kissed her before the list reached the part where fear and faith started arm wrestling.

"Tomorrow," he echoed.

She fell asleep fast, her body finally cashing checks her mind had been writing all day. Jake lay in the dark and traced the outline of the near miss in his head: the lane change, the red lights, the jerk to the shoulder, the gravel like hail. He pictured what it would have looked like if he hadn't turned in time, and he had to breathe through it twice before his pulse slowed.

He thanked God for the shoulder. He hated that it felt like a warning.

Sometime in the unmarked middle of the night, a soft sound at the window drew him up on one elbow. Not a knock. Not a scrape. A tap, like something light had struck the glass and then thought better of it.

He waited. Nothing. The city hummed the way it always did.

In the morning, he forgot to mention it. Emileigh forgot to mention the nightmare where she was late for a wedding that wasn't hers. They both drank their coffee a little faster than usual and decided not to wonder why.

On the street, the day looked ordinary again. It wasn't. But it looked that way.

They got in the car. Buckles clicked. The engine turned.

They had no idea how close "almost" could live to "after."

Chapter Twenty-Eight

Tahlia texted at 8:12 a.m., a number Jake hadn't seen in years:

We need to talk. It's about Mitch. And... me.

He stared at the screen long enough for the coffee to go cold, then typed back, Ten minutes. 5th & Peachtree. He didn't tell Emileigh. Not yet. He told himself he wanted facts before he brought more smoke into their home.

Tahlia was already there when he arrived, leaning against the brick like a memory he'd left in a different version of himself. Same eyes. Same control in her shoulders, like she could will the day to obey.

"Jake." She tried to smile. Didn't finish it. "You look good."

"Say what you came to say."

A beat. Then: "Mitch and I... it wasn't just a fling. We ran hot for a while. I kept him close after it burned out." She swallowed. "Closer than I should have."

His jaw tightened. "Why?"

"Because," she said, quiet, "I wanted you back. And I knew he wouldn't let you get comfortable with anyone else if I... nudged him."

Traffic hissed over Peachtree, buses exhaling at the curb. The city seemed to step back to give the words room to land.

"So the flowers?" Jake asked. "The venue calls? The music?"

"I fed him information," she said. "Where were you. What mattered to you. He did the rest." She lifted a hand, let it fall. "I thought I could control it. I thought I was just... slowing you down. Until I couldn't stop it anymore."

Jake laughed once—no humor, all hurt. "You used him to use me."

"I used *him* because I couldn't stand the idea of you choosing someone else." Her chin shook, then steadied. "And it was wrong. I know that now."

"Why tell me?"

"Because he's past me now." Her voice thinned. "He's not taking cues. He's… enjoying it. And when a man like Mitch enjoys the game, somebody gets hurt." She took a breath that sounded like surrender. "I have proof he spoofed numbers, called the venue, and sent the bracelet. I can show you."

Jake looked up. "Show me."

She pulled a slim folder from her bag: a florist receipt with cash and phone order scribbles; a venue call log with a blocked number timestamped the morning they toured; screenshots of messages to a bandleader with the exact song request. At the top of one page: a selfie of Mitch in the shop mirror, uncaptioned, the florist's logo behind him.

"He used my contacts sometimes," Tahlia said, eyes on the folder. "But the plays are his now. He thinks I'm soft. He thinks I won't go to the police because I'll go down with him." She finally met Jake's eyes. "I will. If that's what it takes."

He exhaled slow. The pieces aligned with a click he could feel in his bones—how every 'coincidence' felt like choreography.

"Emileigh didn't relapse," she said, and the way she said Emileigh's name told him this wasn't a favor, it was a confession. "I've been cruel. But I'm not going to let him finish what I started."

Jake took the folder. His hands were steady. His voice wasn't. "You're going to tell her."

"I will," Tahlia said. "But first... there's one more thing. He's planning something tonight. I don't have the details, just the place. Atlantic Station—Blue parking deck, near the 17th Street side. Sunset." She hesitated. "Don't go alone."

"Then you call the cops."

"I can. I will." She nodded. "But Mitch is fast. If he thinks he's cornered, he'll pivot. I wanted you to have the target before he moves it."

Jake stepped back, pulse drumming. "If you're lying to me—"

"I'm not."

He slid the folder under his arm. "Then get clean. Tell the truth. To the police. To Emileigh. To yourself."

Her eyes glistened; she let it happen. "I'm trying."

He left without looking back.

***

Emileigh noticed immediately—the hum under his skin, the way his keys hit the bowl with more force than necessary. "What happened?"

He thought about lying and found he didn't have the energy. "I met Tahlia."

Her face changed—surprise, pain, the old name traveling through memories she'd tried not to keep. "Why?"

"Because she finally told the truth." He laid the folder on the table and walked her through it: the florist, the venue, the band. His voice stayed even. His hands didn't.

When he finished, she was breathing like she'd run upstairs. "So it wasn't me," she said, not as a question but as a verdict.

"It was never you," he said, and meant it, and hated all the ways he'd given doubt a chair anyway.

She touched the ring, then him. "What do we do?"

"Police, first," he said. "Then, Pastor. Then—" He checked the time. Sunset is still hours away. "There's a spot at Atlantic Station—Blue deck. Tahlia says he's planning something. I'm not letting him dictate our life anymore."

"I'm coming with you."

"No," he said, soft but solid. "If he wants disorder, I'm not giving him a crowd."

"I'm not letting you go alone." Steel in her voice. "We do this together."

He thought of the almost-crash, the bracelet on the lobby table, the envelope at her desk. He shook his head. "I need you safe. Please."

"Jake—"

"I'll share my location. I'll be careful. I'll keep the call open in my pocket." His eyes found hers. "Trust me to come home."

She looked at him for a long time, then nodded once. "Then let me do one thing." She picked up her phone. "I'm calling Pastor. And I'm driving you there. You won't be alone until you have to be."

He wanted to argue. He didn't. "Okay."

***

They prayed in the car on 17th Street, two blocks from Atlantic Station's Blue deck, the skyline rising clean against a sky that threatened late-afternoon thunder. Simple words, little and strong. Emileigh's hands were warm around his.

"Call me when you're done," she said. "Or I'm coming to find you."

"I will." He meant it.

He stepped out into the air that smelled like hot concrete and ozone. The deck swallowed sound—tires squealing, a MARTA bus sighing somewhere on the bridge, voices bouncing off concrete.

His phone buzzed as he walked. Unknown number. Transcription unavailable. He didn't answer.

The Blue deck level he chose was mostly empty— weekday lull—just a few cars and the hum of fluorescent lights. He scanned the edges, every pillar a maybe, every echo an old habit.

"Predictable," a voice said behind him.

Jake turned.

Mitch leaned against a concrete post like he was part of it, hands in pockets, sunglasses on, though the light was flat. The smile didn't reach his cheeks.

"Thought you'd bring backup," Mitch said. "Tahlia loves a crowd."

"So do cowards," Jake said. "This ends."

"Ends?" Mitch looked past him toward 17th Street, as if something out there might be funny. "You got engaged and thought the movie rolled credits. That's cute."

"Walk away," Jake said, stepping closer.

"From what?" Mitch's mouth twitched. "You, pastor's boy, finally came to play."

Jake's phone buzzed again. He ignored it. Somewhere nearby, a delivery bay clanged, a cart rattled, a car alarm chirped and went silent.

"Last warning," Jake said, voice low.

"Then take it," Mitch said, pushing off the post just enough to share breath. "Warn me."

They stood there, two men held together by a woman they loved for opposite reasons, the city thrumming around them.

Jake's phone buzzed a third time—longer, insistent. He glanced down and saw Emileigh's name.

He stepped back to answer. Mitch's smile edged colder.

"Run along," Mitch said. "Wouldn't want you to miss your bedtime story."

Jake brought the phone to his ear. "I'm okay," he said quickly. "I see him. I'm leaving in two minutes."

"Don't goad him," she said. "Please."

"Two minutes," Jake repeated, and ended the call. He pocketed the phone, heart pounding harder now that he'd heard her voice.

When he looked up, Mitch was gone.

Jake scanned the deck—pillars, ramps, the low wall that opened toward Central Park at Atlantic Station. Nothing. Just the thud of his pulse and the airy whine of the lights.

He waited sixty seconds. Ninety. Two minutes.

Then he turned toward the exit and headed for the street.

He didn't see the black SUV until it slid out from behind a delivery truck and matched his pace, window rolling down just enough for a camera lens to pop like an eye.

He didn't bother to hide his face.

He just kept walking, jaw tight, eyes forward, the choice already made: go home, lock the doors, file the papers, refuse to flinch.

Behind him, the shutter clicked three times. Somewhere, a message prepared itself with a timestamp it would lie about.

Jake pulled onto 17th, then Peachtree, both hands firm at ten and two, determination burning clean through the noise.

He was going home.

He didn't see the thunderheads building over Midtown.

Chapter Twenty-Nine

Tahlia's second text came just after noon:
I'm going to Emileigh. She deserves the truth from me.

Jake stared at the message until the words stopped swimming. He typed Do it and hit send before he could soften it.

He told himself this was good—clean air, clean lines. He told himself the ground might finally stop tilting.

***

They met on the steps of the High Museum, white walls soaking up the sun. Emileigh came with the Pastor's assistant, a woman with steady eyes who stood a polite distance away, headphones in, an anchor disguised as company.

Tahlia didn't waste time with pleasantries. She apologized—plain, unadorned—and then laid out what she'd done and what Mitch had done since: the florist, the venue, the band, the calls, the little "accidents" shaped to look like fate. She handed over copies of the receipts and screenshots. She didn't make excuses.

Emileigh listened without interrupting, palms flat on her knees to keep them from shaking. When Tahlia finished, the city noise rewove itself around them—buses sighing, a scooter whining down Peachtree, a MARTA train whispering beneath the street.

"I'm not going to tell you I forgive you today," Emileigh said, voice level. "But I'm going to tell the truth with you. And we're going to end this."

Tahlia nodded. "I'll go to APD with you. I'll put my name on everything."

They spent an hour at the Midtown precinct, filing supplements to the report: dates, call logs, the bracelet, the venue manager's note. A detective with a soft drawl and a hard pen took it all down.

"Keep your phones on," he said, sliding a card across the desk. "If he escalates or steps on the order, call 911 first, then me."

Outside, Tahlia turned to Emileigh, eyes glassy. "I'll testify. Whatever it costs."

Emileigh let a beat pass. "Good," she said. "Because it's going to cost."

They parted with a brittle peace. Tahlia walked toward the Arts Center station, head bowed. Emileigh texted Jake: With Tahlia. We filed more. Headed home. I love you.

I love you, he wrote back, and for the first time in days, he felt the words hit something solid.

Mitch

The first time Tahlia tried to bring him to heel, he'd played along. It had amused him. Now it bored him.

He sat in the back of a rideshare on Spring Street, watching the city slide by. On a burner phone, he queued a message. He'd already done the homework—downloaded an app that could mask a number with another, cropped a few pictures from the Blue deck into something suggestive, and changed a timestamp.

He typed:

From: Tahlia

To: Jake

I tried. She went back. Twelve Midtown—Room 1412. If you hurry, you'll see it yourself.

He attached a photo: a woman from behind with Emileigh's height and hair, stepping into an elevator at Atlantic Station—just blurry enough to be certain if you wanted to be.

He added a second image: the bracelet on a hotel table, two glasses sweating beside it. Cropped tight. No room details to disprove. Perfect.

He didn't hit send yet. Timing was a spice.

Emileigh beat Jake home and started a pot of chili they could eat for two days. The quiet of chopping and sautéing steadied her—the way onions surrendered to heat, the way meat darkened just before it was ready to be left alone.

Jake walked in with flowers—nothing fancy, grocery-store hydrangeas—and a look that told her he had braced for worse at the museum than what he'd heard.

"She did the right thing," he said, setting the bouquet in the sink like it might sprint away.

"She did," Emileigh agreed. "Late, but she did."

He kissed her forehead and reached for bowls. "Let's eat before we fall over."

They were halfway through when Jake's phone vibrated on the counter. Unknown number. Then his screen lit with Tahlia and a preview he didn't want to read and couldn't not read.

I tried. She went back. Twelve Midtown—Room 1412. If you hurry—

His chair scraped tile. Emileigh looked up, spoon midair. "What is it?"

Jake's pulse stuttered. He stared at the name, the words, the photo thumbnail—dark hair, a blue-lit elevator, a silhouette his fear knew by heart.

He lifted the phone slowly, like moving too fast would make something spill. He opened the thread. The second photo loaded: bracelet, glasses, a room table.

His throat burned. "It's fake," he said aloud, as if saying it would erase the images. "It's fake. It's—"

"Let me see," Emileigh said, already reaching. He angled the screen toward her. She took it in, the way a person takes a punch: eyes wide, then narrowed, then dry.

"That's not me," she said, calm as glass. "We just left the precinct—you saw the timestamp. And I don't own that dress."

Jake nodded, hands shaking. "He spoofed her number."

"Call Tahlia," she said, already dialing on speaker.

Tahlia picked up on the second ring. "I didn't send it," she said, breathless, no hello. "Mitch spoofed me. I swear— Jake, Emileigh, I'm at home. I can send you a screen recording of my last hour."

"I believe you," Jake said. He did. But the images had burrowed somewhere old and tender. "He says Twelve Midtown. 1412."

"Don't go," Tahlia said. "Please. That's his trap. He wants you moving—angry, fast, alone."

Emileigh laid a hand on Jake's arm. "We stay put. We call the detective. We lock the doors."

"I know," Jake said. He did. He knew it like he knew his own driver's seat. He also knew the urge to end this with a door knock and a single sentence: *It's over.*

He breathed in, out. "I'm calling the detective."

He called. Voicemail. He left a message, short and clipped. Then he called the non-emergency line and logged the spoof in real time. He did everything right. It still felt like drowning.

They ate two more bites each and gave up. The chili went cold. The sky outside was bruised.

By sunset, Jake was pacing. He told himself he was working the adrenaline out of his body. He told himself that sitting still rewarded Mitch.

Emileigh watched him, the way a person watches a storm roll toward a house they love. "Stay," she said, once.

"I'm staying," he said.

The phone on the counter buzzed again—Unknown—and then a green bubble slid in under Tahlia's message like a worm:

Clock's ticking, pastor's boy. I'd hurry.

Jake's jaw set. "That's him. That's not her."

"I know," Emileigh said. "We both know."

They stood like that, shoulder to shoulder, while the daylight thinned and Midtown's lights came on in patient rows.

At 9:11 p.m., Jake's phone chimed a third time. A map pin dropped, labeled Twelve Midtown – Level 4, with a grainy photo of a sedan that looked like Emileigh's, taken from behind—same model, different sticker on the bumper.

"I'm going to the deck," Jake said. "Not inside. I'll film from the ramp, send the footage straight to the detective. I'll be home in twenty minutes. You can stay on the line the whole time."

"Jake—"

"Twenty minutes," he said. "And then this is evidence, not a story."

He kissed her, quick and hard. He meant to be careful. He meant to be calm. He meant to come right back.

She followed him to the door. "Location on. Call open. No elevators. No rooms."

"Yes," he said, already halfway down the hall. "I promise."

Mitch

On a rooftop two blocks away, Mitch watched the Atlantic Station lights glitter like a fake sky. People were easy. They wanted to move. He didn't need them to run. He only needed them to turn.

He sent one last nudge: a blank text from a third number, nothing in it but a little bell. It would feel like the sound you hear right before a race gun.

Then he put the phone in his pocket and smiled at his reflection in a dark window. No teeth.

"Go on," he whispered. "Be the hero."

Chapter Thirty

Jake took Peachtree to 14th, then cut across toward West Peachtree to avoid the cluster around the Connector. The night had that heavy summer feel that promised rain and then thought better of it. He kept the call open in his pocket, the speaker low enough that he could hear Emileigh breathe.

"I'm here," he said, pulling into Twelve Midtown's garage entrance. "Level 4."

"Okay," she said. "Slow. Film as you go."

He did. He set his phone to record and held it up on the wheel with one hand, tires humming over the painted arrow. The deck looked like every deck—concrete, pillars, the faint smell of oil and someone's cologne hanging longer than it should.

He circled once, twice. No bracelet. No dress. No Emileigh. No Mitch.

He narrated anyway for the camera, timestamp in frame, street noise bleeding through from 17th Street. "No contact. No sighting. Likely spoof and fabricated images. Leaving now."

"Good," she said in his ear. "Come home."

On the down ramp, a coupe whipped past too fast, horn blaring, making him tap the brake and blink away the lurch. He eased out behind it, fed into 17th, and turned onto Peachtree heading south. Lights smeared red and white on the windshield. He breathed. He was going home.

"Almost there," he said.

"Almost," she echoed.

His phone vibrated again. Against his better judgment, he glanced down. A new message from the fake Tahlia thread blinked on the lock screen:

Too late.

He didn't open it. He didn't need to. He flipped the phone face down on the passenger seat and said, "He's bluffing."

"You're almost home," Emileigh reminded him, like a mantra. "Straight shot."

He took Peachtree past 12th, past 10th, where people spilled out of restaurants, and rolled through a stale yellow. His eyes burned. He blinked hard. Tears he hadn't planned to shed showed up anyway, hot and unhelpful.

"God," he said quietly, "help me finish this right."

A sudden screech cut across from his left—a rideshare stopping short at the curb. Reflex made him glance. A flash of motion on the right—a pedestrian darting back from the crosswalk. He corrected, too sharp. The right tires clipped the slick paint of a lane line. The car fishtailed, a slow, sickening slide that felt both endless and instant.

"Jake?" Emileigh's voice rose in his pocket. "Jake—"

He gripped the wheel, tried to feather the brake the way his father taught him in the rain, but the back end swung wider. The median loomed—a low concrete lip that wouldn't forgive.

He saw the curb. He saw the oak beyond it. He saw, in a single, clarifying bead of time, Emileigh's face the first night they prayed together on the 17th Street bridge, city lights caught in her hair.

"I'm sorry," he said—to God, to her, to the part of himself that had almost made it home clean.

The car jumped the lip. The world popped—metal, glass, the obscene hiss of a radiator confessing. The airbag exploded white. Everything went soundless and bright, like the inside of a shell.

The phone flew from the seat and clattered under the dash. On the other end, Emileigh's voice kept calling his name into a pocket of silence that could not answer.

Sirens were somewhere. Footsteps, shouts. A woman saying, "Call 911—oh my God, call." A man's voice: "Hang on, buddy."

Jake's eyelids fluttered once. Twice. The lights above him went tall and fuzzy, then shrank to a pin.

The last thing he felt was the ring of the steering wheel under his fingers. He was holding on. Then he wasn't.

Emileigh

"Jake?" She was already on her feet, keys in hand, shoes half on, the phone pressed to her ear so hard it hurt. "Jake, answer me."

No sound. Then voices, distant and jagged. Then a word that didn't belong to any normal night: "Crash."

She ran, didn't lock the door, didn't think. She took Peachtree like a prayer, calling 911 with one hand and Pastor with the other, begging God out loud in a voice that made people on the sidewalk turn and step back.

Blue lights flashed three blocks ahead, bouncing off glass and tree trunks. She pulled to the curb at a sick angle and ran toward the cluster of strangers making a circle where their fear could stand.

A paramedic knelt by the car, voice steady, hands moving with quiet speed. "Sir? Sir, can you hear me?"

"Jake," she whispered, feeling his name leave her mouth like blood leaving a vein. "I'm here. Please—"

Someone reached out to hold her back. She didn't register who. She watched the paramedics work, listened for a sign, any sign.

One of them looked up at the officer and said a string of numbers that meant time and pressure, and oxygen. The only word Emileigh understood was unresponsive.

The world tilted.

Pastor's voice came through her phone in a hush like velvet. "I'm en route. I'm with you. Breathe, daughter. Breathe."

The paramedics slid Jake onto the board. Lights painted the oak, the median, the broken glass. A siren wound up, high and merciless.

They lifted him into the ambulance. A paramedic paused at the door. "You coming?"

Emileigh nodded and climbed in, knees weak but held up by something older than her fear.

The doors slammed. The siren rose. The city peeled away.

She took his hand, careful of wires and tape, and pressed her forehead to their knuckles. "I'm not letting go," she said, and then to God, Please.

The ambulance leapt forward. The chapter ended.

Chapter Thirty-One

ICU, after midnight

The room hummed with machine patience—soft beeps, a steady breath hiss, the clock's unhelpful march. Fluorescent light flattened everything into simple colors: white sheets, gray rails, the deep brown of Jake's hand under Emileigh's fingers.

Pastor sat in a corner chair with his Bible open to the Psalms, voice low enough to make the syllables feel like warm cloth. "You hem me in, behind and before," he read, and then he prayed it more than said it.

Nurses moved with practiced kindness, checking lines and numbers. A detective had come and gone, notebook tucked under his arm, promising to pull camera feeds from Peachtree and 17th. "We've got the spoofed messages logged," he'd said. "Don't engage at all. Let us build the case."

Emileigh barely nodded. She'd taken off her ring to rub the indentation it left and put it back, like setting a paperweight on a stack she refused to let blow apart. "Jake," she whispered, thumb circling his knuckle. "I'm here."

His eyes stayed closed. The machines kept their calm.

Pastor Rose rested a hand on her shoulder. "We'll keep watch," he said. "And we'll keep telling the truth."

She breathed in, out. "Okay."

Tahlia found Mitch at a two-top facing a glass. The city was a smear of light behind him, his reflection floating like a ghost over the street.

"You did it," she said, sliding into the seat across from him before he could choose the tone. "You split them. Clean."

He leaned back, smirk just shy of smug. "Told you—predictable."

She let out a short, appreciative breath and tilted her head, the way she used to when she wanted him to talk. "Walk me through it."

"Why?" He enjoyed this. "You taught me half of it."

"Because I like hearing the music I wrote," she said, smiling with no warmth. "Start with the deck."

He obliged. "Blue level. Camera angles are trash. Got the lens shot I wanted. The bracelet? Old trick. The florist? Easy. The band? Easier. The texts?" He tapped his phone. "A spoon is still a spoon whether it's silver or plastic. I fed him with both."

"Good boy," she said lightly.

The word landed. He didn't like it. He liked not liking it.

"And the crash?" she asked, casual as lint.

He shrugged. "Didn't plan it. Didn't need to. You spin a top right and the table does the rest."

She clucked her tongue, almost fond. "Still a beta at heart. You only know how to stir water." Her smile sharpened. "But I'll give you this—you stirred it cold."

His jaw ticked. "You needed me."

"Correction," she said, leaning in until he had to hold her stare. "I *used* you. Needing implies equality."

He laughed once, no humor. "You really want to do this?"

"You already are," she said. "And you're telling me because you still want my approval more than you want her."

Silence bloomed, then curdled.

She reached into her purse and set her phone on the table between them, screen dark, lens pointed nowhere. "We're done after tonight," she said, voice soft as a bruise. "I'll take my bow. You'll take your leash."

His eyes chilled. "What leash?"

"The one that makes you perform for praise," she said. "You just did." She stood, the chair's legs sighing against the floor. "Enjoy your victory lap, Mitch."

He watched her go, burning under the compliment he hated. When he glanced down, he caught his reflection again—smaller now, and angrier.

He didn't see that her phone camera had been rolling the whole time.

ICU, near dawn

The hallway clock glowed 4:17. Pastor dozed upright, Bible tented on his chest. A nurse dimmed the room one notch lower and left.

Emileigh leaned close. "Jake," she said softly. "It's me."

His fingers twitched. The monitor's rhythm shifted half a step. She stood, heart in her mouth. "Jake?"

His eyelids fought their way up, heavy and stubborn. The room swam back to him in slow frames—ceiling, light, her face, the ring, the bandage, the ache.

She smiled, already crying. "Hey. Hey, baby. I'm here."

He looked at her like a man waking in a language he used to speak. For a beat, relief broke through—something in his eyes eased.

Then it shuttered.

He pulled his hand back from hers as far as the line would let it. His mouth worked once, twice. The sound came out raw.

"I know."

The two words fell between them like dropped metal.

Her breath snagged. "Know... what?"

He looked past her, not able to hold her face and the thought at once. "About you." His jaw set. "About *him*."

She took a half step back like the air had shoved her. "Jake, no. He—"

The monitor ticked a little faster. A nurse slipped in, read the numbers with a glance, touched a button, and smiled the trained smile of someone who knows when a room is breaking. "Let's give him a second," she murmured.

Emileigh nodded without really nodding, eyes never leaving Jake's. "I didn't," she whispered. "I *didn't*."

He closed his eyes. Whether from pain or refusal, she couldn't tell.

She pressed her palm to the sheet instead of his skin and prayed the shortest prayer she knew. Help.

Tahlia stepped into the early gray and thumbed her phone to life. The recording timer blinked crimson: 00:07:41.

She sent the file to herself, then to the detective with a single line: His admission. All of it.

A reply came faster than she expected.

Received. Meet at 10 a.m. Precinct. Bring the device.

Across the street, a MARTA bus hissed; somewhere, a shopkeeper rattled a gate. Tahlia wrapped her arms around herself as if she could hold the whole city in place.

"Clean," she told the air. "Get clean."

Behind her, a sedan idled too long at a red. She didn't look back.

Pastor stood at the window with his hand on the glass, praying without words. The detective returned with a second card and a different face—intent, wired with purpose. "We've got movement," he said, not yet victory, not yet comfort. "We'll be in touch."

Emileigh nodded. "Please."

She sat again, took Jake's hand again, even if he didn't take hers back. "I'm not leaving," she said, more vow than fact.

The machines kept time. Outside, Atlanta woke up and pretended nothing in it had broken overnight.

Jake opened his eyes once more. For a heartbeat, love flashed clear on the surface like a fish breaking water.

Then the doubt pulled it under.

The chapter closed on the sound of the monitor, steady and uncertain at once. The monitor is not the only thing that is uncertain, Emileigh thought to herself.

www.ingramcontent.com/pod-product-compliance
Lightning Source LLC
Chambersburg PA
CBHW071226300726
48975CB00002B/317